Frederic Hill, Constance Hill

Frederic Hill

An Autobiography of Fifty Years in Times of Reform

Frederic Hill, Constance Hill

Frederic Hill
An Autobiography of Fifty Years in Times of Reform
ISBN/EAN: 9783337098773

Printed in Europe, USA, Canada, Australia, Japan

Cover: Foto ©Raphael Reischuk / pixelio.de

More available books at **www.hansebooks.com**

FREDERIC HILL

AN AUTOBIOGRAPHY OF
FIFTY YEARS IN TIMES OF REFORM.

EDITED, WITH ADDITIONS,

BY HIS DAUGHTER

CONSTANCE HILL.

" Let all the ends thou aim'st at be thy country's,
Thy God's, and truth's."

SHAKESPEARE.

WITH PORTRAITS.

LONDON:

RICHARD BENTLEY AND SON,

Publishers in Ordinary to Her Majesty the Queen.

1893.

TO

THE RIGHT HONOURABLE

CHARLES PELHAM VILLIERS, M.P.,

THIS STORY OF A LIFE

WHICH HAS BEEN MUCH INDEBTED TO HIM

IS

AFFECTIONATELY INSCRIBED.

PREFACE.

SOME years ago a friend suggested to my father that he should from time to time note down the recollections of his long life. This he did; and three years ago he placed his manuscripts in my hands to arrange and edit. Since then I have discovered a large quantity of diaries and contemporary correspondence. These, together with material drawn from other sources, have enabled me to enlarge the more interesting episodes of his life; notably, the periods of the Reform Bill agitation in Birmingham, and of his residence in Scotland. All such matter has been submitted to my father for his approval or criticism, and although he has now completed his ninetieth year, his memory is clear and retentive, enabling him to give useful explanations or to supply connecting links.

The family letters which had to be examined, and from which a selection had to be made, date from 1783, and extend over a period of upwards of seventy years. It is remarkable that the perusal of this correspondence of three generations brought to light no painful secrets nor ill-feeling of any kind, but, on the contrary, left on the mind of the reader a lively sense of the strong affection and trust in one another which prevailed in the whole family. This was a marked feature of the five " Hill brothers," of whom my father is the last survivor.

It has been observed that the first part of a biography is often the more interesting portion of the story. This is true as regards the present " Life," the first fifty years of which were passed during a period of great national changes, both social and political. It has been thought well, therefore, that the autobiographical portion of this work should deal with the period from 1803 to 1853, and that I should briefly describe the period subsequent to that date. Some family incidents of interest previous to 1803 are recorded in the first chapter.

In the chief work of his life, that of Penal Reform, my father encountered much opposition. He has lived to witness great fluctuations of opinion on that important subject; but he has the satisfaction, now in his old age, of seeing the most esteemed of our European and American Penologists advocating the opinions that he formed more than half a century ago, and of seeing public opinion setting in the same direction.

CONSTANCE HILL.

INVERLEITH HOUSE, HAMPSTEAD,
    October, 1893.

CONTENTS.

CHAPTER I.

1803.

CHAPTER II.

1805–1815.

CHAPTER III.

1816–1824.

CHAPTER IV.

1824–1830.

CHAPTER V.

1831–1832.

CHAPTER VI.

1832–1835.

CHAPTER VII.

1835–1836.

CHAPTER VIII.

1835–1839.

CHAPTER IX.

1835-1839.

CHAPTER X.

1839-1840.

CHAPTER XI.

1840-1842.

CHAPTER XII.

1842–1844.

CHAPTER XIII.

1845–1847.

CHAPTER XIV.

1847–1850.

CHAPTER XV.

1850–1851.

CHAPTER XVI.

1851–1852.

CHAPTER XVII.

1853–1893.

CHAPTER XVIII.

1853–1893.

LIST OF ILLUSTRATIONS.

FREDERIC HILL.

CHAPTER I.

1803.

I WAS born on the 29th of June, 1803, at Hilltop, a
house situated at the summit of Gough Street, then
in the outskirts of Birmingham. I was the sixth
child of Thomas Wright Hill and Sarah, his wife,
whose maiden name was Lea.

Our parents frequently related to us incidents
connected with earlier generations of our family;
some of these which I remember I will repeat.

My great-grandfather, John Hill, settled in Kidderminster as a tailor. His family consisted of two
sons and two daughters. His eldest son, James,
my grandfather, who was a baker at Kidderminster,
was a man of independent character. His oven was
heated by fuel which was procured from a wood
belonging to the lord of the manor, a member of

the Foley family. In the canvass for a county election, James Hill was asked to give his vote in favour of this gentleman, but his political principles obliged him to refuse to do so. The consequence was that at the next faggot harvest he was not permitted to be a purchaser, and was thus put to great inconvenience. Firewood could still be obtained, but from a place four miles distant, which considerably augmented its cost. In this difficulty he determined to try an experiment. Coals were plentiful in the neighbourhood, but they had not at that time been used for heating baking ovens. James Hill tried the effect of making his fire partly of coal and partly of wood. The experiment succeeded, and other bakers soon followed his example. The lord of the manor, now finding that he was rapidly losing his customers, sent to offer my grandfather the supply of faggots which had been so curtly refused!

A saying of James Hill's was often repeated amongst his descendants: "There are two kinds of evils about which it is of no use to complain—those which *can* be cured, and those which cannot."

My grandfather died before I was born, but my great-uncle John lived to the advanced age of ninety-six, and one of my earliest recollections is seeing him seated in a large armchair in our parlour.   John Hill was one of those who enrolled themselves as volunteers to fight against the Pretender in 1745.   There is a diary extant which he kept during a visit to London in 1760.   In it he speaks of hearing "dear Mr. Whitfield preach at his chapel in Tottenham Court Road;" and also mentions Mr. Wesley.   Amongst the miscellaneous entries are notes of purchases made on old London Bridge, and also a recipe for a "cordial for the colic," which consists of a great variety of ingredients.   It seems that the sufferer might have to wait some time for his cure, as, when made up, the mixture is to be put aside "to stand for twelve days before being used."   But the most interesting part of this diary is an allusion to the preparations which he witnessed in Westminster Hall for the trial of Lord Ferrers.

Lawrence Shirley Lord Ferrers, Viscount Tamworth, had murdered his steward at Stanton, in Leicestershire, and on the 16th of April, 1760, he was arraigned in Westminster Hall before a vast concourse of people.   Preparations were made for the reception of the Royal Family, all the ambassadors and other distinguished persons, besides the members of both Houses of Parliament and a large number of ladies.   "The grandeur of the scene exceeded all description, and the awful solemnity with which it was conducted was inexpressibly affecting." When the hearing was ended, the lords rose up one by one, beginning at the youngest, and each laying his right hand on his breast, and solemnly bowing, said, "Guilty, upon my honour." Lord Ferrers was condemned to be hanged at Tyburn, and his body to be delivered to the surgeons to be dissected. " The Lord High Steward then broke his staff, to show that his office was ended, and dismissed the assembly." The foreigners were greatly interested in the proceedings. One ambassador exclaimed, " Great God, what laws ! What a people, that thus condemns one of their own body for taking away the life of a common man !" *

We were all taught to respect our great-uncle John Hill, especially in connection with his conduct as a juryman. He had been called upon to serve in that capacity at Worcester, when he alone, of the twelve jurymen, refused to take a bribe. The judge happened to hear of this, and thenceforward, whenever he visited Worcester on circuit, he asked if he should have the pleasure of meeting the honest juror.

A further instance of sturdy independence was furnished by another ancestor.

* See contemporary Memoir published immediately after Lord Ferrers's execution.

The maiden name of my paternal grandmother was Symonds. Her grandfather refused to place his vote at the disposal of a rich relative named Millington, a solicitor of Shrewsbury. In consequence of this, Mr. Millington left his whole fortune to found a hospital, instead of bequeathing it to the Symondses. This institution is still known as Millington's Hospital.

Through this same Sarah Symonds we claim a connection with the patriot John Hampden, whose first wife belonged to the family of Symons, or Symeon, of Pyrton. I may here also mention that we claim a distant kinship with the author of "Hudibras."

Sarah's father, John Symonds, was a religious Nonconformist. When my grandfather, James Hill, proposed for his daughter, he remarked, " Before I give my consent, I must form a judgment of your spiritual state. I request you, therefore, to put up an extemporary prayer." This the lover accordingly did; and as the marriage soon afterwards took place, I conclude that the trial was considered satisfactory.

My great-uncle, the Rev. Joshua Symonds, was a popular Nonconformist minister. He lived at Bedford. The philanthropist Howard was a member of his congregation, but withdrew from it, owing to a difference of opinion upon certain religious tenets. Soon afterwards a parliamentary election took place, in which Howard was a candidate. Mr. Symonds had been so much impressed with the excellence of his character, that, ignoring the diversity of their opinions, he not only gave him his vote, but used all his influence in his favour. The canvass was not successful, but from this time forward Howard became one of his most attached friends. Wilberforce was a correspondent of my great-uncle's, and Mr. Newton, of Olney, the friend of the poet Cowper, was his intimate friend.

My father was named after a relative—Thomas Wright, a Shrewsbury nurseryman, of whom it is told that on his wedding day he took six men with him and planted, in commemoration of the occasion, the lime trees which became the fine avenue known as the "Quarry" (a corruption, I suppose, of the French *carré*). He was reproved for having kept the dinner waiting, and replied that "if what he had done was successful, it would be of far more value than a wedding dinner."

Amongst my father's recollections of his childhood, he used to tell us that he had curly hair, and his mother, who admired his curls, would not allow them to be cut off or hidden; the consequence was that, unlike all his schoolfellows, he did not wear a wig.

He wore leathern breeches, which were very stiff till softened by use. When a new pair arrived the breeches-maker used to put the lad's feet into them, and then, lifting him up by his breeches, would shake him till his legs settled into their proper place.

The household of his parents, James Hill, the baker, and Sarah Symonds Hill, was subject to a strict puritanical discipline. On Sunday the shutters were only partially opened; the family attended chapel three times, and in addition had a sermon read aloud in the evening. It even became a question whether Stackhouse's " History of the Bible " was of a sufficiently sacred character for Sunday reading.

The family stock of books was very limited; but this evil was not, in my father's opinion, without compensation, since, by frequent perusal, he made himself master of their contents. He acquired an intimate knowledge of the Bible, while among the secular works the "Arabian Nights' Entertainments " was his special favourite, a large portion of which he knew by heart. To these works was added another in a somewhat curious way. His father, together with a friend, had been appointed executor to a common acquaintance, recently deceased, who, having been a man of somewhat secluded habits, and of a studious and philosophic turn of mind, was set down by some of the good people of Kidderminster as in league with the evil one. This gentleman had sympathized with my father's love of reading, and had bequeathed him two volumes. But these the co-trustee strongly recommended should be burnt, as they bore a cabalistic appearance, and came from a dangerous quarter. James Hill, however, who was more enlightened than his neighbours, said, "Oh, let the boy have them;" whereupon were put into the lad's hands a "Manual of Geography" and a copy of "Euclid's Elements." Of this latter work the boy became enthusiastically fond. He mastered its difficult problems, and in later years pursued his studies into the higher mathematics.

A strong tie of affection existed between my father and his younger brother Matthew. In 1785 Matthew left home. He sought employment in Scotland, and finally went on to Ireland. My father felt the separation so keenly that, being unable to afford a seat in the mail coach, he walked the whole way from Birmingham to Holyhead (a distance of about a hundred and forty miles), crossed in the packet to Dublin, spent a week with his brother, and returned home in the same way. It was on this occasion that he first beheld the sea. Looking upon it from the Welsh hills, he thought it was a great ploughed field, but, to his surprise, the furrows began to move.

Matthew died in early manhood, to the great sorrow of his brother, whose attachment to him remained undiminished through a long life, and was testified upon his death-bed.

My father became one of a class to whom Dr. Priestley gave instruction in natural philosophy. In 1791, when the Birmingham riots broke out, which at first were directed chiefly against Dissenters, my father and his other classmates offered to defend Dr. Priestley's house. But the doctor thought it wrong to employ physical force even in self-defence, and declined their offer. Dr. Priestley, however, left his home, and took his household to a safer shelter elsewhere. Meanwhile, in spite of his refusal, my father and a few brave companions determined to do what they could to protect the doctor's property. My brother Matthew thus describes what followed :—

"My father barred the doors, closed the shutters, made fast the house as securely as he could against the expected rioters, and then awaited their arrival. He has often described to me how he walked to and fro in the darkened rooms, chafing under the restriction which had been put on him and his friends. He was present when the mob broke in, and witnessed the plunder and destruction, and the incendiary fire by which the outrage was consummated. Lingering near the house, he saw a working man fill his apron with shoes, with which he made off. My father followed him, and, as soon as the thief was alone, collared him, and dragged him to the gaol, where he had the mortification to witness the man quietly relieved of his booty, and then suffered to depart ; the keeper informing my father that he had had orders to take in no prisoner that night."

Not to be wholly baulked in his zeal, my father climbed up a lamp-post to address the angry mob ; but a volley of stones soon put an end to his eloquence.

During the burning of Dr. Priestley's house, one incident occurred which was comically unexpected. The cry of the mob in those days was " Church and King!" and they pretended to consider all Dissenters as disloyal subjects. Dr. Priestley was fond of music, and, as a diversion from his mental labours, used to grind a small barrel-organ. When the rioters had sacked the house, this organ was brought out into the garden and put with other things to be afterwards carried away. Seeing the organ, one of the mob began to turn the handle, when to the surprise of all they heard the loyal air of " God Save the King " !

Matthew continues—

" The mob which had begun by attacking Dissenters as public enemies, burning down their chapels and their houses and making spoil of their goods, soon expanded their views, and gave unmistakable signs that the distinction between Dissenter and Churchman had had its hour, and was to be superseded in favour of the doctrine now so well known, ' La propriété c'est un vol.' When matters came to this pass, the magistrates swore in special constables. My father was one of this body ; and, like his comrades, compendiously armed with half a mop-stick by way of truncheon, he marched with them to the defence of Baskerville House, which was under attack by the mob. The special constables at first drove all before them, in spite of the immense disparity of numbers ; but after a time, becoming separated in the *mêlée*, they sustained a total defeat. Some were very severely bruised, and one died of the injuries which he received. My father, although not conscious at the time of having received a blow, could not the next morning raise his arm. He was always of opinion that if they had had a flag, or some signal of that kind, round which they could have rallied, the fortune of the day would have been reversed."

Baskerville House, after being pillaged and burnt, was purposely left standing for many years to be a disgrace to Birmingham. I well remember its desolate appearance.

The following letter from Dr. Priestley's secretary to my father is in our possession :—

" Mr. Russell presents his compliments to Mr. Hill, and

sends him, at Dr. Priestley's request, a set of his ' Church History ' and also of ' Early Opinions,' of which the doctor requests Mr. Hill's acceptance as a testimony of his gratitude for Mr. Hill's exertions and attentions during the late riots. Mr. R. expects to make an addition to the books now sent, but is unwilling these should be delayed.

" Digbeth, Friday, January 13, 1792."

The two following letters also bear upon this period :—

SARAH HILL (*née* SYMONDS) *to her son* T. W. HILL.

" Kidderminster, July 27, 1791.

" DEAR CHILD,

          "We should be much gratified to receive a line from you when you can write with convenience to yourself. It will be a particular satisfaction to know that the effects of the blow you received upon your arm are quite gone off. I was exceedingly anxious about you when I heard of the late dreadful commotions in and about Birmingham. You won't think I disapprove of your dis-interested spirit and ardent desire to succour your friends, but I feared you should sustain material injury in endeavour-ing to do something where it appeared, by the accounts I heard, nothing was to be done, at least nothing to any purpose. But you on the spot were more capable of judging than persons at a distance, and I am sure you would act consistently with principles that I must approve.

" I think we are much indebted to the kindness of our great and gracious Preserver for that protection which you and other friends experienced when exposed to so much danger from a bigoted outrageous mob. I hope a stop is effectually put to their depredations, and that you will now enjoy peace and tranquillity, though you must and will feel something of the distressing effects for a considerable time. Trade will be injured, and many deprived of those opportunities for attending public worship which they lately enjoyed.

" All unite in love to you.

" From your affectionate mother,

"S. HILL."

Letter from SARAH HILL *(afterwards* MRS. WILLIAMS) *to her brother* T. W. HILL, *written in the autumn of* 1792.

" DEAR BROTHER,

"Having an opportunity of writing post free induces me to write a line to thank you for the letter we received last night. It was a satisfaction to us to hear something of my sister. We had felt anxious about her from the reports a week ago of riotous proceedings at Birmingham, but I trust you will not have any more serious alarms of this kind. By what we hear the C—— and K—— folks seem disposed to court the friendship of you Dissenters in support of the Constitution, etc., etc. I think some of them must be ashamed of their former conduct.

"Parties here seem at present to run high. Three or four informations have been sent, we are informed, to Mr. Dundas of what one body or another has said against the K—— and *Constitewshun.* To-day we received a paper which summoned the inhabitants to meet in order to stop the progress of sedition, and every morning we are serenaded with the chorus of 'God save the King,' by boys who are passing up and down the street.

"In the midst of all this bustle, Truth no doubt is making its silent progress in the minds of men, and though at present apparently clouded with the mists of Ignorance and Wickedness, will, in the end, break forth with the greater luster.

"When I hear or read anything pleasant upon these subjects I seem to want my dearest Matthew to partake with me, as he used always to do, in the satisfaction and joy they afford. At another time, when Bigotry and Despotism seem to spread their baleful influence, I can rejoice in the hope that he was taken from the evil to come, and is gone where 'the wicked cease from troubling.' Oh may my dear and now only brother and myself be enabled to follow him in the path to Heaven! . . .

"I use the freedom of a sister and set down what comes uppermost ; but, allowing for this freedom, I do not think myself authorised to trouble you with bad spelling, bad grammar, or, *if I can help* it, bad sense. Everything of this kind I must therefore beg you to pardon, and, at the same time, to remember that whenever you will take the trouble to point them out to me I shall think myself obliged to you.

"We depend upon seeing you at Christmas.

"Yours affectionately,

"S. HILL.

"Saturday night, 11 o'clock."

My mother's maiden name was Lea. Her grandmother was a woman of sterling character. She had been left an orphan when a child, and was heiress to a considerable property, but her relations trying to force her to marry against her inclination,

she quitted their home, renouncing at the same
time all claim to her fortune.   In the course of time
she married a man named Davenport, and settled in
Birmingham.

Mrs. Davenport lost her life through her heroic
exertions at the time of a fever epidemic in Birmingham.   Her eldest daughter showed herself
worthy of such a mother by her devoted care of
her younger brothers and sister.   She married a
Mr. William Lea, and died before I was born ; but
my grandfather, William Lea, I can distinctly remember.   Near his house there was a sheet of
water called the " Moat," which surrounded an old
mansion.   It was associated in my mind with a
brave act on the part of my grandfather.   Some
years before my birth, William Lea happened to be
passing, when he saw an angry mob throw an old
woman into the moat, in the belief that she was
a witch.   In an instant he forced his way through
the brutal crowd, plunged into the water, and
rescued the forlorn creature.   He was a powerful
man, and the mob made no resistance.   Mr. Lea
took the poor woman to his own house and nursed
her till she had recovered from the effects of her
ill-usage.

My mother inherited her parents' strong character.   While yet a child she gave proof of

courage and sagacity. She was one day on a visit at a lady's house when a violent thunderstorm took place. Clothes were hanging out in the garden to dry, and the lady peremptorily ordered one of her maid-servants to go and fetch them in. The maid, though terror-stricken, prepared to obey; but my mother, pitying her, volunteered to go herself. Not being tall enough to reach the clothes, she was compelled to climb up the tree, to which the line was fastened, in order to let it down. She had scarcely reached the ground in safety, when the tree was struck.

When nursing her mother, who was very ill, the little girl was about to pour out some medicine, when she perceived something strange either in the look or smell of the drug. This she mentioned to her mother, but the latter, being in much pain, said impatiently, "Oh, it is sure to be all right, child; give it me at once." On this, her daughter began reluctantly to pour out the medicine; but the little delay, caused by her prudent hesitation, probably saved her mother's life. At that instant a great noise was heard in the hall, which at once arrested attention, and the doctor, rushing upstairs and into the sick-room, cried out, "Stop!" and, snatching up the glass and bottle, declared the medicine to be poison. It appeared that his assistant, who had compounded it, had made some great mistake, which fortunately the doctor had discovered just in time.

My mother, who was distinguished for her common sense, always encouraged us, even as young children, to overcome timidity. She advised us, when we saw anything at night which was alarming, to go up to it and touch it. This would soon prove to us that there was no cause for fear. As a child, she herself had acted in the spirit of her own instructions. On one occasion a member of a Roman Catholic family told her that on Christmas Eve, at midnight, the cows went down on their knees. The little girl determined to ascertain the truth of this statement. When the next Christmas Eve arrived she sat up till twelve o'clock, and then went out boldly into an adjoining field to watch the proceedings of the cows.

When my mother grew up she became, for a time, nursery governess to a family named Anderton, who treated her with affection and respect. One day, during the Birmingham riots, she was driving with the children in an open carriage, when they were stopped by a party of the rioters, who insisted on her calling out, "Church and King!" This, however, as she was a staunch Liberal and

Nonconformist, she refused to do, upon which some of the men assumed a menacing attitude ; but one of them, who seemed to be in authority, called out, " Leave her alone ! She is a brave young woman ;" and the carriage was suffered to pass unmolested.

Soon after the termination of the riots she was married to my father, Thomas Wright Hill. They lived at Birmingham for a few years, then removed to Kidderminster, and later on to the neighbourhood of Wolverhampton, where they occupied a farmhouse, called " Horsehills," which my father had been able to get on low terms owing to the place having the reputation of being haunted.

My father was acting as manager of a brass foundry in Wolverhampton, and in that capacity had to dismiss a bad workman. The man came one evening to the house and asked for Mr. Hill, and the servant showed him into the parlour, where my father and mother were sitting. The man complained of his dismissal in a surly, dogged tone, and his angry manner alarmed my mother. Looking keenly at him, she noticed something shining in the breast of his coat, and discovered it to be the muzzle of a pistol. With ready presence of mind she turned to my father and asked him to go upstairs and look at the baby, who she fancied was

crying.   Directly he had quitted the room my
mother seized the man by the collar, and exclaiming,
" You villain ! " pushed him out of the parlour,
down the passage, and out of the house.   He was
taken so completely by surprise that he attempted
no resistance.

In the year 1801 our family quitted Wolverhampton and returned to Birmingham, with a view
to my father succeeding his friend, Mr. Clark, in
the management of a school, an occupation better
suited to his tastes and powers than that in which
he had hitherto been engaged.   He took the house
called Hilltop, which I have already mentioned as
my birthplace.

The removal from Wolverhampton to Birmingham and the change in my father's occupation were
measures taken on the advice of my mother, who
in this, as in many other matters, showed the
sagacity for which she was distinguished.   My
father's income being small and our family
numerous, her whole energy came into play in
keeping us all in comfort and respectability.   When
we children were old enough to judge, it was a
matter of wonder to us how she had accomplished
this task.   It was from her that we inherited our
ambition to conquer difficulties and to improve our
position in the world; for my father, although a

man of much talent, originality, and patriotism, certainly was not ambitious.

An amusing instance of the family wish to be foremost was given by Edwin and Rowland when children. They determined that their house should be the first in the square to open its shutters, and the watchman once found them in the road accomplishing this feat at three o'clock in the morning!

In proof of my father's originality, I may state that he was the first person to propose the plan for securing to minorities their fair share of Parliamentary representation. This plan has become known as Hare's system. I have every reason to believe that Mr. Hare (with whom I was personally acquainted) and my father came to the same conclusion independently of one another. The reader will find a detailed account of my father's plan in the " Life of Sir Rowland Hill," by his nephew, Dr. Birkbeck Hill.

My father was also the first to propose the principle on which the present patent law is based, viz. the payment of a moderate sum for a monopoly during a certain small period, with a further payment for any prolongation of the period. My brother Matthew explained this principle to Lord Brougham, who became its strong supporter.

CHAPTER II.

1805–1815.

ONE of the first things that I can remember is being in a go-cart, and attempting to follow my nurse down the cellar steps, and rolling over and over till I reached the bottom. I was much frightened, but fortunately little hurt.

I can also recollect at a very early age riding on my father's back as he swam to an island in a piece of water called "Roach Pool."

The next thing which I recall to mind is an adventure with our butcher's horse. The animal, while tied at our gate waiting for his master, had been teased and pelted with stones by street-boys. I toddled out of the house, and the irritated horse seized me with his teeth and lifted me into the air. I seem to have done the best thing I could, for I vigorously pummelled his nose, which caused him to drop me. On hearing my cries my mother ran to my assistance, and found the skin of my chest torn and bleeding, but happily no deeper injury was inflicted.

Another of my early recollections is being taken by my nurse to see the new police cells then in course of building. In playfulness I was put into one of them, and thus placed for a moment in a position in which I had, in after-life as an inspector of prisons, to visit thousands of criminals.

In the year 1810 the Jubilee of King George III. was celebrated. I can recollect our school having a whole holiday on the occasion. It is remarkable that I have lived to see another Royal Jubilee, that of our gracious Queen Victoria.

My father used to give lectures occasionally on natural philosophy, and although a young child, I was able to take great pleasure in them. The lectures were delivered sometimes in our schoolroom, sometimes at the Philosophical Institute. My brother Rowland acted as assistant on these occasions. It was he who prepared the diagrams, and when electricity was the subject he employed an electrical machine of his own construction.

I have a clear recollection of one effective experiment. The model of a church was placed before us with a lightning conductor attached to the spire.   Presently an imitation thunder-cloud passed over the church, but the church stood safe.   Then the conductor was removed and the thunder-cloud was again brought in contact with the spire, which this time fell in ruins before us.

On another occasion my brother delighted us by a mimic volcano.

Again the electrical machine was used to illustrate my father's lectures on astronomy.   I well remember seeing the constellations of Orion, the Great Bear, and Cassiopeia's Chair alternately represented by tiny sparks of light.

One night, after delivering a lecture at the Philosophical Institute, my father brought some scientific friends home to supper.   The night was dark, and he volunteered to lead the way ; but being absorbed in the contemplation and discussion of some astronomical appearance, he led the whole party into the waters of " Tycell's Pit," a horsepond in our neighbourhood !

At the time I am writing of England was at war with France, and the pressgang was in full force. " Men were kidnapped, literally disappeared, and nothing was ever heard of them again.   The street of a busy town was not safe from such pressgang captures, nor yet were dwellers in the country more secure, so great was the press for

men to serve in the navy after every great naval
victory." It was no wonder that the pressgang
inspired terror. Well do I remember my dread
of it. My mother used to send me sometimes on
errands into Birmingham, and sometimes I went on
business of my own, such as the purchase of seeds
or plants for my little garden, of which I was very
fond. I used to run all the way to the shop and all
the way back again, fearing lest a pressgang officer
might pounce upon me at every turn. I did not
know that I was far too young to be thought of as
their prey. I have no recollection of mentioning
my fear to any one. Had I done so it would have
been quickly relieved. I have since learnt that
children frequently endure terror in silence.

When I was about eight or nine years old I had
an attack of chicken-pox, and was sent afterwards
for change of air to our relatives the Wagstaffs at
Kidderminster. The Wagstaffs were kind, but,
after a time, I found their house rather dull, and
became wishful to return home. But how was
this to be accomplished? The cheapest mode of
transit was by the "Caravan," which plied between
Kidderminster and Birmingham. The fare was
a shilling. As my cash in hand amounted to only
threepence or fourpence, the question was how to
raise the difference. After some consideration I

thought I saw a possible way out of my difficulty. The family were in the habit of playing cards in the evening. Pope Joan was their favourite game —with small stakes. I joined the game, venturing my halfpence with extreme caution till I had made up my shilling, and then firmly declined any further risk. The following morning before the household were awake I slid out, took my seat in the " Caravan," paid my shilling, and arrived at home, to the astonishment of my family!

I have to confess yet another instance of childish gambling. I started a little lottery for my school-fellows, the prizes consisting of small prints placed between the leaves of a book. Each boy who paid a halfpenny was permitted to insert a pin into the closed book, and if in so doing he happened to divide the leaves at the place where I had inserted a print, the print was his. I little thought then of the condemnation with which, later in life, I should regard such gambling practices.

Another and more legitimate plan by which I contrived to make a little money was the formation of a small library, the books of which I let out at a cheap rate to my companions. But my grand resource was a bank. All unconscious as I was of the laws then existing against usury, I advanced little sums of money to my schoolfellows at high interest.

The family being in narrow circumstances, we children had but little pocket-money, and had to eke out our small incomes by work and contrivance. My dear mother, who held the family purse, used to give me a small allowance for sweeping the schoolroom and also for cleaning shoes.

Another duty assigned to me was that of cleaning the chimneys by setting fire to them ; no fear then existing of police interference, or of a race of fire-engines for a reward. Our house, as I have already mentioned, was on the top of a hill, and my ambition was to have all the chimneys on fire at the same time, so that the conflagration might be seen from a great distance.

I remember on one occasion during Christmas-time going out on my own account to sing carols in the streets of Birmingham, and thereby earning some pence, which I brought home with no small pride.

My sister Caroline (three years older than myself) and I saved up our money for many months, and at last were able to purchase Miss Edgeworth's " Parent's Assistant." Our edition consisted of six small volumes, half-bound, and cost fifteen shillings. We procured it by order from London, and its arrival gave us unbounded satisfaction. This work, together with many others by the same author, have given me unceasing pleasure throughout my long life. I have lately reperused the story of "Simple Susan," which in this, my eighty-eighth year, I have read with the fullest enjoyment.* I rejoice to say that the love of Miss Edgeworth's stories is inherited both by my children and grand-children.

Another favourite of my childhood was Mrs. Barbauld's "Hymns in Prose." I recollect, how-ever, that in one of them a difficulty occurred to me. The author speaks of a united family where "if one is sick they mourn together, if one is happy they rejoice together." What would they do, I thought, if one were sick and another happy at the same time ?

When I was about ten years old I had one of the greatest disappointments I ever experienced. During the long wars fast-days were appointed, and these fast-days served as general holidays. For one of these it had been arranged that a barge full of holiday-makers (including myself) was to go by canal to a place called Tarlibig, where a lift had been constructed to serve the purpose of a lock. An interesting part of this journey was to be the passage of the barge through a long tunnel, where there was no towing-path, and where

* This was written in 1890.—ED.

boats were propelled by men lying on their backs and pushing with their feet against the roof. It was summer-time, and we were to start early in the morning, and to be out all day. Each family had got ready its share of provisions, and I remember starting from home in high expectation. At the gates of the wharf, however, we were met by the dismal tidings that an order had been received from the canal committee forbidding the excursion. No reason was given for this order; and it was not till a considerable time afterwards that it was found to be religious intolerance, the canal directors having learnt that many of the intending excursionists were Dissenters.

In the year 1813 the East India Company's monopoly of the importation of tea was abolished. I remember the matter being much talked of, and people expressing great alarm at the possible effects of the change. It was believed that the " Hong merchants," as they were called, would be ruined, and the tea trade annihilated. Many were the groanings over all this ; but the monopoly ceased, and from that day no more was heard of the wrongs of the Hong merchants. With this exception the East India Company continued to enjoy the monoply of trade with the East till the passing of the Reform Bill of 1832.

The winter of 1813–14 was marked by a long and hard frost—the longest and most severe I can remember. It began early in December and continued till the following March. The Thames was frozen over, and so thick was the ice that an ox was roasted whole upon it.

Near our house (Hilltop) there was a little smithy, to which I often went in the evening to watch the blacksmith at his work, though his business consisted only of the monotonous occupation of making spurs. The interest which children take in watching any creative work has often impressed me with the idea that provision should be made for their having regular opportunities of witnessing such processes. Formerly, I believe, more artisan's work was carried on in the open air in England than is now the case; but I was much pleased when paying a visit to Antwerp to see the people working both in their shops and in the streets, and this with a neatness in their persons, materials, and tools which made me imagine I was witnessing a theatrical performance!

How well I remember—as who does not?—my first going to the play. The piece was *Macbeth*, and it may be judged how young I must have been when I state that, looking down from the gallery, I supposed the actors to be all of them children.

I now began to read Shakespeare for myself. My eldest brother Matthew expressed surprise and satisfaction at finding me so employed, but his pleasure was somewhat modified by my remarking "that I left out all the long speeches"!

It is curious how a trifling circumstance will sometimes remain fixed in the memory. One day when Rowland had taken me for a long ramble, and we were trudging home somewhat tired, we were overtaken by a gentleman in a chaise. He pulled up his horse and asked us if we should like to have a lift. We gladly accepted his offer, and during the drive had a good deal of pleasant talk with him. When we reached the place where we had to alight we thanked the stranger for his kindness, whereupon he answered, "Pray don't thank me; I would not have been deprived of the pleasure of your company for a *shilling!*" We thought this a great compliment, and were much gratified.

Shenstone's Leasowes, or *the* Leasowes, as we always called it, was a place of delight to me. It is situated about six miles from Birmingham, on the way to Hagley. The undulating ground was well suited to the poet's purpose, and Shenstone showed himself a true lover of nature, as well as a first-rate landscape gardener, by the way in which he arranged his grounds. The place abounded in beautiful walks, babbling streams, waterfalls, grottoes, and pretty points of view, where seats were placed for the convenience of visitors. Some of the seats had well-chosen lines of poetry placed over them, others were dedicated to Shenstone's friends.

I never inquired as to the extent of the Leasowes, for I should have regarded such an inquiry as an attempt to reduce poetry to prose. Moreover, there was nothing in the place to suggest such an inquiry, for though no artifice was apparent, no boundary could be seen.

Excursions to the Leasowes, with some of my brothers, sisters, and schoolfellows, carrying our dinner with us and spending the whole day there, were always looked forward to and enjoyed with a keen relish.

The following epitaph on Shenstone was said to have been written by a Frenchman :—

> " Beneath this plain stone
> Lies William Shenstone ;
> His Leasowes *rurals*
> Give *récréations plurals.*"

I well recollect witnessing the ascent of an air-balloon from Birmingham Heath, where a great crowd had assembled to see so unusual a sight.

The aeronaut was a Mr. Sadler, possibly the same whose balloon in 1785 was the first to ascend from Birmingham. The day was fine, and the appearance of the balloon, as it rose up into the air, with the sun shining upon it, was to me grand and beautiful. Its safe descent was announced to us some hours later by the arrival of a messenger in a post-chaise and four.

Dr. Darwin has well described such a scene in his " Botanic Garden," when speaking of Mont-golfier's balloon—

> "So on the shoreless air the intrepid Gaul
> Launched the vast concave of his buoyant ball ;
> Journeying on high the silken castle glides
> Bright as a meteor through the azure tides."

My brother Arthur (five years older than myself) and I slept in the same dormitory. After we were all in bed he used frequently to relate one of the tales in the " Arabian Nights' Entertainment." He told the stories well, and we were all much interested; so much so that it was a wonder to me, when his voice became drowsy, how such stirring matter could possibly allow of his being inclined for sleep!

My chief companions and schoolfellows, besides my youngest brother Howard, were Edmund Clark, Howard Luckock, and Samuel Thornton. Edmund Clark was a boy of talent and genuine humour, and was a general favourite.   He became, ultimately, a barrister with prospects of success, but illness undermined his constitution and brought him to an early grave.   Howard Luckock and Samuel Thornton were kind-hearted and pleasant companions.   Both lived to an advanced age, but of all the four I am the only survivor.

When I was about twelve years old, some plays written by Arthur were performed in our large schoolroom.   The scenery, which I remember regarding with great admiration, was designed and painted by Rowland.   I recollect, especially, a skeleton wood scene which I was employed to cut out.

On one occasion we acted Miss Edgeworth's spirited drama of *Eton Montem*.   The part of " Talbot" was taken by Samuel Beale, who afterwards became distinguished in relation to railways and as member of Parliament for Derby.   The part of " Rory O'Ryan " was assigned to Edmund Clark.   I myself played that of " Wheeler."

My mother had occasion, at rare intervals, to go to London.   When on one of these visits she joined a party of friends in a boating excursion upon the Thames.   In those days old London Bridge was still standing.   Its arches were numerous and very narrow; their piers, consequently,

much impeded the passage of the stream, so that
at mean tide the water rushed through them with
great velocity. The watermen were proud of accomplishing the feat of "shooting London Bridge,"
but the danger of such an undertaking can readily
be imagined. Indeed, there is an old proverb to
the effect that "London Bridge was made for wise
men to go over, and fools to go under."

My mother suddenly became aware, when it was
too late for remonstrance, that they were fast
approaching one of its narrow arches. At the
same moment she observed the boatman take
from his breast a "caul," the sailor's charm
against drowning. Her usual courage did not
forsake her. She sat calm and collected till the
danger was past. I well recollect her relating this
adventure.

Margate and Aberystwyth were the two seaside places of resort most accessible, in those days,
from Birmingham. My mother visited both occasionally with some of the children. The journey
from London to Margate was performed by water
in the Margate *Hoy*, as the vessel was called. If
the wind were adverse, the journey frequently
occupied as much as three days or even more; the
captain always carrying provisions for that time.
I have heard my mother speak of the monotonous

cry of the seaman as he reported the soundings—
" Five fathoms and a large half twain."

My mother had a decided taste for music, but
the only indulgence of this taste she allowed
herself was attendance at the triennial Musical
Festivals in Birmingham. These she greatly
enjoyed.

I well recollect the publication of " Waverley,"
the first of Walter Scott's admirable series of novels,
in the autumn of 1814. My uncle Thomas Lea,
who lived in Scotland, used to send us the books
as they appeared. They came by sea (the cheapest
mode of transit). As soon as they arrived they
were read aloud to eager listeners.

Another event connected with the year 1814
stands out clear in my memory; this was the
general rejoicings in Birmingham in honour of the
peace concluded by the allied powers upon
Napoleon's abdication at Fontainebleau, previous to
his being sent as a prisoner to the Island of Elba.
The whole town was illuminated, and we boys did
what we could on the occasion. My brother
Rowland prepared a transparency, which was put
up in front of our house with lights behind it. If
I remember rightly, it represented the figure of
Britannia.

The peace, as is well known, was of but short

duration. Napoleon made his escape from Elba, and the episode of the hundred days ensued.

The very name of "Boney" had long been a bugbear to me and my young companions. I could gather from the conversation of the elders that there was always an apprehension of invasion, and preparations for such an event went on around me. A stout band of volunteers was being formed in Birmingham, and my father had all his pupils, as well as his own sons, drilled; for he considered it the duty of every man and boy in the united kingdom to qualify himself to defend his country. I used to hear many expressions of defiance of the French, and of faith in the patriotism and courage of the English.

Well do I remember the arrival in Birmingham of the news of the victory of Waterloo. Every one was aware that a great battle must be taking place, and while the result was yet unknown, we were all on the tiptoe of eager expectation. On the morning of the day when decisive news was expected, many people stationed themselves far out on the London road to get the first view of the approaching mail-coach. When at last it dashed into Birmingham, covered with waving boughs of laurel, there was a great shout of joy and triumph.

It is difficult, in our present times of peace, to

realize how long those wars had lasted, and what a relief to the whole country was caused by their termination.

I remember my father's telling me, when he was about seventy years of age, that during one half of his whole life this country had been at war.

By one of the many changes which have taken place since I was a boy, Birmingham has been relieved of the necessity of sending its prisoners for trial to Warwick.   In those days, and indeed till long afterwards, one might hear boys in the streets, at the close of the Assizes, calling out, "Here's a full, true, and particular account of all the criminal prisoners that *was* tried, cast, quit, and condemned before my Lord Judge at Warwick 'Sizes!"

In the year 1815 I saw two men standing in the pillory in the Birmingham market-place.

It was several years later than the period I am writing of that I went to see Warwick Gaol.   In the large yard, where the prisoners passed most of the day, I beheld a considerable number of men walking about, unemployed, and all of them in chains.   There was a dungeon many feet beneath this yard, where the wretched prisoners passed the night still in chains.

During times of dearth bread riots were common, followed by attacks on bakers, hucksters, and farmers. On one occasion there was a curious attempt of the mob to fix the rate of prices. A body of men seized on the loads of potatoes brought into the Birmingham market, and their leaders, having fixed on a price which they considered proper, though much below the actual value, they sold all the potatoes accordingly, and handed over the proceeds to the owners. The result of this proceeding was that for a whole month afterwards not another potato was brought to the Birmingham market, and the article could not be obtained at any price.

Rick-burning and the destruction of machinery were of frequent occurrence. An ignorance of political economy which led, in part, to these offences was not confined to the class which made the attacks, for it disgraced the Statute Book, as shown by the law declaring the practice of "fore-stalling and regrating" (buying goods on the way to market and reselling them) to be illegal. The judges, when passing sentence on any one convicted of these practices, used to dwell on the enormity of the prisoner's offence.

In my youth there lived, on Birmingham Heath, a man named Booth, who, to the knowledge of every one, carried on the trade of uttering false money, both coins and banknotes. The feeble police had several times attempted his arrest, but in vain.   He had built himself a house which he had strongly fortified, and it was not till a detachment of cavalry was brought into action that his career was stopped, and he was brought to trial, convicted, and hanged.

In 1817 a murder was committed in Birmingham which excited a widespread sensation.   On the 26th of May, a beautiful young woman named Mary Ashford, in her twentieth year, went to a dance at Erdington without proper protection.   She left the festive scene at a late hour, accompanied by a young man named Abraham Thornton, a farmer's son in the neighbourhood.   They were last seen talking together at a stile, but next morning she was found dead in a pit of water ; and there were fearful evidences that she had been murdered.   General suspicion pointing to Thornton ; he was arrested and tried for murder at Warwick Assizes in August ; but, though strong circumstantial evidence was given against him, the defence, which was an *alibi*, obtained a verdict of " Not guilty."   The feeling of surprise and indignation at his acquittal was so intense that a new trial was called for, and an appeal was entered against the verdict by William Ashford, the brother and next of kin to the murdered girl.   Thornton was again apprehended and sent to London in November, to be tried before Ellenborough and the full Court of Queen's Bench. Instead of regular defence in arguments, evidences, and witnesses, Thornton boldly defied all present modes of jurisdiction, and claimed his right, according to ancient custom, to challenge his accuser to fight him, and decide his innocence or guilt by the "Wager of Battel." His answer to the question of the court was, "Not guilty, and I am ready to defend the same by my body." He accompanied these words by the old act of taking off his glove and throwing it down upon the floor of the court. At this stage of the proceedings, William Ashford, who was in court, actually came forward, and was about to accept the challenge by picking up the glove, when he was kept back by those about him.

With what wonder did the assembly, and indeed the nation, ask, "Can a prisoner insist upon so obsolete a mode of trial in such a time of light as the nineteenth century?" But with greater wonder and regret was the judgment of the court received; for, after several adjournments, it was decided in April, 1818, that the law of England was in favour of "Wager of Battel;" that the old law sanctioning it had never been repealed; and that, though this mode of trial had become obsolete, it must be allowed. Thornton was therefore set at liberty.

At the beginning of the next Session of Parlia-

ment, the Attorney-General brought in a bill for the
abolition of this monstrous process of " Wager of
Battel," which of course was passed.

William Ashford lived till 1867, a strange link
with the Middle Ages and their romancers.

CHAPTER III.

1816-1824.

THE year 1816 was very wet and bad for agriculture. The corn did not ripen properly, and I can remember that our bread was marked by streaks, showing its unwholesome quality. The price of wheat rose to a hundred shillings the quarter. Great distress prevailed, greater than can be readily imagined in these days of free trade and easy access to the stores of foreign countries. But a new hope was gradually gaining around—the hope of Parliamentary Reform. Far off indeed, seemed the possibility of its accomplishment, but many stout-hearted men were working for that end.

Hampden Clubs had already been formed in almost every town of importance, with the express object of fostering a desire for reform and educating the people in politics. This was not done, however, without violent opposition from the Tories, and on February 17, 1817, a Secret Committee of the House of Commons urged Government to break up the clubs. The time, however, for such arbitrary acts had passed by, and the clubs were not interfered with.

The members of the Birmingham Hampden Club, of which Mr. George Edmonds was chairman, sent a requisition to the High Bailiff of Birmingham on the 20th of January, to call a meeting of the inhabitants to

" declare to the Legislature the unexampled distress in which the people were involved, and to petition that every practical retrenchment in the national expenditure might be made as a mode of present alleviation, and that a Reform in the House of Commons should be instituted without further delay as the best security against similar calamities in future."

The High Bailiff refused to call the meeting. The members then began to consider the question as to whether they should call the meeting on their own responsibility. No large gathering had taken place in Birmingham since the riots of 1791, when the popular feeling was fiercely anti-democratic. Could the people be trusted, at a time of national distress and excitement, to maintain order?

I well remember Mr. George Edmonds coming to our house to talk the matter over with my father and my elder brothers, and their all being strongly in favour of holding the meeting. Soon afterwards it was convened in an announcement, which was preceded by a copy of the requisition, to the following effect:—

"The High Bailiff having refused to comply with the above requisition, we, the undersigned inhabitants of Birmingham, do invite our fellow-townsmen to meet on Wednesday next, January 22, 1817, on the open ground to the left of St. Paul's Square, called Newhall Hill, to take into consideration the important objects of the requisition.

"The chair will be taken at twelve o'clock."

Here follow forty-eight signatures; among them is that of my brother Edwin.

The meeting was held, and although it was attended by a great concourse of people, no disorder occurred. I can recall the striking effect of the sea of black hats as seen from the speakers' platform. Mr. Edmonds, as well as many other friends of Reform, spoke eloquently and were listened to with a profound attention broken only by cheers. A petition in favour of Parliamentary Reform was adopted, and ordered to be presented to the House of Commons

by Peter Moore and Joseph Butterworth, members
for Coventry.

Two years later a still more important meeting
was held by the Reformers on Newhall Hill.   This
took place on the 20th of July, 1819.   The leaders
on this occasion were Major Cartwright, Messrs.
Edmonds, Wooler, Maddocks, and Lewis.   A resolution was passed to elect Sir Charles Wolseley
as the "legislatorial attorney and representative"
in Parliament of the town of Birmingham.   This
was done as a protest against the gross injustice
of leaving large towns unrepresented, while a great
portion of the House of Commons was elected by
close and rotten boroughs.   Wooler, in the course
of his speech, observed

"that their petitions had hitherto been easily disposed
of, but that by embodying the principle and sending up Sir
Charles Wolseley instead of the petition, the task of the
honourable House would not be quite so easy.   They will
not," he added, " be able to lay Sir Charles so quietly upon
the table nor under the table."

Sir Charles Wolseley accepted the post offered
to him.   The Government became alarmed, and
resolved to prosecute Major Cartwright and his
friends for sedition.   Meanwhile, at a great meeting
held in Peter's Field, Manchester, a most arbitrary
act was perpetrated by the yeomanry in firing upon

the assembled crowd, although no offence had been committed. Six persons were killed and a large number wounded. This was known afterwards as the " Manchester Massacre." It aroused a strong feeling of indignation throughout the country.

In the autumn of this same year (1819) my brother Matthew was "called" to the Bar. A few months later he was retained for the defence of Major Cartwright, who, together with the other leaders of the Newhall Hill meeting, was brought to trial on a charge of sedition. My brother was cautioned by some of his fellow-barristers that, if he accepted this retainer, he must give up all hope of rising in his profession, for he would always have the Bench against him. Matthew, however, acting on a feeling of duty, stood firm and accepted the proposed brief.

"The trial took place at Warwick at the summer assizes of 1820. The jury was, of course, special ; and such was the character attributed to these bodies, that Sir Francis Burdett had recently declared, 'according to the prevalent manner of constituting special juries, he believed that Abel would be convicted of the murder of Cain, if such were the issue proposed for trial.' It is not surprising, therefore, that, in spite of an eloquent defence on the part of the counsel for the accused, a verdict of 'guilty' was returned against all the defendants. The verdict was appealed against, and the case came on some months later before

the Court of King's Bench. Matthew's speech upon the
'infamous practice of packing juries' made a powerful impression. Finally, judgment was again given against the
defendants. Major Cartwright was fined a hundred
pounds without imprisonment, the others being sentenced
to various periods of detention in Warwick Gaol.

"Before he left the court, Major Cartwright produced
from one of the pockets of his waistcoat, which he wore of
an unusual size, a large canvas bag. From this he slowly
counted one hundred pounds in gold, observing that he
believed they were all '*good sovereigns.*'" *

In 1819 our family moved from Hilltop in Birmingham to the neighbouring village of Edgbaston.
I may here mention our various occupations at this
period. Edwin, who came next in age to Matthew,
posessed decided mechanical talent. He was aiding
our friend Mr. Phipson in the management of a
rolling-mill. Rowland and Arthur were engaged in
the school, while Caroline assisted her mother in
domestic affairs. I came next to Caroline. For
three years past I had been an assistant teacher.
On my reaching the mature age of thirteen, Rowland had decided that my schoolboy life must
come to an end, and that I must now assist in
the instruction of others ; such were the necessi-
ties of the family. In spite of my youth, I felt

---

* See "Memoir of M. D. Hill," by his daughters, R. and
F. Davenport Hill.

much interest in the school and in the improvements in its management which were introduced. At about the same age (thirteen or fourteen) I taught arithmetic in Miss Chubb's "School for Young Ladies." The girls worked separately, and I remember I walked round and overhauled their calculations. If they thought me an impudent fellow, they did not give vent to their opinion.

Younger than myself were my brother Howard, my special companion, and my sister Sarah. Both these, unhappily, died in early life.

At Edgbaston we had built a more commodious school-house, on plans made by Rowland, which we named Hazelwood; hence the appellation of the "Hazelwood System."

To Rowland is chiefly due the honour of founding the system. Its most prominent features were: (1) self-government and mutual responsibility; making the school, in fact, an enlightened republic; (2) fixed standards of merit instead of competition as a test of success; (3) the abolition of all arbitrary punishments (including corporal punishment), for which natural penalties were instituted.*

A striking instance of the good result of following a boy's natural bent was afforded in the case

---

* For detailed account of the Hazelwood System, see "Life of Sir Rowland Hill," by Dr. Birkbeck Hill.

of my friend, Mr. Follet Osler, F.R.S., the well-known glass manufacturer, a successful student of several branches of science, and the inventor of the anemometer. His father was wedded to the old plan of education, and wished his son's training to be purely classical ; but seeing the boy's scientific talents so much developed at Hazelwood, he happily abandoned his original plan.

The Honourable Montagu Villiers (afterwards Bishop of Durham) spoke, at the school distribution of testimonials in the year 1846, of his own impression of our system of education, and expressed great gratitude for its benefits. He said that

"when he first came to Hazelwood he had few thoughts beyond self ; that he found a very different feeling pervading the community of which he had suddenly become a member —the boys aiding one another, the elder ones assisting the younger, and all receiving constant assistance and kindness from the conductor and teachers. He learnt, for the first time, what responsibility was, and what powerful motives it might give to the performance of good acts."

In 1822 Matthew, assisted by Rowland and Arthur, brought out a book entitled " Public Education," which made the novel plans of our Hazelwood System generally known.

Matthew sent a copy to Jeremy Bentham, and so interested was the great philosopher in the work

that he invited the author to come and see him.
This was the more flattering, as Bentham's society
was sought by persons of distinction of all nations,
but few obtained access to him. From this time,
for four or five years, Matthew usually dined with
Bentham once a week.

"In conversation with his host he learnt that Bentham
obtained from Dr. Priestley the doctrine which he made the
basis of his writings, namely, that the object of all government and of all social institutions should be—' the greatest
happiness of the greatest number for the greatest length
of time.' " *

"Public Education" was reviewed largely by
the newspapers and magazines of the day, but an
article which appeared in the *Edinburgh Review*
was especially instrumental in arousing a keen
interest in our school. The book was translated
into several foreign languages.

"The result was that crowds of persons came from the
Continent and from all parts of the British Isles to inspect
the school, some of whom remained many days on the
spot, or returned again and again to familiarize themselves
with the system it described. New institutions, on the
model of Hazelwood, were established. One of these,
opened in the neighbourhood of Stockholm—named, after
the founders of Hazelwood, ' Hillska Skola '—acquired

---

* See " Memoir of M. D. Hill."

high repute. Pupils from abroad, then far more rare in England than at the present day, sought admission at Hazelwood. Through Bentham's influence several youths were sent from Greece to be trained in the principles of liberty. Many came also from the new Republic of South America, then throwing off the bonds of Spain." *

We had, indeed, applications to receive many more pupils than it was possible for us to accommodate.

Taking the names of some of the visitors to Hazelwood, as well as I can recollect, in the order of their arrival, they were Mr. Thelwall, Mr. Hone, the poet Campbell, De Quincey, Wilberforce, Joseph Hume, Lord Clarendon, Mr. and Mrs. Grote, and Ramahoun Roy.

Mr. Thelwall told us the story of his trial for high treason, his life depending on the issue. He described the eagerness with which he scanned the face of each juryman as he ascended the steps to the jury-box, and his sudden feeling of relief and security as he saw one whose open, honest, and intelligent countenance satisfied him that *he* would be no party to an unjust verdict.

Mr. Hone, well known for his parodies and political caricatures, was an excellent narrator, and he thrilled us all by his account of Eliza Fenning (a poor housemaid, charged with an attempt to

* See " Memoir of M. D. Hill."

poison her mistress), her trial before the Recorder of London, John Sylvester (known by the sobriquet of " Black Jack "), her conviction on the flimsiest evidence, and her condemnation and execution.

It will be remembered that Hone himself was brought to trial on a charge of blasphemy in relation to his parodies. The presiding judge on the first day's trial was Mr. Justice Abbot, who was mild and fair ; but on a verdict of " Not guilty " being returned, the imperious Chief Justice, Lord Ellenborough, took his place, in the full expectation, probably, that he should be able to bully the jury into a verdict of "Guilty." He treated Hone with haughty sternness, not even allowing him to sit down, although he was ill, and had to conduct his own case. This circumstance, however, Hone declared, so roused his indignation as to give him, for the time, unwonted strength. The result of the second day's trial was again a verdict of " Not guilty ; " and when the Government, in despair, abandoned the case, it was stated that Lord Ellenborough felt deeply mortified, and took the matter so much to heart that his health was affected. Letters written at this time by Lord Ellenborough to Lord Sidmouth bear out this theory. In any case, there is no doubt that a year afterwards Lord Ellenborough died. His funeral procession, curiously enough, passed by Hone's house on the anniversary of the trial, and it was reported that Hone rose from his seat and let down the blinds.

In later life Hone became a zealous Methodist.

De Quincey, who wrote an excellent review on "Public Education" in the *London Magazine*, also visited Hazelwood.

The venerable Wilberforce, whose noble and careworn countenance I well remember, was principally attracted by the extent of freedom which was allowed to the boys.

Thomas Campbell dined one day at our house. Something in the course of conversation caused my father to quote his guest's well-known line—

"Coming events cast their shadows before,"

observing at the same time that it had always struck him as a beautiful conception, both true in fact and highly poetic. Campbell responded that he considered that line as one of the best, if not the very best, he had ever written. Glancing at Sir Walter Scott's "Life," I see that he too admired this particular line; and quoting it to Washington Irving, said, "What a grand idea is that!"

Campbell delivered a series of lectures in Birmingham. One of these I heard, and greatly enjoyed. Among the auditors on that occasion was Maria Edgeworth, whom I then, for the only time in my life, had the pleasure of seeing. A few years later her friend, Captain Basil Hall, visited Hazelwood, and gave the boys an interesting lecture upon the nature of the trade-winds, introducing a spirited account of some of his adventures at sea.

About this period we had become acquainted with Colonel Nichol. This gentleman had seen a great deal of service, having been in more than a hundred battles. He had travelled so much as to have visited almost every part of the world. He had been governor of Ascension Island, which was garrisoned when Napoleon was a prisoner at St. Helena. The island was without water, but Colonel Nichol, by boring through the rock, obtained a good supply. To this day ships call at Ascension Island for water. New Zealand he knew well—a country at that time very little frequented. He spoke highly of its qualifications as a place of residence, especially with regard to climate, being free from all extremes of heat and cold. So much, indeed, had he been struck with the advantages of the country, that he, together with some fellow-officers, determined, if possible, to make a settlement there. At the close of the great continental war in 1815, Colonel Nichol and his friends made

an application to Government for a very moderate
sum of ready money to enable them to carry out
their project, undertaking at the same time, in
lieu of this, to forego their claims to half-pay. But
"red-tapism," which even now has not ceased to
exist, caused their offer to be curtly refused. Had
it been accepted it would have caused a material
saving to the Government.

Another of our acquaintances was Dr. Blair,
whose character was a counterpart, to some extent,
of "Forester," in Miss Edgeworth's admirable
story bearing that name. His mother was a lady
of property, who kept a closed carriage, a luxury
which was then very uncommon in Birmingham.
She wished her son to ride in it, but he always
preferred walking, trudging along with his sturdy
stick, or rather club. His mother sometimes gave
directions to her coachman to walk the horses by
his side, in the hope that, for very shame, he would
get into the carriage ; but this he persistently
refused to do.

On one occasion, when we were desirous of
assisting a friend in obtaining some medical appointment, we applied to Dr. Blair to compose our
circular. He good-naturedly undertook the task,
but his scholarly precision soon brought him to a
standstill. He confessed he could not make up his

mind whether at one part of the document he should use the word "that" or the word "which." As despatch was important, one of us was obliged to take the work from the doctor's hands.

Dr. Blair was a great chess-player, as was also my father, and the two used sometimes to play together far into the night. Indeed, on one occasion, when the servant came downstairs in the morning to open the shutters, she found the two gentlemen, wholly unaware of the passage of time, still engrossed in their game.

Another anecdote connected with my father we heard from an intimate friend of the elder Charles Matthews, named Hamilton Reynolds. It was Mr. Matthews' practice, when performing in his "At Homes," to look round the theatre for some especially responsive listener. He told Mr. Reynolds that there had been an elderly gentleman in the Birmingham Theatre who showed the keenest enjoyment, and had a remarkably hearty and sonorous laugh. He added, "I could act anything to that old gentleman. I would give him five pounds a night if he would come always." On comparing time and place, the "old gentleman" proved to be my father.

Our family were acquainted with the celebrated Dr. Parr. I was very young at that time, but I

remember once to have seen him. My eldest
brother, who knew him best, used to tell us of his
sayings and doings. The doctor was a great
stickler for the observance of old customs, and, in
virtue of this feeling, he always had an assembly of
his parishioners in the grounds of his rectory on
May Day, and there was much dancing round the
Maypole and other amusements, the doctor being
always present and a delighted observer. On one
of these occasions he was seated with a tankard of
ale before him, and he called to a little chimney-
sweep and said, "Tell the people Dr. Parr drinks
their good health;" upon which the little fellow
mounted on a chair and piped at the top of his
voice, "People! people! me and Dr. Parr drinks
your good health!"

On another occasion, at a dinner-party, a young
minister having spoken in disparaging terms of
Hume, the historian, Dr. Parr called to Mr. Joseph
Parkes, "Joe, did you hear that? Don't tell
anybody!"

Dr. Parr stood up for the old practice of school-
flogging. At a large dinner-party the same young
man was laying down the law against it. The
doctor, unable to restrain himself, cried out, "Sir,
it is flogging which makes the scholar, it is flogging
which makes the soldier, it is flogging which makes

the statesman, and it is the *want* of flogging which makes you—what you are!"

But the best and most honourable of Dr. Parr's utterances was at a public dinner at Birmingham at the time of the riots of 1791. The toast of "Church and King" having been proposed, the doctor rose, and, turning his glass upside down, exclaimed in a loud voice, though the words might have cost him his life, "I will not drink that toast; it means a Church without the gospel, and a king above the law."

My brother Matthew, who had joined the Midland Circuit, used to regale us, from time to time, with stories of odd evidence, strange verdicts, mock-trials for breaches of professional etiquette, and the sayings and doings of Bench and Bar.

The senior barrister of the Midland Circuit was a King's Counsel named Clarke, a dull speaker, though he was often successful in gaining verdicts. In a trial in which he was engaged he thought that there ought to be a reference instead of the case being decided by the Court, but the solicitor came to say that his client would not agree to a reference. Upon this Mr. Clarke told the solicitor to bring the man to him, and then said to him, "Sir, you are a d—d fool, and if you don't consent to a reference I shall use *strong* language."

On one occasion Henry Brougham, having come

down to Warwick "Special," Mr. Clarke, who was opposed to him, had the temerity to make him the butt of his own poor wit. Brougham in reply began, "My lord, for a full half-hour have I been exposed to the shafts of my learned friend's wit, and that is no *laughing* matter."

Matthew used to tell a melancholy story of a series of lawsuits coming on year after year, which had their origin in a bitter feeling of hostility between the wives of the rector and the squire of the same parish, the two husbands being dragged into the fray. The first offence was given by the squire's lady, who, in speaking of a dinner at the rectory, described the soup-tureen as "scanty," an expression which was regarded by the rector's spouse as a reflection on her hospitality. The feud thus begun took various shapes. Sometimes the right to possess a small piece of valueless ground was contested, or some other matter equally contemptible; but, however worthless the cause, the disputants were continually coming into court. The poor rector was compelled to sell, one by one, almost every valuable possession, then, in effect, to mortgage his living, and finally was brought to utter ruin. The struggle ended in both rector and squire being confined in Northampton prison for debt at the suit of the solicitors.

CHAPTER IV.

1824–1830.

In the year 1824 I had a short tour in France with
my brother Rowland. We went first to Boulogne
to visit an old acquaintance, Monsieur Chevalier,
who had lived many years in Birmingham as a
teacher of French. Originally he had been brought
to England as a prisoner of war; but when the war
was over, and he was set at liberty, he came to live
at Birmingham, where, in due time, he fell in love
with an English lady and married her. This lady
had a claim to a valuable estate, and the prosecution
of this claim was one of the first lawsuits in which
my brother Matthew was engaged. The suit
continued long with varying success, but at last the
two parties concerned agreed to divide the property.

Monsieur Chevalier acquired a full knowledge of

our language, and became fluent in its use. He was even heard to declare that if he had to address an audience whom he wished to convince, he would rather speak to them in English than in French, owing to the greater force of the English language. This statement coming from a Frenchman was certainly remarkable.

While at Boulogne we went to see the column which Buonaparte, with the vanity and impudence which were two of his characteristics, had erected to commemorate his expected conquest of England. Desiring to ascend the edifice, we looked about for the person in charge, and found the following notice for the information of English travellers: "The keys of this column find themselves all around the corner."

At an inn not far from Paris the owner sold English stout, which was thus advertised: "Ici on vende le *strong*."

It would seem that the French are still content to make use of very imperfect English translations; for, more than forty years later than the period of which I am writing, a nephew of mine, when travelling in France, saw this notice put up in a railway carriage: "It is defended to put no heads and no hands out of no windows."

I was one day riding in a diligence when the

passengers, supposing that I did not understand their language, began to talk about me. One of them remarked that I was evidently a sulky Englishman, and that he would lay a wager that if we travelled together a hundred miles I should not utter a word. Preserving silence until we approached the place where I intended to alight, I suddenly gave them a volley of French. Their horror-stricken countenances and apparent efforts to recall what they had said were most amusing.

During our stay in Paris there was a debate in the Chamber of Deputies. We had no difficulty in procuring good seats, the accommodation for visitors being greatly superior to that provided in our own House of Commons. This was particularly the case, I observed, with regard to ladies.

When we entered financial matters were under consideration which seemed to excite little interest. Large sums of money were voted away with scarcely an observation; but at length the debate became personal, on the question of whether one of the speeches delivered should, or should not, be printed. All apathy at once disappeared, and gave way to an angry and animated discussion. Amongst those who offered themselves as speakers was the well-known politician, Benjamin Constant. He began to mount the steps of the rostrum, but, being old and lame, his progress was slow; meanwhile a younger deputy, opposed to him in politics, ran up the steps on the further side, got possession of the rostrum, and began to address the assembly. Poor Benjamin Constant, unable to get a hearing, was obliged to sit down on the steps he was climbing. Thus I lost the chance of hearing him speak.

Rowland and I called upon the Marquis Voyer d'Argenson, or, as he preferred to be called, Monsieur d'Argenson, who had recently, when in England, visited Hazelwood. He received us kindly, and afterwards introduced us to the family of the Duc de Broglie, into which he had married. He must, I presume, have been the son of the Voyer d'Argenson who, in an early stage of the French Revolution, was one of the moderate and wise leaders of what was then not a revolutionary but a reform movement.

At the time of our visit to Paris the Rue de la Paix was the only street which was provided with a footpath. At night the city was lighted by dim oil-lamps which were suspended by ropes across the streets.

A couple of years later I paid a second visit to France; this time in company with my brother Arthur. We went first to Guernsey and stayed a week or so with the head of the Civil Government

—the " Bailiff," as he is called—our able and enlightened friend, Mr. Daniel de Lisle Brock.

I was much struck with the happy signs of abundance, comfort, and contentment in the island; and I wrote a description of its social conditions, which afterwards appeared in the *Examiner* newspaper, and from which I quote the following :—

"Why is it that within so short a distance of places where the pining labourer is but half fed and half clad, the man of Guernsey should have a well-stored board and abundance of clothing? The climate is not peculiar; the land is not remarkably fertile. How is it, then, that Guernsey should be so much ahead in the career of happiness? *Guernsey has superior laws, superior institutions.* And the state of things is one among the thousand proofs that have been given, that the prosperity and happiness of a people are much more dependent on its laws, institutions, and the manner in which the government is carried on, than on climate and fertility of the soil. . . .

"One of the most striking changes which the visitor, whether from England or France, observes on his landing, is the entire absence of beggars. A tradesman, who had been established at St. Peter's Port for upwards of thirty years, assured me that during the whole period of his residence in the island he had never once seen a beggar. For myself I neither saw nor heard of one; and I was satisfied, from all I learned, that a beggar is in Guernsey a being of a past age, a creation of history—a fit subject for the speculations of the antiquary. . . .

"There are many causes which co-operate in preventing any numerous class of the people of Guernsey from sink-ing into that state of poverty which leads to crime and misery. In the first place, all the necessaries of life are exceedingly cheap. Wheat, for instance, during the last twenty years has been about two-thirds of its price in England. I need scarcely say that our Corn Laws do not extend to Guernsey.

"In the year 1821, when the rigour of the English Corn Laws was greatly increased, it was intended to extend these laws to Guernsey and the other Norman Isles; but the inhabitants bestirred themselves, and succeeded in warding off this terrible blow to their prosperity. For their success in this struggle they were, in a great measure, indebted to the exertions of Mr. Brock, of Guernsey.

"The people of the Norman Isles are not only allowed to import corn for their own use, from wheresoever they choose, but are permitted to export all the corn they grow themselves to England; so that there is the singular anomaly, constantly going on, of corn from the Baltic, sailing by the coast of England to supply the people of the Norman Isles, to enable them to send to England the wheat which is growing at their own doors.

"There is no law of primogeniture in the islands; and, next to the equal division of property, I may mention the abundance of paper-money in Guernsey as a great cause of prosperity. The paper-money is issued by the Government of the island, and in the following way. When any great undertaking has been determined on by the States (as the representatives of the people are called), such, for instance, as the opening of new roads, there is immediately an issue of one-pound notes. These notes are sent out as the work proceeds and as money is wanted. When the undertaking is completed, and begins to yield an income, the notes are gradually bought in again and new undertakings are commenced. The notes are not payable on demand; indeed, the Government has not even an office at which they can be presented. Nevertheless the notes are never refused. The people find by experience that their representatives do not issue the notes in greater abundance than the demand for them justifies, and consequently no depreciation in their value is to be feared. Moreover, the purposes for which the notes are issued are of advantage to every man in the island, so that every one looks upon them as coming from a bank in which he is a partner. Here, then, in the little island of Guernsey, we have, perhaps, the only instance in the world of a really national bank; a bank in which the whole property of the State is the security, and the profit of which is shared by the people at large.

"By means of this truly healthy currency, undertakings of great magnitude (considering the size of the island) have been executed during the last few years; but improvements have not been brought about without opposition from the ignorant. So indignant was an old farmer at the innovations which were setting in on every side, that, on his death-bed, he left positive orders that his coffin should not pass over a single yard of the new roads. His orders were obeyed, and the bearers had to engage in a kind of steeplechase, clambering over hedges and across ditches, to get to the place where the poor man's body was to be laid.

"In nothing are the inhabitants more to be congratulated than in the administration of their laws. In Guernsey every man can procure real, substantial justice at his own door, at his own time, and at a trifling expense."

We left Guernsey in a sailing-vessel, together

with a few other passengers, as there was no steam
communication in those days with the islands.

Arrived at St. Malo, we were at once subjected
to the ordeal of the custom-house—a much more
severe affair at that time than it is now. If our
party had been a gang of felons we could not have
been more scurvily treated. We were paraded
through the town to the place of examination,
headed and followed by a band of officers with
drawn swords, and surrounded on all sides by a
crowd of idle gazers, about as ceremonious in their
remarks as idlers usually are. Such treatment of
travellers was not, however, confined to the Continent. I remember once landing at Brighton when
a custom-house officer, after satisfying himself that
my hat contained nothing but its legitimate furni-
ture, and that my pockets were equally innocent,
proceeded to examine my boots! I frankly own
that, feeling as I did the absurdity of the whole
affair, I had great difficulty in keeping my foot in
a due state of quiescence during the examination.

St. Malo was fortified, and at nine o'clock its
gates were closed for the night, and no one was
allowed even to walk in the streets without carrying
a lantern.

During our visit an alarm of fire occurred at the
very inn in which we were staying. This caused

great excitement. With all speed the town fire-engine, a lumbering, rickety concern, was fetched and set to work ; but it was so leaky, and so much water squirted out at the sides of the hose, that but little could have reached the house. This, however, was of small importance, seeing that after all it was found that it was not the house, but a chimney only, that was on fire. This discovery changed the nature of the excitement, for now everybody was embracing everybody else, and congratulating each other on their wonderful escape. The end of this strange scene was the dispersion of the crowd by the soldiers when it was deemed that the people had been assembled long enough.

Nothing else remains in my memory till we reached Paris. At the place where the diligence stopped there were many clamorous emissaries from the various hotels eager to secure our luggage and our persons. To get quit of these men I announced that we were going to the Hôtel de la Marine.

"Alas!" exclaimed one of them, "I am sorry to inform you that that hotel has been lately burnt to the ground."

Hoping there might be some mistake, I remarked, "But there may be more than one Hôtel de la

Marine in Paris.   At the hotel that I am speaking of the head waiter is a black man."

"Yes, truly," he replied; "he was killed in the fire."

Shocked at this intelligence, we agreed to go to our interlocutor's hotel, and were conducted thither by him.   We soon had reason, however, to be much dissatisfied with our new quarters, and happening, the following day, to be walking down the Rue Vivienne, we saw, to our great surprise, the Hôtel de la Marine standing safe and sound, and at the door our friend the black waiter!   With much indignation at the trick that had been played upon us, we hurried back to our new inn, packed up our clothes, and proffered payment for the couple of days that we had been there.   But the landlord refused to accept this, and declared that he would not allow our luggage to be taken away unless we paid for a whole week.

I now sallied out in quest of a *juge de paix* to whom to apply for redress.   On my way I met a young man, whom I asked for the address of a *juge de paix*, and stated to him our case, about which he expressed sympathy and indignation.   He said that it happened singularly enough that he was himself the secretary of a *juge de paix!* Whilst we were talking we were joined by another young man, and to him the first repeated my narrative, adding that what especially excited his wrath was, that such a deception should have been practised on a *foreigner*. The two young men pressed me to let them show their feelings in the matter by calling for a bottle of wine at a neighbouring *cabaret*. To this I assented. We drank our wine and had a cheerful chat, at the end of which my entertainers, to my surprise, hastily withdrew, leaving me to pay the bill, as much chopfallen, no doubt, as was Gil Blas after receiving similar treatment.

Arthur and I now agreed to call in the aid of our friend Monsieur d'Argenson. He readily undertook the matter, and made arrangements for our appearing with him before a *juge de paix*. This we accordingly did, and our dishonest landlord, having received notice, was also there, together with his pretty wife, whom he cunningly brought with him. When we had stated our case, and the landlord had replied, the *juge de paix* proceeded to deliver judgment, which he did in our favour. At this stage of the little drama, however, the pretty wife stood up and made a pathetic protest against the decision. Whereupon his worship unhesitatingly altered it, and ordered us to pay for five days.

To return to home affairs. In the year 1826

the last State Lottery took place. Government had already attempted to regulate and afterwards to abolish private lotteries. Not content, however, with ceasing to encourage gambling by having a lottery of its own, it went from one extreme to the other—no uncommon thing in legislation. If foolish people like to gamble, they should, I think, be allowed to do so, and to suffer the consequences. Indeed, in some way or other the spirit is sure to manifest itself, and if it be made contrary to law, to folly is added the evil of law-breaking.

The laws that affect the treatment of the insane are, happily, very different now from what they were at the time of my youth, when much cruelty was practised through sheer ignorance. An acquaintance of ours named Steer had a friend who was subject to occasional fits of insanity. When these occurred, he was taken to the lunatic asylum of his district and there bound to a seat on a pivot, which was whirled round and round till he became insensible.

Mr. Steer himself had a strange adventure with his friend. They were sleeping in the same room, when Mr. Steer was awakened by feeling his face in a fiery heat. Opening his eyes, he saw a shovel full of live coals which his friend was waving over his face—" to warm him," as he explained. Mr.

Steer, with calm presence of mind, thanked him, and said " that was quite enough." At this moment the watchman in the street below drawled out, " Past three o'clock, and a starlight night!" upon which the lunatic rushed to the window, threw up the sash, and exclaiming, " Confound you! what are you making that noise for?" dashed the burning coals at the head of the poor watchman.

Speaking of watchmen reminds me of a Bill which was introduced into Parliament, to compel watchmen to sleep six hours in the day, so that they might be fit for their night duty; whereupon a gouty member rose and requested that *his* name might be inserted in the Bill, as he had not enjoyed such a sleep for many a long year.

In 1826 the Society for the Diffusion of Useful Knowledge was formed. Matthew and Rowland were amongst the original members of the committee, and Edwin joined them a year later, on his removal to London.

In Charles Knight's *Plain Englishman* an article had appeared so far back as 1822, headed " Diffusion of Useful Knowledge." This was the name chosen for the new society. Mr. Knight had already projected the issue of a series of popular works by first-rate authors. His friend Matthew Hill introduced him to Brougham, and a committee was soon at work. It represented almost every creed, and included distinguished statesmen and men eminent in every branch of learning. So prompt was it in action, that the first publication, No. 1 of a series of fortnightly sixpenny numbers, forming the "Library of Useful Knowledge," appeared in March, 1827. This was Brougham's "Discourse on the Objects, Advantages, and Pleasures of Science."

The aim of the society in its fullest scope was to promote a love of freedom and of peace by educating the people and elevating their tastes.

The "Library of Useful Knowledge" soon reached a circulation of nearly twenty thousand. The "Entertaining Library" which followed was equally successful. The *Penny Magazine* appeared at the end of March in the next year. Very soon the sale of a single issue reached two hundred thousand. The brothers Chambers anticipated this magazine a few weeks by their admirable *Journal*, the first number of which had come out in February; but its price was higher, and it was not illustrated. The great success of the *Penny Magazine* led to the publication of the *Penny Cyclopædia*. The *Saturday Magazine* of the Christian Knowledge Society appeared a few months later; other similar publications followed, and cheap serials, combining instruction and amusement, rapidly became abundant.[*]

It was not till many years later than the period of which I am now writing that I became acquainted with the family of Cowper, into which I ultimately married ; but it is pleasant to me to know that at this time my future wife and her family were taking a lively interest in the same objects that were occupying our minds. Professor Cowper was largely contributing to the diffusion of cheap literature by means of his admirable printing machine, which had supplanted the old hand-press.

Among the many evil practices which have been abolished during my lifetime is the practice of duelling. Most of my contemporaries must remember, as I do, tragic stories of friends or acquaintances who had duels forced upon them by their country's code of honour, which was at variance with their country's laws.

My brother Matthew wrote an article against duelling, which appeared in the first number of *Knight's Quarterly Magazine*, in the year 1823. He suggested that after every duel, whether fatal or not, an inquest should be held into the circumstances of the quarrel, with the view of discovering and punishing the aggressors. It was pointed out

[*] See " Memoir of Matthew Davenport Hill."

that, if this course were adopted, "that noxious animal, the *bully*, would become extinct." When this essay was written, the anomaly with respect to military men was still more extreme than that which prevailed among civilians. The Mutiny Act made it even possible for an officer to be punished for *not* fighting a duel, although the rules of the Horse Guards forbade duelling.

It was not till the year 1843 that duelling was finally abolished, when the death of Colonel Fawcett, by the hand of his brother-in-law, produced so great a revulsion of feeling that public opinion would no longer sanction such outrages.*

In the year 1829 the Government, under the leadership of the Duke of Wellington and Sir Robert Peel, brought forward and carried the Bill for Catholic Emancipation. By doing so they gave great offence to many of their supporters and to a large part of the population generally. A great meeting was held on Pennenden Heath, in Kent, to protest against the measure.

What little lay in my power to do towards influencing public opinion in Birmingham in the right direction I did by writing a pamphlet, addressed to my fellow-townsmen, entitled "Freedom to Catholics Consistent with Safety to the State."

* See "Memoir of Matthew Davenport Hill."

Another matter which interested me at this period was the question of wages. In 1830, at the request of a Parliamentary friend, I made some inquiries into the working of what is called the "Truck System"—that is, the paying of wages (in part at least) in "kind" instead of in money. The subject was about to be brought before Parliament. The evidence which I collected, by visiting iron works and other places, where large numbers of workmen were employed, convinced me of the benefits of the system both to master and man. The action which Parliament took ultimately was to make the Truck System illegal. Such State interference in freedom of contract is, in my opinion, always mischievous.

CHAPTER V.

1831–1832.

The great Reform Bill—Birmingham Political Union—Thomas
Attwood—Lord John Russell—Family action—Contempo-
rary letters—Mr. Scholefield—Earl Grey—Public readings
—Triumphal procession.

THE question of Parliamentary Reform had taken
a firm hold of the public mind by the beginning of
the year 1831. The period being one of national
crisis, we held a family council to determine what
action duty to our country called upon us to take.
All agreed that one member should be spared from
the work of the school and set at liberty to take an
active part in the coming struggle. I was chosen
for this purpose. Without loss of time, therefore,
I enrolled myself as a member of the Political
Union, an association which had been started in
Birmingham as early as January, 1830. Mr.
Thomas Attwood, a banker whose name soon rose
into great prominence, was its president. With
him and the other leaders of the Reform movement
I soon became personally acquainted.

The Political Union was joined by a large number of the inhabitants of Birmingham and its neighbourhood. A medal was struck, which its members wore as a distinguishing badge. It was suspended to a ribbon of the Union Jack colours. The accompanying engraving is taken from one of these medals in my possession.

THE SAFETY OF THE KING AND
OF THE PEOPLE.

THE CONSTITUTION, NOTHING
LESS, NOTHING MORE.

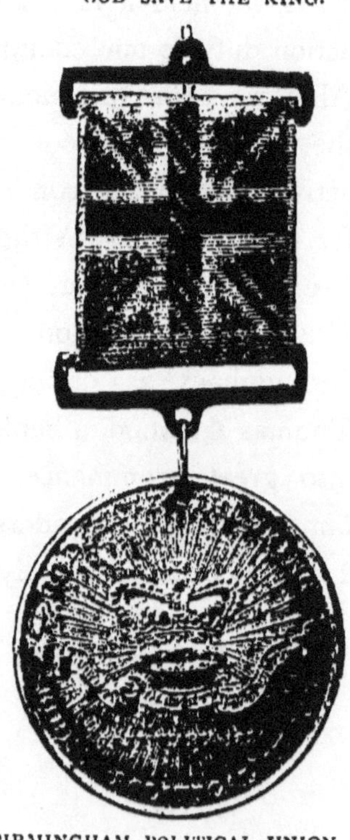

GOD SAVE THE KING.

BIRMINGHAM POLITICAL UNION.
UNITY, LIBERTY, PROSPERITY.

Associations similar to the Birmingham Political Union were rapidly forming all over the country.

The Grey Ministry was at this time in power, and we had, therefore, a favourable Government to deal with; but at any moment this Ministry might be ousted. There was a prospect of a severe struggle. The chief cause of apprehension was the part which the Duke of Wellington might deem it his duty to take; while the question as to whether the army would consent to act against the people, or would refuse to do so, was much discussed.

Another ground of apprehension was the conduct of the extreme Democratic party, under the leadership of "Orator" Hunt. Of this party few, happily, showed themselves in Birmingham.

On the 1st of March of this year (1831) the Reform Bill was introduced into the House of Commons by Lord John Russell. My brother Matthew was in the Strangers' Gallery on that memorable occasion. Describing the scene to us afterwards, he stated that when Lord John rose to propose the measure he was greeted with shouts of derisive laughter from the Tories. But the Bill was received very differently by the Liberals and by the nation at large. It was hailed with a burst of enthusiasm, soon followed by the cry of, "The Bill, the whole Bill, and nothing but the Bill!"

The extreme Radical party, indeed, denounced the measure as not going far enough, but by the large and more intelligent portion of the Liberal party it was warmly approved. The amount of political power which it transferred from persons who were irresponsible to men elected by the people quite satisfied them. They were also, no doubt, influenced by that instinctive dislike to great and violent change which happily distinguishes our race, and which secures us against such terrible and bloody disasters as have befallen the French.

The following is part of a letter written by me at this time to my brother Rowland :—

"Hazelwood, March 1, 1831.

"MY DEAR ROWLAND,

"We shall have a town's meeting to-morrow called by the Political Union.

"I rode down to town after I received your letter, and accompanied young Attwood to a meeting of the Council. Attwood and all others agree in the advisability of confining their attention and support to the measure of Reform brought forward by the Ministers.

"The meeting will take place as usual at Beardsworth's, but it is thought probable that even his immense building will not be capable of receiving the tide of people that will be ready to pour into it. An address will be voted to the King and Ministers expressive of delight and gratitude, and offering the assistance of all attending the meeting. Probably there will be fifteen or twenty thousand even at this short notice. The greatest enthusiasm prevails.

"The Union will proceed to the meeting with music and banners and every symbol of joy.

"If the first reading of the Bill passes successfully, there will be a general illumination.

"Mr. Scholefield showed me, in private, a letter he had received from Earl Grey, whom he knows personally. Scholefield had written to him expressive of his joyful concurrence in the measure proposed, and Lord Grey writes in answer to say that Ministers will exert themselves to the utmost to carry it. I hope to God they will have firmness enough to dissolve Parliament if the Bill be rejected.

"I believe that the most effectual means of assisting the cause at this juncture is to aid the Union with money. It is so important as an example as well as in itself. Its income is great, but its expenditure is great also. Thomas Attwood told me, a short time ago, that in the last year they had expended £1500 in printing alone.

"There must be no delay in whatever is done.

"Yours truly,

"FREDERIC HILL."

Soon after the second reading of the Bill (though it was carried by one vote) the Ministers found themselves opposed by a majority in the House of Commons. The result was a dissolution of Parliament. This took place on April 22, "after a scene of bellowing and roaring and gnashing of teeth on the part of the adversary in both Houses, which it was almost frightful to look at."* Lord

* See Cockburn's "Life of Lord Jeffrey."

Brougham, speaking in the Upper House, with peculiar emphasis called the Parliament "pro- *rogued.*"

On June 14 Parliament was again summoned, but now the Whigs had an overwhelming majority. Still there was a hard battle to be fought over the details of the Bill, and it was not finally passed till September 21.

On October 7 the Bill was thrown out by the House of Lords. Upon this a strong feeling of indignation was felt throughout the country; and now began a state of public excitement such as I have never witnessed either before or since. Many people apprehended a civil war.

Immediately after the rejection of the Bill, Mr. Attwood wrote an address to the people of Birmingham, which was placarded and widely circulated, and which had at once a calming and reassuring effect. It began, I remember, with these words:—

"Peace! Peace! Peace!

"The King is firm, the Ministry are firm, and the House of Commons is firm; why then should there be fear?"

The last sentence was as follows:—

"Friends and fellow-countrymen, listen to us. The sword must not be drawn in England. The terrible knell

of the tocsin must not sound.   The tears of the widow
and orphan must not mark our course.   We will have no
barricades.   Without blood, without anarchy, without
violation of the law, we will accomplish the most glorious
reformation recorded in the history of the world." *

In the " Life of Lord John Russell," by Spencer
Walpole, we find the following passage.   After
speaking of some disturbances in the country which
had taken place upon the rejection of the Reform
Bill by the House of Lords, he goes on to say—

"More significant than these disturbances was the
attitude of the great meetings which were everywhere
summoned to denounce the Lords and to support the
Administration.   At Birmingham, in particular, the head-
quarters of the Political Union, a gathering which was
computed to comprise a hundred and fifty thousand
persons voted an address to the Crown, expressing alarm
at the awful consequences which might ensue from the
failure of Reform, and praying the King to create as many
peers as might be necessary to carry the measure.   The
persons present pledged themselves to pay no taxes if
Reform were not passed, and, in the mean time, they
accorded their thanks to Lord Althorp and Lord John
Russell."

Lord John replied in a letter which became
famous—

"I beg to acknowledge with heartfelt gratitude the
undeserved honour done me by a hundred and fifty

---

* See "A Century of Birmingham Life," by J. A. Langford.

thousand of my fellow-countrymen. Our prospects are obscured for a moment; but I trust only for a moment. It is impossible that the whisper of a faction should prevail against the voice of a nation."

At this time I received the following letter from my Guernsey friend, Mr. Daniel de Lisle Brock :—

"Guernsey, December 24, 1831.

"DEAR MR. HILL,

"You say truly that the times are critical—they never were more so ; but I have great confidence in Lord Grey. I had many conversations with him on business twenty-five years ago on an occasion of importance, when he was introduced to me by his father, then the Governor of this island. I never left the present Lord Grey but with renewed impressions of his strong mind and quick intellectual capacity. . . . He must have more moral courage than any public man of modern days, from his very attempt to effect so great a purpose. . . . You inhabitants of Birmingham must be found worthy of him and of the position in which you have placed yourselves. You must afford a bright example to the rest of England. All eyes are directed towards you. . . .

"Yours truly,
"DANIEL DE LISLE BROCK."

As the spring of 1832 approached, and the prospects of the Reform Bill seemed now hopeful and now gloomy, the general excitement increased.

The Council of the Political Union gave notice that a great open-air meeting would be held on

May 7, at the foot of Newhall Hill, for the purpose of passing resolutions to urge the House of Lords to pass the Bill. The branches of the Union in the neighbourhood of Birmingham were invited to attend, and all supporters of Reform asked to be present.

An enormous concourse of people assembled, amounting, it is said, to two hundred thousand.

"The banners and bands of music formed not the least remarkable or attractive features of this extraordinary awaking of the people. It was a grand and sublime sight, which those who witnessed will never forget. Mr. Attwood was in the chair, and before the business commenced these two hundred thousand voices sang the spirit-stirring hymn by the Rev. Hugh Hutton, 'The Gathering of the Unions'—

CALL.

"Over mountain, over plain,
      Echoing wide from sea to sea,
Peals, and shall not peal in vain,
      The trumpet-call of Liberty!
Britain's guardian spirit cries—
Britons, awake! awake! arise!

"See rises from the bed of fame
      Each chief of glorious Runnymede,
With Hampden! history's noblest name—
      They call us to our country's need.
They call, and can we heedless be?
No! for we must, we will be free.

> " But not to war and blood they call,
>   They bid us lift nor sword nor gun ;
> Peaceful but firm join one and all
>   To claim our rights, and they are won.
> The British Lion's voice alone
> Shall gain for Britain all her own.

ANSWER.

> " Lo, we answer, see ! we come !
>   Quick at freedom's holy call
> We come, we come ! we come, we come !
>   To do the glorious work of all.
> And hark ! we raise from sea to sea
> Our sacred watchword, Liberty !

> " God is our Guide ! from field, from wave,
>   The plough, the anvil, and the loom,
> We come our country's rights to save,
>   And speak a tyrant faction's doom !
> And hark ! we raise from sea to sea
> Our sacred watchword, Liberty !

> " God is our Guide ! no sword we draw ;
>   We kindle not war's fatal fires.
> By union, justice, reason, law,
>   We claim the birthright of our sires !
> And thus we raise from sea to sea
> Our sacred watchword, Liberty ! "

In the petition to the House of Lords this great meeting prayed them not to injure or mutilate the Bill ; and anxiously and earnestly implored the Lords "not to drive to despair a high-minded, generous, and fearless people." Then followed one of the most solemn spectacles ever seen. Mr.

Thomas Clutton Salt, acting, as it were, on a sudden inspiration, took off his hat, and, the vast multitude following his example, he made them repeat after him the Union vow. Thus from the two hundred thousand assembled arose in unison, like the solemn voice of the sea, these words: "In unbroken faith, through every peril and privation, we devote ourselves and our children to our country's cause." *

At the very time that this patriotic meeting was being held, Government was sustaining a serious defeat in Parliament. On the 9th Earl Grey resigned.

The historian of the "Thirty Years' Peace" thus describes the scenes which followed the resignation of the Whig Ministry:—

"The excitement in the provinces was, if possible, even more threatening than in London. Birmingham was at that time looked upon as the head-quarters of Reform ; and the movements of the Political Union, presided over by Mr. Thomas Attwood, were deemed of great importance both by the friends and the opponents of Reform. The news that the Reform Bill was in fact defeated, and that Lord Grey had resigned, instantly excited not only the more ardent reformers of the town, who had hitherto constituted the Union, but stirred up the whole population, timid and fearless, eager and apathetic, alike ; and they in

---

* See "A Century of Birmingham Life," by J. A. Langford.

various ways made manifest their anger and their determination. Placards were exhibited in the windows, some of which were in these words :—

NOTICE.

NO TAXES PAID HERE
UNTIL
THE REFORM BILL IS PASSED.

Others stated, ' No taxes paid here in money, and no goods bought distrained for taxes.' And, as was the case in London, immense numbers of persons to whom political agitation was disagreeable, and who, therefore, had hitherto abstained from taking part in it, now joined the Political Union. Catholic priests and grave Quakers ostentatiously enrolled their names in the books of the Union, stating that they did so in order to preserve the peace ; for anarchy and confusion, they asserted, ' were certain unless the Reform Bill was instantly carried.' Deputations from the surrounding towns came hurriedly to Birmingham, as a centre, in order to concert measures in this dangerous crisis. A meeting was held and a petition was proposed. Mr. Edmonds read the resolution passed by the Council, and having urged upon the assembly the observance of ' legal, peaceable, firm, and determined conduct,' he proceeded to move the petition to the House of Commons, the adoption of which was seconded by Mr. Scholefield, who announced that at the close of the proceedings, a deputation, of which he had the honour of forming a part, would leave Birmingham for London, to communicate the opinions of the vast multitude he then addressed to the members of the legislature. . . . The delegates who brought this petition to London were next day present at various public meetings held in the metropolis.   Their presence excited still more the enthusiasm of the people."*

On the 11th I received the following note from Mr. Charles Jones, a member of the Council of the Political Union :—

"May 11, 1832.

"MY DEAR SIR,

"I have just received a packet from Manchester.   There has been a meeting there, and a petition adopted and signed in *three hours* by 21,000 persons, which was instantly forwarded by express to London.

"We are still receiving great accessions to our numbers. Pray come this afternoon—the Council meets at half-past four for the purpose of signing an address to his Majesty. I am happy to inform you several persons will attend, to promote the good work which your patriotism suggested yesterday respecting the funds.

"Yours truly,
"C. JONES."

Letter from M. D. HILL.

"Chancery Lane, Thursday, May 11, 1832.

"DEAR FREDERIC,

". . . Nobody here seems to doubt but that the King must give way.   I have been to a district meeting of the Finsbury division, and spoke.   It was held near Islington, and attended by 20,000 people.   Joseph Hume was in the chair; all went off well. . . . We have very good reason for believing that the army would not fight

---

* See " A Century of Birmingham Life," by J. A. Langford.

for the Tories.   I trust the people of Birmingham will not lose their patience yet.

> "Yours very truly,
>> "M. D. Hill."

Three days later I wrote to Matthew :—

> "Birmingham, May 14, 1832.

"Dear Matthew,

> "The excitement is greater than it has been since Thursday.   I think that was the day the news of the resignation came, but my mind is in such an excited state that I cannot answer for dates.

> "Mr. Scholefield attended the Council to-day to give an account of his reception in London.   The audience (at least five hundred in number) was quite touched with his account of his interview with Lord Grey, and gave the old lord three hearty cheers.

> "Many donations were announced—among others one of £20 from an old schoolfellow of Mr. Attwood's.   The Council spent a great deal of time in discussing the merits of 'The Covenant.'   The great question is, Shall we go for the Bill, or for more than the Bill?   Attwood, Edmonds, and several others are for abiding by the Bill.   Jones and others are for going for more.   I expect that the Bill will have the day.

> "The middle classes are, I think, becoming rapidly prepared as a whole body to refuse the payment of taxes.

> "The general expectation here is that the Duke will instantly resort to violent measures.   An arrest of all the members of the Council is looked upon as a probable measure.   I much fear that the people will not be able to restrain themselves in this case.   Would to God that the

organization had been effected! I want the Council to publish an address stating clearly the possible measures which the Duke may resort to, and the precise steps which the people should adopt in each case.

"Attwood appears to be quite equal to the post in which circumstances have now placed him. He is as calm and clear-headed as ever; and his advice to the people is very judicious. He is determined, if possible, to keep strictly within the law. The other members of the Council show no signs of flinching. New members, too, are crowding to the Union.

"Yours truly,
"Frederic Hill."

Same date.

"Dear Rowland,

". . . God knows when this political excitement will be over, now that a sword has been appointed Prime Minister of England. The people here are in a fever of excitement; the shopkeepers say that nothing is being done. This morning an idle report got about that the Duke of Wellington was at the Swan. A great crowd instantly assembled. The proprietor of the inn sent down to Mr. Attwood to come and assure the people that the Duke was not in his house. Mr. Attwood was not yet come to town, but fortunately Mr. McDonnell (a Catholic priest) was at hand, and satisfied the people that the traveller who was supposed to be the Duke was not he. The gentleman was a Colonel O'Brien, and he stated himself to be a staunch reformer.

"The Council of the Union has been sitting to-day, but has not adopted any measures. The time was partly occupied by Mr. Scholefield's account of his reception in London, as one of the deputation.

" You talk of a physical struggle. I hope you discourage
the idea as far as possible. We are much safer in every
respect on other grounds. In *moral* force the Tories are
miserably feeble ; let us, then, defeat them *there*. I have no
doubt they will do their best to decoy the people into
acts of violence, but non-payment of taxes will bring the
rascals to. The Council discourage all idea of a physical
struggle unless the Duke's party are the aggressors. The
great ,thing to keep the people quiet is to keep them
employed. I propose that a number of pieces of waste
ground, large courts, etc., should be taken, and that every
evening, when the papers come in, they should be read and
commented on, and a closing address made enforcing
order. If you like the idea, perhaps you can carry it into
effect in London. I shall try to do so here. But I am
not yet on the Council, so that I cannot move rapidly.
Attwood told me I was elected last Saturday ; but it was a
mistake, notice only having been given. The situation is
one of great responsibility, but I am inclined to accept it.
The election will be made to-morrow evening.

" Yours truly,
" FREDERIC HILL."

On the following day I became a member of the
Council of the Political Union, and I immediately
brought forward the plan proposed in the foregoing
letter. It was received with approbation, and
measures were at once taken to carry it into effect.
The public readings were announced beforehand
by bills put up in conspicuous places in Birmingham.
One of these bills is still in my possession, of which
I give a facsimile.

Public Reading

OF THE

NEWS.

In order to satisfy the eager desire of the Public to learn the News of the Day, and with a view of preventing the circulation of incorrect reports, arrangements have been made for

READING

THE LONDON

NEWSPAPERS

PUBLICLY,

Every Evening at a Quarter-past 7

AT THE FOLLOWING PLACES:

**Cooper's News-Office, Union-street,
Front of the Old Wharf, and
The Corner of Regent Place, Caroline-
street, St. Paul's.**

The Public Reading will begin

THIS EVENING,

Friday, May 18, 1832.

BARLOW, PRINTER, BENNETT'S HILL.

These public readings were fully appreciated. They appeased the general craving for news at a time when there was no electric telegraph, and when the want of cheap newspapers and of education made it difficult for a large portion of the public to obtain correct information for themselves. The working men were now content to remain quietly at their employment during the daytime, instead of leaving it to seek for news. I myself was one of the readers. I frequently addressed audiences from the steps of St. Philip's Church. They were, invariably, both orderly and attentive.

Letter from ROWLAND HILL.

"May 15, 1832.

"DEAR FREDERIC,

"Your plan of a public reader is excellent, and I will try what can be done towards initiating it here. . . .

"Sunday's *Spectator* contained a glorious account of the 'Gathering of the Unions' at Birmingham. It should be read to the people. . . .

"What a pity the late Ministers opposed the flogging abolition Bill! It would be well for all Reform Associations to declare their intention of requiring a Reform Parliament to abolish corporal punishments in the army.

"Yours,

"R. HILL."

Letter from M. D. HILL.

" Chancery Lane, May, 1832.

" DEAR F.,

"... I have been to Westminster, and have read your letter to the Chancellor's secretary, he himself being engaged in hearing appeals in the House of Lords. He and every one else to whom I have shown it appear greatly struck at the dignified firmness of the Birmingham people.

" I think your plan of public readings admirable. It ought to be adopted throughout the kingdom.

"... To-night we hold an adjourned meeting in our parish, at which I mean to propose a Parish Convocation, to organize the inhabitants to collect subscriptions.

" I mean to print my speech if I succeed, and I will send you some copies for distribution. ...

" Peel has twice refused office, but is expected to relent. The Tories talk of passing the Bill with but little alteration. No dissolution is expected to-day, at least.

" Yours,

" M. D. HILL."

The following is a contemporary account of the state of public feeling in Birmingham at this time :—

" The population of the town during Monday last continued in a highly excited and feverish state, arising out of the events of the preceding week. Every kind of employment appeared to be altogether suspended ; the streets were crowded from morning until night, and the greatest avidity to obtain fresh intelligence was everywhere exhibited. The Council of the Union met in the forenoon, and, it becoming known that they were preparing a Declaration for publication against the proposed Ministry, the vicinity of the place of meeting became an object of attraction, and crowds of persons remained constantly on the spot. In the course of the day great accession was made to the members of the Union, and the streets were paraded by many of the newly enrolled members with music, banners, etc.; no attempt at disorder, however, took place. . . . The Declaration, issued by the Council of the Union, appeared upon the walls, and was eagerly read by the populace. This document, after reciting the grounds on which it rested its alarm at the report of the Duke of Wellington's appointment to the Ministry, observed—

"'For these and various other reasons we hereby solemnly declare our fixed determination to use all the means which the constitution and the law have placed at our disposal, to induce his Majesty to reject from his Councils that faction at the head of which is the Duke of Wellington . . . and we declare our firm conviction that the public excitement and agitation can never be allayed until the great Bill of Reform shall be carried into law by that Administration by whose wisdom and virtue it was first introduced. These are our fixed and unalterable sentiments; and we hereby appeal to our fellow-countrymen throughout England, Scotland, and Ireland, and we confidently call upon them to unite with us, and to sign this our solemn Declaration in support of the liberty and happiness of our country." *

---

* See "A Century of Birmingham Life," by J. A. Langford.

The very morning after the day on which this meeting was held affairs underwent a sudden and unlooked-for change. News arrived at an early hour on Wednesday, May 16, that the Duke of Wellington was unable to form a Ministry, and that Earl Grey and his colleagues had returned to power. This welcome intelligence was conveyed to Birmingham by Mr. Joseph Parkes, who "travelled by post express down from London with the news, distributing printed slips to the effect that Earl Grey was again in power—scattering them by the roadside and amongst the population of every town and village in the way." The public joy on this occasion can never be forgotten by those who, like myself, witnessed and shared in it.

The following letter from me to my brother Matthew may give to younger generations some idea of it :—

" Birmingham, May 16, 1832.

"DEAR MATTHEW,

"I hope that the torrent of joy has not wrecked your nervous system. Never was there such a change from gloom and anxiety to bright prospects and security. Thank God, the strain on the patience and self-control of the people is loosened. I greatly fear they could not have forborne much longer. The ecstasy into which we here are thrown is, I suppose, but the counterpart of the state of things with you. Poor Edmonds! When I met him this morning his eyes were red with weeping; the news had quite overpowered him. Parkes reached Birmingham soon after six. He aroused Jones by a quarter past, who hurried to the churches to give orders for clamming the bells and hoisting flags from the steeples. Luckily the Royal Standard, which had been had from Somerset House for the great meeting yesterday week, was still in Birmingham. It has been all day streaming from the top of St. Philip's Church—a noble sight!

"Of course dispatches were instantly sent off to Mr. Attwood. Joe Parkes himself was the bearer of the glad tidings. With as little delay as possible placards were posted against the walls proclaiming the joyful news, and inviting the inhabitants to go *en masse* to conduct Thomas Attwood into town. When I found that all arrangements had been made in Birmingham, I galloped back to Hazelwood. We had the phaeton immediately prepared, blue rosettes to the horses' heads, and, with my mother, Sarah and Ellen, and some of the youngsters in the carriage, I drove off to join in the procession. The place of rendezvous was the Five-ways Turnpike, but many thousand people went the whole of the way to Mr. Attwood's house. The procession, consisting of from twenty to thirty thousand people, marched on to Newhall Hill, where in a short time we had from fifty to sixty thousand. Good resolutions and addresses have been adopted, and Attwood and Scholefield go up to London this evening with them.

"Father is better. How can any one be otherwise!

"Yours truly,

"FREDERIC HILL."

The triumphant procession described in my

letter entered the town by Smallbrook Street, and advanced through High Street, New Street, and Newhall Street, to Newhall Hill. Preparations had there been made to hold a congratulatory meeting. On the arrival of Mr. Attwood he was at once called upon to take the chair, amidst the enthusiastic cheering of the crowd. But before proceedings commenced he turned to the Rev. Hugh Hutton and requested him to offer up a prayer of thanksgiving. In an instant there was the hushed silence of deep feeling whilst the preacher, in the name of that vast multitude assembled, returned thanks to the Almighty for "the great bloodless victory" that had been achieved. Mr. Attwood made an eloquent speech, in which he said that Earl Grey "had been carried back—as he should be carried back—on the shoulders of the people into his Majesty's Councils," adding "that by patience, fortitude, and a strict regard to law, they had gathered up strength that had proved omnipotent."

The Reform Bill passed the House of Lords on the 4th of June, and on the 7th received the Royal assent. Thus was accomplished the greatest political change, without bloodshed, that was ever made, as far as my knowledge goes, in England or in any other country; a change which has been productive of vast improvements, and which for more than thirty years maintained its peaceful course without material alteration.

Birmingham was now entitled, for the first time, to be represented in Parliament. Her two candidates were Mr. Attwood and Mr. Scholefield. The nominations took place on December 12, when my father had the honour of proposing Mr. Attwood.

At this very time Matthew was standing a contested election as candidate for Hull. My father wrote to him on December 12 :—

"Attwood and Scholefield are chosen without opposition. God speed you at Hull! It was my task this morning to propose Attwood. I was listened to by twenty-five thousand people, they tell me."

And a few days later he wrote again—

"They have made me chairman of Attwood's Committee. I am glad that you liked what I spoke at the town's meeting. All I said came from the heart, as prompted by a sincere affection for liberty, goodness, and truth. Still the fervour of delivery was not less because Attwood and Birmingham had common cause with Hill and Hull."

CHAPTER VI.

1832–1835.

My brother Matthew had been invited to represent the borough of Hull in the Liberal interest. His candidature was successful.

"The first subject to which he turned his thoughts on becoming a member of the Legislature was one which his professional duties had brought painfully under his notice—the anomaly of refusing to Counsel in felonies the right to address the jury, whilst it was permitted in other classes of offences."

Matthew had never forgotten Hone's description of the judicial murder of Eliza Fenning (already alluded to), and the deep impression it made upon him bore practical fruit in his first session in Parliament.

"Had Eliza Fenning been tried in Scotland or in the British Colonies, in the United States or in any other country in the civilized world, or, indeed, had she been charged in England with only a misdemeanour, her Counsel might have addressed the jury. The caprice of the English law, in this latter respect, would have been absolutely ludicrous had it not involved consequences so tragic."

When giving evidence on this subject, my brother said—

"I am charged with holding up my stick at another; he prosecutes me for a common assault; my Counsel may speak for me the whole day; but let that stick have a nail at the end of it, and let me be accused of puncturing my opponent with it, and my supposed offence becomes a felony; then, my life being at stake, my Counsel cannot speak." *

A Bill was introduced into Parliament for a change in the law which Matthew did all in his power to promote, but it encountered much opposition, and was not finally passed till three years later.

I am tempted to quote my brother's words on one other subject of even greater importance— namely, the Abolition of Slavery in our Colonies. Speaking on the question of compensation to the West India planters, Matthew said—

* See "Memoir of M. D. Hill."

"Let me congratulate the House that the slave does not add to our difficulties by himself demanding compensation ; for I confess I know not how we should resist his claim if he said to us, 'I have been kept in bondage during the best years of my life. I have been compelled to labour, not for myself or my children, but for a hard taskmaster, who, with the value of my toil in his pocket, comes before you to demand compensation. If, then, you have money to spare, pay me first.'"

We were all proud of Matthew's many talents, and were ready to help him, whenever it was possible, in his efforts for the protection of the injured and for the promotion of the public good. Many years later Rowland wrote to him, saying, "The members of our family have always been ready to assist one another, consequently each has worked with the combined force of all ; but you have been the pioneer for us all."

"The glorious Reform Bill," to use my father's words, stood "as a mighty organized body ready for working incalculable good." My brothers and I seized the occasion of its advent to devise and discuss with one another many a project of Reform, as the following letters will show :—

From ROWLAND HILL.

"Bruce Castle, February 10, 1832.

"DEAR FRED^c.,

"What is to be done with Ireland is really a most difficult question. No doubt justice in the first instance, and I should say a complete wiping away of the Protestant Church Establishment. But we must not expect everybody to adopt the decided measures we may think best. And having done this, what next? The habits of the people, resulting from a long system of mismanagement, would not at once change, and the murders and burnings must not be allowed to continue. It is manifest, I think, that the people are not honest enough for trial by jury; and I am very much inclined to advocate a sort of despotism, responsible, however, to the English Parliament. Still I would try, *in the first instance*, the removal of all unjust institutions; but I would *prepare* to follow up this with very strong measures of coercion. . . .

> "Yours affectionately,
> "R. Hill."

From the same.

> "Bruce Castle, May 8, 1832.

"Dear Fred^c.,

"I send you for perusal a letter from Malthus. I had written to him requesting his acceptance of 'Home Colonies,' and expressing a hope that I had correctly interpreted his evidence. . . .

"Among various plans, consider this—To try to obtain the management of some cotton works. Educate the children well. Let all engaged devote part of their time to agriculture for the sake of health. Keep the mills at work from early in the morning, say four or five, till late at night, say nine or ten, without any interruption, employing two sets of workpeople. Form a town of the work-people, making use of improved arrangements, etc. This plan would, I think, afford employment for the various talents of the family, in the improvement of the machinery, education and management of the workpeople, etc., and would be attended with increased economy in the production of cotton. By having a great number of persons under our control we should be able to try many of the co-operative plans. . . . The changes connected with the restrictions on trade which must speedily follow a reformed Parliament (the upsetting of the East India Charter, Bank Charter, the Usury Laws, Corn Laws, duties on the productions of other countries, etc., etc.) must give an impetus to those trades which are most advantageously followed in this country.

" Yours,

" R. HILL."

The pamphlet " Home Colonies " referred to in the foregoing letter was written by Rowland at the request of Lord Brougham, and was published in 1832.

The objects of the plan were the "gradual extinction of pauperism and diminution of crime."

The following year there seemed a likelihood of our being able to give these schemes a practical trial.

A commission had been appointed to inquire into the abuses which had arisen in the administration of the Poor Law. Among those who gave evidence before it was the Rev. H. P. Jeston, Vicar of Cholesbury, near Tring. He described in a striking manner the deplorable condition to which these abuses had reduced his parish. Much of the land had ceased to be cultivated, and misery was visible on all sides.

Rowland writes to me.

"Bruce Castle, April 30, 1833.

"DEAR FRED^c.,

"Turn to page 86 of the Poor Law Report and read the account of the parish of Cholesbury, Bucks. You see that the whole parish (a small one) may be bought for about £2000. What think you of buying it? . . .

"I have written to Mr. Jeston for further information, and if his reply is satisfactory I think of riding over to see the place. Edwin thinks highly of the plan. I should like to know your opinion, and that of Arthur and father. By establishing a kind of pauper colony we might, I think, at once get rid of the rates and obtain a good rent for the laud. At the same time we might establish the truth of our opinions on the subject of Home Colonization.

"Yours,

"R. HILL."

We took up the matter with every intention of carrying it through, but, unfortunately, there proved to be an insurmountable difficulty opposed to our scheme. In the middle of the town of Cholesbury there was a public-house, the centre of drinking and disorder, whose owners positively refused to treat with us on any terms for its purchase. Convinced as we were that all our efforts for the reform of the place would be vain so long as this public-house remained open, we reluctantly abandoned our design.

I may here mention that thirty years later I became intimately acquainted with Mr. Jeston, for whom I entertained a warm esteem.

Letter from EDWIN HILL.

"Bruce Castle, May 19, 1832.

"DEAR FRED^c.,

"As you are a member of the Council (of the Political Union), will you consider the propriety of a petition for ameliorating the condition of the army and navy by the introduction of a system of treatment fit for intellectual beings?   Objects of immediate concern—abolition of impressment and flogging; secondly, introduction of adult education—regimental libraries and institutions like Mechanics' Institutions.   We, the people, have been almost at the mercy of a body of men who know little or nothing but the art of destroying others.   When we put arms into the hands of men, we should also put knowledge into their heads, and a love of virtue, if possible, into their hearts.   If we could do this an army would not be the dangerous thing it is.   I think this important and well timed, and, if well managed, it will tend to conciliate the soldiers and sailors; and the people are likely to feel the necessity of the measure from having just seen the sword almost drawn over their heads.

"Yours affect^{ly}.,

"E. HILL."

From the same.

" B. C., August 13, 1832.

" DEAR FRED^c.,

"Rowland says you have spare time. I think something will be done soon by Government in the matter of general education. Should you like to lay down clearly a few of the broadest principles which should govern such a proceeding? Such a work would probably be very useful. The chief points would be the mode of holding the managers to responsibility as respects the efficiency of their teachers and the economy with which it would be carried on. This branches into your favourite subject of municipal government.

"Do you think your idea of allowing foreign representatives to sit in our Parliament could be brought forward well now? There is much exasperation against Nicholas on the score of Poland, and against the Kings of Prussia and Hanover and the Emperor of Austria for their attempts to put down the Press in Germany. I think anything which showed how the States which are governed by representatives of the inhabitants could be brought to coalesce, and thus to form a compact opposing body, would be cordially welcomed if not too startling in its nature; or, rather, if not put forward in too startling a form, for people start more often at manner than at matter.

"Yours affectionately,

"E. HILL."

I adopted the suggestion thrown out by Edwin, and after collecting a great deal of information as to the state of education in Great Britain, on the Continent, and in America, I wrote a book entitled

" National Education, its Present State and Prospects." In my introduction I remark that " the subject of education has at length acquired a strong interest in the public mind," and that even " the timid and feeble-minded are finding out that the imagined monster on which they had not dared steadily to fix their eyes is, in fact, a most friendly and benign power. In a word, that popular knowledge, instead of being a source of danger and insecurity, is the best guarantee for public tranquillity and the rights of property."

Whilst the work was still in progress I received a kind and encouraging letter from our friend Mr. Charles Knight, who offered to publish it. This he did in 1836.

Amongst private letters which followed the appearance of " National Education," the name of one writer is of general interest. Joanna Baillie wrote to my sister-in-law, Mrs. Matthew Hill, to tell her of Lady Byron's interest in the book. She goes on to say—

" Will you have the goodness to let Mr. F. Hill know this, and thank him again for his goodness in bestowing upon me this copy of his useful and able work, which I have read with much interest ? It is cleverly written, and in a candid, good spirit, and will, I hope, make a beneficial impression on the public."

The subject of currency first interested us during this period. My brother Edwin and I entered into a series of discussions upon it with each other. We invited Rowland to join us, but he had too many other matters in hand to be able to do so. Edwin and I both gradually formed opinions which remained unchanged in after-life, and which we have advocated as occasion offered. One of these was in favour of a paper currency. Many years later Edwin published his work upon the "Principles of Currency, Means of securing Uniformity of Value and Adequacy of Supply."

In the year 1832 we established what we called the "Family Fund." Its object was to secure every member of our family (five of whom were now married) from pecuniary anxiety. The necessary expenditure of each branch of the family was assessed, and half the remaining surplus income, in each case, was handed over annually to the "Family Fund." Its management, together with the selection of investments, was entrusted to me.

This fund continued in being for twenty-four years; at the end of which time the general condition of our family had so far improved that all pecuniary anxieties had disappeared. The balance, which had much increased in amount, was then divided ; each person's share being in proportion to his original contribution.

On the dissolution of the "Family Fund" we issued a short printed address to the " Junior Members of the Hill Family," to explain to them the nature of this fund. The address is signed by my four brothers and myself, and bears the date of July, 1856. It closes with these words :—

"In such a union, beyond the mere material benefit, there naturally arises a moral influence of considerable power, and of this we have experienced the advantage, our connection having been sufficiently close to give each of us, in a great measure, the benefit of the experience, knowledge, and judgment of all the others, and to secure to each that friendly advice of which every one, some time or other, stands in need.

"We attribute such success as has attended our family very much to the spirit of co-operation which was recommended to us by our parents during their lives and on their death-beds ; and which we, in turn, living and dying, would recommend to our successors."

In 1833 the repeal of the Corn Laws began to be widely discussed. My friend Mr. Charles Villiers was the first person, according to my recollection, to bring the subject before the House of Commons. I had furnished him, previously, with some information on the subject, and had made a calculation of the loss to the country caused by those bad laws. My calculation was founded on the price of bread and flour in the Channel Islands (to which the Corn Laws did not extend) as compared with the whole estimated cost of bread and flour in this country. My estimate was not, of course, more than a rough approximation, but it showed the annual loss to this country to be, at least, ten millions sterling.

It is well known how Cobden and Bright came forward as champions of this great cause. Writing many years later, Cobden's biographer relates that—

" strange as it may appear, they both at different stages of the Corn Law agitation contemplated withdrawal from the great movement. Both had worked hard for years to overthrow the gigantic evils of the Corn Laws, and yet success seemed distant. Bright had lost his wife (in September, 1841), and was cast down with grief. Cobden visited him in the midst of his despondency, spoke kind words, and then recalled to his mind the thousands of poor widows and children who, at that moment, were starving for bread through the cruel laws against which they two had been so long protesting. ' Come with me,' he said, ' and we will never rest till we abolish the Corn Laws.' John Bright rose to the summons." *

The long struggle for the repeal of the Corn Laws is matter of history. Enemies of all classes

* See " Richard Cobden," by F. Bullock.

had to be fought.   The Tories were against it, and many among the working classes were also against it, as they feared, in their ignorance, that cheap bread would cause low wages.   Even Lord Melbourne, in the House of Commons, said that "any man who could seriously advocate the repeal of the Corn Laws must be mad."

It was not till the year 1846 that the measure was finally carried.

To return to my own personal narrative.

In the year 1827 a branch of our school had been started at Bruce Castle, Tottenham, near London, and six years later it was deemed advisable for the whole school to remove thither.   We therefore quitted Birmingham and came to reside at Tottenham.

I had assisted my father and brothers in teaching ever since I reached the age of thirteen.   I enjoyed my work, but I hoped for a different career in the future.

Even in early boyhood I had conceived a strong wish to obtain some day a useful and important post under Government.   When I first mentioned my ambition to my brother Matthew, he laughed and said, "You remind me of the boy who wished to be apprenticed to a bishop."   However, I continued to cherish the idea, and when, in 1833, the family had but one school to manage instead of two, my assistance was no longer necessary, and I began to consider what steps I should take towards gaining my object. I determined, on Matthew's advice, to be called to the Bar to facilitate my entrance into the Civil Service, and to that end entered my name as a student of Lincoln's Inn.

Being "called" in those days was a very different affair from what it is now. No study of the law was required, and there was no examination. When, some time later, the last of the prescribed dinners had been eaten, I was conducted to the upper end of Lincoln's Inn Hall and introduced to one of the benchers. A manuscript was then placed in my hands containing the opening part of a trial, and I was desired to read it aloud. I had scarcely, however, uttered a few words when the bencher made me a slight bow, which indicated his perfect satisfaction in my legal acquirements, and was also a sign that the ceremony was concluded.

In the year 1834 I was fortunate in obtaining the post of parliamentary secretary to Mr. Sergeant Wilde (afterwards Lord Truro), who was an intimate friend of my brother Matthew. In this capacity I had to furnish Mr. Wilde with accurate information upon any subject on which he intended to speak, and at his request I used to draw up, as a kind of brief, a statement of the various points at issue.

In 1835 the Duke of Richmond introduced into Parliament and carried a Bill for the appointment of inspectors of prisons. At the suggestion of my friend Mr. Charles P. Villiers, I applied for one of the nominations. The appointments rested with Lord John Russell, then Home Secretary. My application was supported by many influential friends ; amongst these were Sergeant Wilde, Joseph Hume, Charles P. Villiers, Joseph Scholefield, J. Brotherton, Edward Baines, and Thomas Thornely (all members of Parliament). Thus my long-cherished desire to obtain a Government post, with a field for administration, seemed likely to be fulfilled.

Well do I remember the arrival of the letter from Lord John Russell informing me that I was appointed an inspector of prisons. I was sitting reading in Matthew's chambers in Chancery Lane, and such was my delight that I skipped about the room for joy, and, tradition says, jumped over a chair !

At my interview with Lord John Russell he said to me, " Mr. Hill, I have chosen Scotland as your chief district, because there is most work to be done there, and I know you will do it."

The counties of Northumberland and Durham were also to be under my supervision.

I am tempted to insert a kind note which I received from Mr. Sergeant Wilde on my resigning my post as his parliamentary secretary.

> "Temple, October 10, 1835.

"My dear Hill,

"... I cannot part with you without assuring you that the communication between us has been a source of unmixed satisfaction to me, and the interruption is matter of regret, as I have had great reason to appreciate highly your intelligence, attention, and kindness to me.

"I remain

"Very truly yours,

"Thos. Wilde."

Soon after receiving my appointment I met Mr. Robert Owen, the well-known enthusiast. He accosted me with these words: "Now, Mr. Hill, I have one piece of advice to give you, which is, that you begin by telling the prison authorities that up to this time they have been entirely in the wrong." I need scarcely say that I did not adopt this mode of ingratiating myself with my official coadjutors.

Before leaving London I visited some of our prisons and houses of refuge.

My visits to Newgate caused me to become acquainted with Mrs. Fry. On one occasion I was present when she addressed the female prisoners, who were all assembled in a large room for that purpose. The address consisted almost entirely of selected portions of the Bible, which she read slowly and in a fine melodious voice, pausing every now and then to give her hearers time for reflection. Her manner was very impressive; I noticed that many of the women were moved to tears.

In the course of conversation afterwards Mrs. Fry told me of her first experiences in visiting Newgate. When she asked for permission to visit the female prisoners the officer in charge, though granting her request, strongly advised her against such a proceeding, warning her that she would probably be attacked and robbed. Undaunted, however, Mrs. Fry carried out her intention, and she assured me that, far from being attacked, she met with respect on all sides.

She found the poor women all idle. No work was provided for them. Her first efforts were directed to remedy this great evil.

I asked Mrs. Fry what she found to be the chief thought of a prisoner under sentence of death shortly before her execution. Her reply was: " I grieve to say that commonly the chief thought relates to her appearance on the scaffold, the dress in which she shall be hanged."

Mrs. Fry gave me a book written by her brother, Mr. Joseph John Gurney, entitled, "Notes on a Visit made to Some of the Prisons in Scotland and the North of England in Company with Elizabeth Fry." It was published in 1819. A terrible picture is there drawn of the condition of some of our prisons.

I received the following note from her with the book :—

"Upton Lodge, 17th instant.

"DEAR FRIEND,

"I am glad to say I have found one of our books on the Scotch prisons that my brother, J. J. Gurney, and myself visited in 1819. Of course, since that period there are in some great alterations, but improvements are yet much needed in most of the jails in that country.

"I hope thou wilt have a useful and profitable expedition.

"And believe me, under esteem,

"Thy friend,

"ELIZ^TH. FRY.

"P.S.—I have forwarded other books that may amuse thee on thy journey."

CHAPTER VII.

1835–1836.

Arrival in Edinburgh—John Archibald Murray—First tour of
inspection of prisons.

I left London by the stage-coach on the 30th of
October, and, travelling without stopping on the
road, reached Edinburgh on the 1st of November.
It was evening when the coach drew up at an inn
on the northern side of the North Bridge, and I
was much struck by the sight of the towering mass
of the Castle rock with its twinkling lights.

I slept that night at an inn in Prince's Street,
and early the next morning walked over the Calton
Hill and Arthur's Seat, my mind filled with their
associations and delighted with the magnificent
views.

I had a cordial reception from the Lord Advocate,
Sir John (afterwards Lord) Murray, who was a
friend of my brother Matthew's. From the first
day of my arrival his house was thrown open to me,

and thus began a friendship which lasted to the end of his life, and which was a source of much pleasure and profit to me. Sir John Murray took a great interest in prison reform. I obtained at once from him useful information respecting the leading men in Scotland, and, in a few days' time, he called a meeting of the whole body of the principal local judges, or sheriffs-depute, as they are called, to confer with me respecting the prisons. They gave me a friendly and gratifying reception, as did afterwards the sheriffs-substitute in their various districts.

I began my first tour of inspection within a week of my arrival in Edinburgh.

I knew beforehand that the Scotch prisons were in a bad state, but the picture that gradually unfolded itself before my eyes was far worse than anything I had anticipated.

Mrs. Fry, who visited them in the year 1819, thus describes the Scotch gaols :—

"The construction and management may be shortly enumerated as follows: No airing-grounds ; no change of rooms ; tubs in the prisoners' cells for the reception of every kind of filth ; black holes ; no religious services ; jailers living away from their prisons, consequently an impossibility of any inspection and an almost total absence of care ; free communication through the windows with the public."

She goes on to speak of the dirty straw for bedding, the unglazed windows, the cold, damp cells, and the hopeless, idle condition of the unfortunate inmates.

This, then, is what I saw, with but few exceptions, when, sixteen years later, I entered on my duties as inspector.

Referring to my early reports, I find every circumstance of importance recorded.

The prisons, as buildings, were utterly unfit for the use to which they had been applied. Many were old houses out of repair, and were as insecure as they were unwholesome resorts for human beings. Some of the cells were actually vaults below ground, that during rainy weather were a foot deep in water.

In these places criminals were herded together, young and old, good or bad, without any distinction as to their various offences, and were left to corrupt one another. No work was provided, and they passed their time in idleness, drunkenness, and gambling.

The aphorism still held good in Scotland that "the country at great expense kept State schools for immorality."

The Sheriff-Substitute of Dundee told me that he had great reluctance in sentencing a person to even a short period of confinement in the gaol of his district, as he felt in so doing he was "condemning the offender to the loss of every good trait that might remain in his character."

At Inverness a youth named Mackintosh was sentenced to death for killing a fellow-prisoner in a quarrel about a bottle of whisky. I happened to reach Inverness just as his trial ended. I consulted the judge (Lord Mackenzie) on the propriety of petitioning for the life of Mackintosh on the ground of his having been corrupted by the bad state of the gaol. He approved, and the result was that the lad's sentence was commuted.

The prison-keepers were quite unequal to their difficult task. Their pay was so small that able, well-educated men were not obtainable. In one of the smallest prisons, that of Crail, in Fife, the gaoler's yearly salary was only one pound. The gaolers, in many cases, did not live in the prisons, but merely visited them in the daytime. With but few exceptions there were no female officers, so that the women were entirely under the charge of men.

In many cases the prisons were a nuisance to the neighbourhood, owing to the profane language that was shouted to persons walking beneath the walls.

Communication was carried on, to a great extent, with the outer world, so that the prisoners had no difficulty in obtaining whisky, or even tools to enable them to escape. At Huntly Gaol it was found impossible to keep a prisoner in safe custody unless an officer on guard was constantly with him. At Kinross I found that the gaoler, who lived at a considerable distance, was indebted for the safe custody of the criminal prisoners during the night to the vigilance of the debtors. Observing a bell-rope hanging near the entrance of their room, I inquired its use. "Oh, sir," replied the gaoler, "that is for the debtors to ring the alarm-bell when any prisoner is trying to get away."

It appeared that this gaoler was sometimes compelled to get his good friends, the debtors, to protect him against personal violence. On one occasion they informed him that two of the criminal prisoners had armed themselves with bars, which they had forced off their iron bedsteads, and were ready to attack him and seize the keys. The gaoler and the debtors, however, being prepared for the encounter, went into the cell and compelled the men to surrender.

An odd instance of escape from this same prison came to the knowledge of Lord Moncrieff, when he was Sheriff of Kinross-shire.

"There was a culprit, a native of Alloa, who was thought to be too powerful for the gaol of that place; so they hired a chaise and sent officers with him to the gaol of Kinross, where he was lodged. But before the horses were fed for their return he broke out. He waited till the officers set off, and then returned to Alloa, without their knowing it, *on the back of the chaise* that had brought him to Kinross *with them in it.*" *

At Brechin Gaol I found a wretched vault below ground, called by the prisoners the "black hole," still in use, although it had been pronounced by the sheriff to be "unfit for a dog." The prison was very insecure. I was told that on one Sunday morning there was a great commotion in Brechin Church. The magistrates were called from their devotions by a messenger who entered, post haste, to inform them that *all* the prisoners had run away!

At Kirkwall, in the Orkney Islands, the gaol formed the basement and the second story of the town-house. In wet weather the rain came freely through the roof into the upper cell; but bad as was the condition of this room, it was a region of comfort compared with the lower cells, which I found cold and damp, though it was summer when I visited the place. In the winter, the gaoler told me, the floors were often covered with water.

* See Lord Cockburn's "Circuit Journeys."

In this wretched building I found a young woman. The cell was so dark that I could not see her clearly, but I observed that she had a dirty and forlorn appearance. I asked her when she had last washed herself, and her answer was, " Last week " !

These prisons, bad as they were, had not even a deterrent effect upon criminals. Their insecurity, and the absence of anything like discipline, made them welcome refuges to the most depraved as well as to the homeless petty offenders, who had no poorhouse to shelter them.

I have already spoken of the absence of all classification of the prisoners. At Inverness I found two men shut up together day and night, one of whom had committed some trifling theft, while the other had killed his wife in a drunken brawl. This last, after an imprisonment of only six months, was to be again let loose upon society.

In another cell of the same prison I found a man of a very different stamp. His appearance indicated that steady character and intelligent mind so often met with in Scotland. I was surprised to see him in prison. On inquiry I found he was a native of Skye, and that he had been sent over to the gaol at Inverness for selling some goods by auction without a licence. Probably the offence was committed in ignorance of the state of the law. I made inquiries as to his allowance for food, and learnt, to my surprise, that he was receiving none whatever, and was wholly dependent for subsistence upon the charity of his fellow-prisoners. On his entering the prison, some weeks previously, his petition for food had been sent to the Board of Excise, but no answer had as yet arrived. I was told that another man, who had been recently confined on a charge of private distillation, had remained there for more than three months without receiving any allowance for food. I found, on the contrary, that the criminals were getting sixpence a day for this purpose with perfect regularity.

At Tain I was again surprised by the respectable appearance of one of the prisoners—a young fisherman. The cause of his imprisonment was a curious one. He believed his boat to have been bewitched, so that his fishing was spoilt, and that the only way to break the spell was to draw blood from the witch. He told me he "didna prick the auld wife mair than was just absolutely necessary"!

The laws concerning debtors, at the period of which I am writing, were peculiar. In the case of an escape of a debtor the town authorities became liable for the whole amount of his debts, and this liability held good even in the event of his being recaptured. An instance of the kind occurred in the Forfar Gaol. Two debtors ran away; but, probably finding their own homes still less comfortable than their prison abode, they voluntarily returned. The creditors, however, having learnt what had taken place, at once commenced proceedings against the town for the amount of their claim, and the magistrates were glad to compromise the matter by the payment of seven hundred pounds.

A curious instance occurred at Dingwall, where the prison formed part of the town-house. A debtor who had not escaped, nor even desired to do so, was judged, from a legal point of view, to have run away. What happened was as follows :—A public meeting had been held in the court-room which adjoined the debtor's cell, and the gaoler had given the prisoner leave to attend it. This fact coming to the knowledge of the creditor, he at once threatened the bailies with an action for the whole amount of the debt, and they were obliged to pay it.

After a time this gaol was closed for repairs, and when these had been effected an application was made to the Court of Justiciary to again legalize the building for the reception of criminals. But the bailies took care that no request should be made concerning the reception of debtors. Knowing as they did that the prison was still insecure, they determined to run no risk of again paying other people's debts ; compared with that danger they evidently looked upon the escape of criminals as a trifling matter.

In Scotland the cost of maintenance of a prisoner had to be defrayed by the inhabitants of the particular district in which the crime was committed. These districts were so small that it was often better for the little community to let an offender escape altogether than to incur the expense of his detention.

In those days large bands of vagabonds called "tinkers" used to wander about the country committing thefts and depredations on all sides. I heard many heavy complaints against them, and learnt that farmers and other persons living in retired places found it their best policy to overlook many offences rather than to bring the hostility of the gang upon them by sending for the police ; a force which, in the rural districts, moreover, was often very insufficient. A gentleman, living near Arbroath, told me that a gang of these tinkers settled themselves upon his property and became a great nuisance.   He sent a warning to them that if they did not depart at once he should call in the police; to which they coolly replied that they should remain where they chose, but added that if he would give them half the money that it would cost him to employ the police they would consent to go.

When the tinkers carried on their lawless traffic in the towns, the usual plan was to have them arrested and locked up for the night, but early on the following morning to have them conducted beyond the boundaries of the parish and then set at liberty, in the hope that their next offence would be committed in some other district.   This plan, however, proved of little avail, for the band was so numerous that by the time the last in the chain had left a town on one side, the first had generally completed his tour, and was ready to enter it on the other.

The clashing interests of counties and burghs gave rise to endless disputes, and was constantly tending to prevent the adoption of a good and uniform system of prison discipline.   The difference which existed in the treatment of prisoners in various parts of the country was almost equivalent to a variety of laws respecting the same offence; so that a man was frequently punished, not according to the magnitude of his crime, but according to the latitude and longitude of the place where his crime was committed.

The appointment of the county prison keepers was in the hands of the Commissioners of Supply, as they were called. These were, for the most part, country gentlemen, who had no knowledge on the subject of prison discipline. The burgh prison keepers were appointed by the burgh magistrates, or "bailies." These bailies were unpaid officials, quite ignorant of prison matters, and were under no controlling authority. The result can be easily imagined. Most of the keepers had no idea of any duty beyond the safe custody of their prisoners, and some of them presented examples of drunkenness and profligacy as bad, perhaps, as could be found amongst the prisoners themselves.

My earliest efforts at reform were directed to bringing these abuses to an end. I had much opposition to encounter. I remember one instance in which the bailies were deaf to my representations, and persisted in retaining a bad keeper who had formerly been their boon-companion. I had, however, made the discovery that this man was selling spirits to the prisoners, which act was a criminal offence. I therefore declared to the assembled bailies that if he were not discharged before I left the committee-room, I should write to the Lord Advocate to request that the keeper might be brought to a public trial. Upon this the order for his dismissal was given at once. Notwithstanding their defeat, however, the bailies ventured to appoint a new keeper of equally bad character, but on my warning them that full particulars of their action would be given in my report to the Secretary of State, they threw down the cards, and in a sullen manner told me to choose a keeper myself.

I may here mention a method for detecting falsehood which I sometimes employed. When I had reason to believe that an officer was telling me an untruth, I required him to look me full in the face and repeat his statement. I never knew an instance in which a guilty person could do this without flinching. Some years later I learnt from Mr. Scrimgeour, the manager of the Union Bank of London, that he had adopted the same plan for detecting fraud, and had found it successful.

I took care that my inspections should be un-expected. Not only was the day unknown, but even the hour. I sometimes made my appearance at the prison gate at five o'clock in the morning, and sometimes after nightfall. I remember one instance in which I rang the door bell as the clock was striking the hour of midnight. A keeper would sometimes remark, " If I had only *known* of your coming, sir, I would have had everything in nice order."

Amid the general state of wretched mismanagement which my first tour of inspection revealed, I had the pleasure of finding one prison in a very different state. The Glasgow Bridewell, owing to the individual effort of one man of an enlightened mind, of sterling worth and great benevolence, presented a scene of order and moral improvement. Its able governor, Mr. Brebner, together with these excellent qualities, possessed much insight into character. I was indebted to him for important aid in obtaining good prison officers.

I must make one more exception to my general condemnation of the Scotch prisons. The Aberdeen Bridewell, though not to be compared with the Glasgow Bridewell, was in a better condition than that of the rest of the gaols.

One of the means which I adopted for obtaining a constant knowledge of the state of each of the prisons, was to require the governors to send me a monthly report. In this they had to answer a number of specific questions prepared by me. I encouraged them, at the same time, to add other information, and to make any suggestions that seemed useful.

On the 3rd of February, 1836, I forwarded to Lord John Russell my first " Report on the Prisons of Scotland."

In this report I had given a detailed account of the various abuses which existed, together with a list of the remedial measures which I proposed.

Amongst these I suggested that the management of all the prisons in Scotland should be placed under one directing authority to be appointed by Government, and that the cost of the prisons and prisoners should be defrayed out of one general fund.

I proposed that the principle of entire separation of prisoner from prisoner should be immediately carried into effect, and should be provided for in the construction of all new prisons.

I urged the employment of female officers to attend on the women.

I advised the introduction of profitable labour (all prisoners being required to work), and suggested that such trades should be taught as would enable them to earn an honest livelihood on leaving prison.

I also proposed that a general refuge should be provided for juvenile offenders after they had left prison, and that an asylum should be erected for the reception of all criminal lunatics.

CHAPTER VIII.

1835–1839.

Edinburgh society in its second famous period—Lord Jeffrey,
Lord Cockburn, Lord Murray, and others—James Aber-
cromby on Peel's character—Sydney Smith and Mr. Home
—Mrs. Fletcher—Mrs. Siddons—The " Bride of Lammer-
moor "—The brothers Chambers—David Roberts, the painter
—Miss Stirling Graham's " Mystifications."

On finishing my first tour of inspection of the
prisons I took up my residence in Edinburgh.

In those days, before the age of railways, Edinburgh was, as it were, a place set apart, enjoying
its own peculiar characteristics and unaffected by
the centralizing tendencies of London.

"Philosophy had become indigenous in the place, and
all classes, even in their gayest hours, were proud of the
presence of its cultivators. Thus learning was improved
by society, and society by learning, and, unless party spirit
interfered, perfect harmony and, indeed, lively cordiality
prevailed." *

Edinburgh was the field, too, of Sir Walter Scott's
genius—a genius which had made the old town

* See Cockburn's " Life of Jeffrey."

famous throughout the civilized world. But the figure of the author with the " high Goldsmith forehead, the unkempt locks and the halting limb," had disappeared when I came to Scotland. His spirit, however, still seemed to linger in his "own romantic town." Sir Walter lived in the affections of all who had ever known him, and I heard stories of him and references to him on all sides.

Had I received my appointment but a few years earlier, I should have had official relations with the author of " Waverley," and must then have had the happiness of knowing him personally.

One of the most prominent figures in Edinburgh society, as I first knew it, was Lord Jeffrey. Three years before my arrival, the great battle for Parliamentary Reform had been fought and won ; and " to no individual had the country looked for guidance so much as to Jeffrey." After the passing of the Reform Bill he was elected, together with Mr. James Abercromby, to represent the city of Edinburgh in Parliament. Mrs. Fletcher, in her interesting autobiography, thus describes the scene of the election :—

" It was during the winter of 1832–3 that the hustings were erected for the first time at the Cross of Edinburgh, for the popular election of the members for the city under the new Reform Bill.

"At length, in December, came the day of election, and we were kindly invited by the Lord Advocate and Mrs. Jeffrey to their house in Moray Place, to see the members brought home in triumph. The citizens of Edinburgh did themselves honour in choosing two such representatives as James Abercromby, the Speaker of the House of Commons, and Francis Jeffrey, then Lord Advocate ; men not less eminent for their talents than for their public spirit and courage in supporting the cause of civil and religious liberty, both in and out of Parliament. . . . It was a glorious sight for us to see these truly honest men borne home amidst the acclamation of tens of thousands of their grateful and emancipated countrymen. We stood by them on the balcony of Mr. Jeffrey's house while they shortly returned thanks to the people."

To this account Mrs. Fletcher's daughter adds the following note :—

" Lord Cockburn was more excited by joy on that day even than we were. I well remember his way of rushing into the drawing-room and looking round the crowd of Whig ladies and girls who were present, and calling out, ' Where's Mrs. Fletcher ? She's the woman that I want.' And when my mother came from the window to meet him, they clasped each other's hands and had a good 'greet' together. But not many words were said before there was a call for 'Cockburn' from the crowd without, and he went to the balcony to respond to the call, and made a short speech of deep feeling which was cheered long and loudly."

Mrs. Fletcher I knew well. Her husband, Archi-

Yours very sincerely
Eliza Fletcher

bald Fletcher, who had died in 1828, was almost the father of Burgh Reform in Scotland. Lord Cockburn thus describes him :—

"A pure and firm patriot, never neglecting any opportunity of resisting oppression, ashamed of no romance of public virtue. In all his patriotism he was encouraged by his amiable and high-minded wife, of whom Lord Brougham says, most justly, that 'with the utmost purity of life that can dignify and enhance female charms, she combined the inflexible principles and deep political feeling of a Hutchinson and a Roland.'"

To return to Lord Jeffrey. His great powers of mind shone brilliantly in his conversation.

Nothing could be further from the truth than the idea which prevailed at that time in England that he was dogmatic, sarcastic, and regardless of the feelings of those with whom he conversed. I experienced nothing of the sort, but found him, on the contrary, affable, lively, and kind.

His intimate friend, Lord Cockburn, says—

"Speaking seemed necessary for his existence. The intellectual fountains were so full that they were always bubbling over, and it would have been painful to restrain them. But, amidst all his fluency of thought and all his variety of matter, a great part of the delight of his conversation arose from its moral qualities. Let him be as bold, as free, and as incautious and hilarious as he might, no sentiment could escape him that tended to excuse inhumanity or meanness, or that failed to cherish high principles and generous affections. Then the language in which this talent and worth were disclosed! The very words were a delight. Copious and sparkling, they often imparted nearly as much pleasure as the merry or the tender wisdom they conveyed. . . . It may appear an odd thing to say, but it is true that the listener's pleasure was enhanced by the personal littleness of the speaker. A large man could scarcely have thrown off Jeffrey's conversational flowers without exposing himself to ridicule. But the liveliness of the deep thoughts and the flow of the bright expressions that animated his talk seemed so natural and appropriate to the figure that uttered them, that they were heard with something of the delight with which the slenderness of the trembling throat and the quivering of the wings make us enjoy the strength and clearness of the notes of a little bird."

My friend Mr. Francis Home,* a man of ardent feelings but courtly manners, was once travelling by stage-coach from Edinburgh to London, when, at the dinner-table of a wayside inn, he fell in with a tall portly gentleman who had lately joined the coach. Mr. Home let fall some expression which showed whence he came, whereupon his fellow-traveller turned to him, saying, " I perceive, sir, that you have just come from Edinburgh. Pray how's little Jeffrey ? "

Mr. Home, almost aghast at such a question,

* Pronounced in Scotland *Hume.*

replied, "Sir, when I left Edinburgh *Lord* Jeffrey was very well; and, sir," he added, looking his companion full in the face, "I have yet to learn that a great mind is always to be found in a bulky body."

A peal of genial laughter was the only reply from the tall portly gentleman, who was none other than Sydney Smith. He at once entered into conversation, proposed that they should ride together inside the coach for the remainder of the journey, and on arriving in London invited Mr. Home to visit him.

I was glad to learn from Lord Jeffrey that his views on the subject of the Poor Law coincided with my own, and that he did not hold the opinions of the Malthusians, then very prevalent in Scotland.

With Lord Cockburn I had much intercourse. He was a man strong both in head and heart, and was, like Jeffrey, one of the foremost leaders of the Scotch Whig party. His face was a striking one, with "his clear eyes and grand forehead."

I remember his telling me that when he was at the Edinburgh High School he was "the dunce of his form"—a fact showing either a wonderful subsequent growth of intellect, or else a great blunder on the part of his teachers; a blunder suggesting the suspicion that they may have had a greater claim than himself to the dunce's cap.

My friend Mr. Simpson used to tell a story of Cockburn and Telford, the engineer. Cockburn had possessed himself by chance of a copy of doggerel verses which Telford had written when a young man, and of which he was heartily ashamed. The more his fame increased the more desirous Telford became that these verses should be buried in oblivion. At times the worthy engineer was inclined to be dogmatic in company, and on these occasions Lord Cockburn, who had learnt every line of the unlucky poem by heart, used, by some bold stroke, to make occasion to quote them, ushering them in with the words, "as the delightful author of So-and-so says," or, "as is well expressed in those beautiful lines." Instantly poor Telford became mute, all spirit left him, and he was perfectly subdued. The talisman never failed, and at last Telford implored Cockburn's mercy.

I recollect a conversation with Lord Cockburn on the subject of the payment of procurators fiscal by fees. I mentioned to him that in talking with prisoners I not unfrequently found that they entertained a belief that the cause of their being in gaol was the desire of the "fiscal" to put a fee of two guineas into his pocket. This evil, I thought, might be readily obviated by paying the procurators a fixed salary instead of fees on conviction. Although Lord Cockburn, as a judge, had necessarily much to do with criminals, he said that the idea I had thrown out was quite new to him, and that he would carefully consider it. Some time afterwards the practice of paying procurators fiscal by fees was discontinued, and payment by salary was substituted.

It is to Lord Cockburn that we owe the preservation of the grand open view of the Castle rock from Prince's Street. Had it not been for his exertions houses would have been built on what is now Prince's Street Gardens. He endeavoured also to preserve the fine trees dotted about the city from the axe. It is reported that on one occasion he exclaimed, " I would as soon cut down a burgess without a fair trial as cut down a burgh tree ! "

Mr. James Abercromby, the Speaker of the House of Commons, was the third son of Sir Ralph Abercromby, who defeated the French in the battle of Aboukir. I had much intercourse with him a few years later, when, as Lord Dunfermline, he became a member of the Board of Directors of Prisons. I made notes of several of our conversations. One of these was on the character of Sir Robert Peel. Lord Dunfermline's view of it was new to me. He said that though Peel had been brought up with Tory prejudices, and was tricky in obtaining his ends, he believed his tendencies to be Liberal, and considered that his aspirations were all good. He said he never knew a man who had a greater dread of responsibility, and he added that he knew no one who was less able to bear up when he felt that he was in the wrong. As Speaker, Lord Dunfermline had a full opportunity of observing the countenances of the leading members. He said that when Sir Robert Peel was about to speak on some motion against his conscience, the writhings of his features were pitiable to behold. Lord Dunfermline felt sure that he would ultimately give up the Corn Laws.

I may here mention that my friend Dr. Johnson, of Birmingham, who was physician to Sir Robert Peel's father, and saw a good deal of Sir Robert as a young man, had formed exactly the same estimate of his character.

Speaking of the ventilation of the House of Commons, Lord Dunfermline mentioned that at one period he had been oppressed, day after day, by a husky cough and headache, for which he knew not how to account. At last an honourable member made this startling announcement: "Mr. Speaker, I have to inform the House that we shall soon all be killed!" He went on to explain that Dr. Reid's newly introduced hot-air apparatus had got out of order in the absence of its inventor, and that it was, upon Dr. Arnott's authority, making the atmosphere so dry as to be most injurious to life!

Lord Dunfermline spoke of political opinion depending greatly upon people's trades. When he first stood for the representation of Edinburgh, it was found in canvassing the city that, as a rule, the shoemakers were Liberals, while the butchers were Tories; that the grocers were, almost to a man, Liberals, while the hairdressers were Tories; and, again, that the carpenters were Liberals, while the milkmen were Tories.

Mr. Andrew Rutherford, who became Solicitor-General for Scotland in 1837, I knew. It was mainly to him that Scotland owed her emancipation from the old unjust laws relating to land. Some years later he was raised to the Bench as Lord Rutherford.

I have already spoken of the kind welcome which I received on my first arrival in Edinburgh from the Lord Advocate, Sir John, afterwards Lord

Murray, and of my high esteem for his character. At his hospitable house I had the pleasure of meeting with the most distinguished men of Edinburgh society. This "marvellously genial person," whose qualities were "good nature, a love of humour, and particularly a love of pleasant society," formed a central figure round whom they all gathered, and their welcome of myself verified Burns's lines—

> "Thy sons, Edina, social, kind,
> With open arms the stranger hail."

Sir Walter Scott alludes to John Archibald Murray in his diary for the year 1827 :—

"Went to dine with John Murray, where met his brother (Henderland), Jeffrey, Cockburn, Rutherford, and others of the file. Very pleasant ; capital good cheer and excellent wine ; much laugh and fun. I do not know how it is, but when I am out with a party of my Opposition friends the day is often merrier than when with our own set. Is it because they are cleverer ? Jeffrey and Harry Cockburn are, to be sure, very extraordinary men ; yet it is not owing to that entirely. I believe both parties meet with the feeling of something like novelty. We have not worn out our jests in daily contact. There is also a disposition on such occasions to be courteous and, of course, to be pleased."

And, again, speaking of a similar gathering, he writes—

"We had a very pleasant party. The Chief Commissioner was there, Admiral Adam, J. A. Murray, Thom. Thomson, etc., etc. ; Sir Adam predominating and dancing, what he calls, his 'merry andrada' in great style. In short, we really laughed, and real laughter is a thing as rare as real tears. I must say, too, there was a *heart*, a kindly feeling prevailed over the party." *

Mr. William Murray of Henderland, alluded to above, was Sir John's elder brother. He had inherited the family property of Henderland. He lived with Sir John and Lady Murray, and was, like his brother, possessed of fine qualities in mind and heart.

Lady Murray made an excellent hostess, kind, courteous, and attentive to all her guests. She was an accomplished musician. Her performance on the pianoforte was of a high order. When I first knew her and her husband there was a fourth member of the household who was most tenderly beloved by all; a fine, handsome, promising boy, their only child. But, unhappily, he died when about twelve years old.

All that I ever heard of Sir John Murray redounded to his honour. On one occasion an old lady who had quarrelled with her adopted heir bequeathed her entire property to Sir John. When the will was read he found himself, to his great

* See Lockhart's " Life of Sir Walter Scott."

surprise, possessed of wealth, while the heir-presumptive found himself penniless. Sir John made inquiries into the character of the young man, and receiving satisfactory answers, he quietly transferred back to him the whole property. Soon after this a lady called upon Sir John's mother, and, indignant at what seemed to her an act of quixotism, demanded, "Do you know what your son John has done?"

"Yes," replied Mrs. Murray; "and he would not have been my son John if he had done anything else."

Mrs. Murray lived to the advanced age of nearly a hundred. She had a clear memory for bygone events, and could describe accurately the striking scenes of the Rebellion of 1745. She was a niece of Chief Justice Mansfield.

Sir Adam Fergusson was a marked figure in Edinburgh society. He was the lifelong friend of Sir Walter Scott, and was one of the very few persons to whom the "Great Unknown" confided the secret of the authorship of "Waverley." Scott says of him, "He combined the lightest and most airy temper with the best and kindest disposition."

Referring to my journal, I find the following:—

"Dined at Mr. William Chambers's, and met Sir Adam Fergusson. Sir Adam, though an old man, has much of the animation and fire of youth, and he told stories of fifty years since as if they had occurred yesterday. The conversation happened to fall upon Home, the author of the tragedy of 'Douglas,' with whom Sir Adam was well acquainted. He said that no man could be more unequally matched in a wife; Mrs. Home having neither taste for literature, nor the slightest appreciation of literary men. She was infirm in health and very deaf, and she spent the greater part of the day on the sofa chewing nutmegs, always keeping a nutmeg and grater in her pocket. Soon after 'Douglas' was published, an enthusiastic admirer of the play made a journey from London to Edinburgh on purpose to see its author, and great was his disappointment on reaching Home's house to find that he was away from Edinburgh. The servant asked him if he would like to see Mrs. Home, and he was taken upstairs, picturing as he went the lovely being a poet's wife must be. Her unprepossessing appearance dispelled his illusions, but he sought, by his enthusiastic admiration of her husband, to touch the feelings of the wife. Not one remark could he get, an occasional grunt being her only rejoinder. Much daunted, the gentleman sat silent, when the lady, with some spark of animation, asked if there were any prospect of a peace. 'Yes,' he answered, glad of some conversational question; 'there is every hope that a glorious peace will soon be concluded.'

"'Oh, aye—will it mak' ony difference in the price o' nut*mugs?*'

"This was too much for the visitor, and he hastily withdrew."

Mrs. Siddons was a frequent guest of Home's, and it was at his house that Sir Adam often met her. He said he never saw her smile but once, and then she laughed outright. It was at the dinner-table. Mr. Home asked Mrs. Siddons what wine she would drink, and upon her saying that she preferred porter, he told a servant-boy to go and fetch "a little porter." The boy soon returned, ushering in a little man with straps and badge complete, exclaiming, " This, sir, is the smallest porter I could find."

I became acquainted with the Honourable Mrs. Stewart Mackenzie, a daughter of Lord Seaforth. I met her first at the house of Lord Mackenzie, the son of the author of the " Man of Feeling." I was told that all the members of Lord Seaforth's family were distinguished for their talents, and certainly I found this to be the case as regarded Mrs. Stewart Mackenzie.

I well remember a conversation we had about Sir Walter Scott. She told me that one day, when she happened to be out driving with him, Sir Walter told her, in his powerfully graphic way, the story of the " Bride of Lammermoor." When it was finished, they were both silent for a time. Then Mrs. Mackenzie exclaimed, " Horrible—truly horrible ! I hope that story will never appear in print."

Nevertheless at no distant time it did appear

in print, as one of the Waverley Novels. "But," added Mrs. Mackenzie, "so firm was my belief, at the time, that Scott was not the author of the novels, that even this event did not shake my conviction."

Soon after my arrival in Edinburgh I had the happiness of forming the friendship of William and Robert Chambers. Like all those who desired the spread of knowledge, I had felt grateful to them for the excellent work they were doing in producing good and cheap literature. Their admirable *Journal* appeared as early as February, 1832, and was the forerunner of the mass of cheap publications which gradually followed in its wake.

The story of the lives of the two brothers, as told by William Chambers, is a most interesting and instructive piece of biography. It shows what talent, united with striking worth and indomitable energy, can accomplish in the face of what would seem, to ordinary men, insurmountable difficulties.

I became most intimate with Robert, and at his house, in the society of his excellent wife and many mutual friends, I had very pleasant intercourse.

During the greater part of my residence in Edinburgh, his sister, Miss Janet Chambers, was also a member of the household—a lady conspicuous for her racy Scotch humour, her musical talents, and her warm heart. In 1846 she was married to Mr. Henry Wills, who held an important position on the *Daily News*, then recently started, and who was afterwards editor of *Household Words*. The wedding had to take place in London, as Mr. Wills could not be spared from his responsible post. I happened to be one of a small band of intimate friends who conducted the lady to the steamboat, which was lying off Newhaven, and which was to convey her to England. This little incident was most kindly remembered by her for nearly half a century. Her death, which has recently occurred, deprives me of one of my last surviving Edinburgh friends.

I became acquainted with Mr. Charles Maclaren, the first editor of the *Scotsman*. He had accomplished a great work for reform in spreading Liberal opinions in Scotland, when the only existing organ for such opinions was the *Edinburgh Review*. But the *Review* appealed to a more exclusive set of readers. It "was a sort of bishop over the faithful few, whilst the *Scotsman* was a missionary to the unconverted many."

When Charles Maclaren first launched the *Scotsman*, in 1817, the people of Scotland "were absolutely without voice either by vote or by

speech. Parliamentary elections, municipal government, the management of public bodies—everything was in the hands of a few hundred persons,"
who "took their directions from the Government
of the day or its proconsul. Public meetings were
almost unknown, and a free press may be said to
have never had an existence."

There was no respectable opposition paper till
the appearance of the *Scotsman*.*

Mr. Maclaren was a man of most varied knowledge, which he continued to improve by means
of extensive reading to the very end of his life.
His favourite pursuit was geology, and he spent
many an hour wandering along the hills about
Edinburgh, hammer in hand, adding to his collection of fossils. He was a most amiable man.

I find the following entry in my diary:—

"*Edinburgh, November* 26, 1835.—Passed the evening
at the Lord Advocate's, where there was a large party;
among others, Mr. Wigham, a quaker gentleman, to whom
I had a letter of introduction. We had much conversation upon prison matters. At parting Mr. Wigham said
to me, 'What can I do to forward thy views?'"

He became one of my most intimate friends.
I can never forget his kindness, and that of Mrs.

* See "Memoir of Charles Maclaren."

Wigham, when they nursed me through a severe illness.

Mr. Wigham was a staunch Liberal. In 1840 he nominated Mr. (afterwards Lord) Macaulay as member for Edinburgh, and two years later became chairman of the Anti-Corn Law Association. But although he took a deep interest concerning the public welfare, there was an absence of all hot discussions or asperity of argument in his household.

William Chambers, describing it, says—

"The members of the family seemed to live in an atmosphere of perfect composure. . . . All matters treated of bore reference to something practically good, connected with social progress. A visit to their house was as soothing as a perusal of the fifth chapter of Matthew. I always came away the better for what I saw and heard."

At Mr. Wigham's house I had the pleasure of meeting, on one occasion, Mr. William Lloyd Garrison, the ardent abolitionist, and hearing from him an account of the state of the anti-slavery question at that time in America. I also met Mr. Frederick Douglas, the negro who had effected his escape from slavery, and whose interesting "Life" has since been written.

Among my earliest friends in Scotland was Mr. James Simpson, Advocate.

He was well known as an able and interesting lecturer, and also as the author of " Paris after Waterloo," in which he gave a vivid account of a visit to the scene of the great battle, and afterwards to Paris, while the news of the victory was fresh in all minds.

Among the subjects to which Mr. Simpson directed his mind were those of medical jurisprudence and the treatment of criminals; and he was one of the first, if not the very first, to show the many points of resemblance between crime and insanity. In one of our conversations he made the far-seeing remark that, in his opinion, "a prison should be like a hospital; to which persons are sent, not for a fixed period, but to be cured."

To an

"ardent interest in everything that related to the welfare of his race, Mr. Simpson united so happy a power of public speaking that in moving large bodies of men to enlightened and virtuous action he was almost unrivalled. His admirable lectures on ' Education ' and ' Sanitary Reform,' delivered in most of the large towns of the kingdom, will be long remembered. . . . He never failed in the moral courage necessary for telling his hearers, whether of the upper or lower classes, of their faults ; but he did it in so kind a spirit, and often with so playful a wit, that he never seemed to give offence."

Mr. Simpson was asked on one occasion, by

the artisans of Edinburgh, to repeat a course of lectures on the " Formation of Character and on Social Improvement " which he had delivered twenty years previously.

"Those who formed the deputation stated that they made this request because they felt they themselves had been 'better men, better husbands, better fathers, for having heard those lectures,' and that they were now desirous that their children should partake of the same benefit. On Mr. Simpson inquiring what assurance they had that the lectures were generally desired, they produced in a few days a requisition to him with three thousand signatures.

"An entertainment, perhaps the first of its kind, was given by the working class of Edinburgh to some members of the higher grades on the occasion of presenting Mr. Simpson with a piece of plate as a memorial of their gratitude. The person who was deputed to deliver it (a letter-carrier) concluded his short speech with these words: 'Still come among us, and still will we sit at your feet and learn; and when that time comes when all that is earthly must pass away, rest assured that, be it the marble or the heather that covers your grave, the poor man's tears will water it.'" *

Mr. Simpson's daughters inherited their father's large-hearted benevolence as well as his ready wit. Many were the happy hours that I spent in the society of these friends.

* See obituary article in the *Spectator* of September 17, 1853.

Speaking of Mr. Simpson brings me naturally to speak of the brothers George and Andrew Combe, with whom he was intimate, and of whom I saw much during my residence in Edinburgh. Both were noted men of the time. George Combe was the ardent disciple of phrenology, and one of its first promulgators. I did not share his opinions on this subject, but I valued his practical views on the development of mind and character.

Andrew Combe was the author of an able treatise on "Physiology applied to the Preservation of Health." The brothers resembled each other in their amiable dispositions as well as in their marked talents. "There was more than fraternal affection between them; there was devotion to each other. Whatever occupied the one interested the other; whatever troubled the one distressed the other."

George Combe married the daughter of Mrs. Siddons. She had a striking countenance, having inherited her mother's lustrous eyes. Mr. Combe, who had recourse to phrenology even in the choice of his wife, thus describes her on their marriage in 1833:—

"Our feelings and perceptions are so truly in harmony that one would think we had been bred together during life. This is the result of similarity of combination of brain. Her anterior lobe is large, her Benevolence, Conscientiousness, Firmness, Self-esteem and Love of Approbation are also amply developed; while Veneration and Wonder are equally moderate with my own. It is too soon to boast, but I have a full conviction that our happiness will be permanent, and I reckon myself to have set a practical example of my philosophy in marrying such a woman." *

Dr. Andrew Combe's health was not robust, and in order to enable himself to fulfil the duties of his profession, he laid down rigid rules for his daily conduct. I recollect that one of these rules was, "At 11 a.m. always to be lively;" accordingly at that hour the doctor was to be found capering about his room!

Mr. Peter Nimmo, the private secretary of Lord Murray, was a man of very attractive qualities, with whom I had constant intercourse.

He introduced me, on one occasion, to David Roberts, the painter. This delightful artist was of humble origin, but was never ashamed of it, and showed every filial respect and attention to his shepherd-father and his mother. The old couple were visiting their son when he had a party of brother artists and others at his house. Mr. Nimmo, who had some chat with them, expressed a hope that they were enjoying their visit. The

---

* See "Life of George Combe," by Charles Gibbon.

old shepherd replied, " Ou, we're weel eno' wi' our Davy and his friends ; but they talk of their picturs and picturs and picturs just as if they were saw many sheep ! "

Dr. Alison I knew and greatly respected. Many a talk we had together on his favourite subject of a Poor Law for Scotland ; our opinions coinciding.

Another friend was John Hill Burton, who afterwards became a prominent figure in Edinburgh society. The racy sayings of the learned historian and author of the " Book Hunter " will long be quoted. Between his family and mine a close friendship existed, and is now carried on by our descendants.

An account of Edinburgh society, as I knew it from 1835 to 1847, would be incomplete without mention of a lady whom I met occasionally, who had acquired much local celebrity—Miss Stirling Graham, of Duntrune. Duntrune was her estate in Forfarshire, where she usually lived, but whence she came to Edinburgh for the winter seasons.

This lady, though confining the exercise of her talents to private life, possessed the powers of a consummate actress ; and her impersonation of various characters, especially of old Scotch women, afforded amusement to a large circle of friends, and may be said to " have kept the town in a pleasant kind of buzz." So popular, indeed, were these performances that in later life she was urged to publish an account of them. This she did, in a small volume entitled "Mystifications," which, though first issued for private circulation, soon afterwards appeared before the public, edited by Dr. John Brown.

Unfortunately the work is now out of print, and therefore rarely to be met with.

In his preface the editor gives the following extract from one of Sir Walter Scott's Journals :—

"*March 7*, 1828.—Went to my Lord Gillies' to dinner and witnessed a singular exhibition of personification by Miss Stirling Graham. She went off as to the play, and returned in the character of an old Scotch lady. Her dress and behaviour were admirable and the conversation unique. I was in the secret, of course, and did my best to keep up the ball, but she cut me out of all feather. The prosing account she gave of her son the antiquary, who found an auld wig in a slate quarry, was extremely ludicrous, and she puzzled the Professor of Agriculture with a merciless account of the succession of crops in the parks around her old mansion house."

On leaving the party, Sir Walter, bending down to the ear of the old lady, addressed her in these words : "Awa, awa, the deil's ower grit wi' you !"

Miss Stirling Graham, in writing of her impersonations, remarks, " The cleverest people were the easiest mystified. Indeed, children and dogs were the only detectives."

The following is her own account of the most celebrated of her performances, somewhat abridged :—

"Visit to Mr. Jeffrey.

" At the theatre one Saturday evening, in the year 1821, Mr. Jeffrey requested me to let him see my 'old lady ;' and, on condition that we should have some one to *take in*, I promised to introduce her to him very soon. Accordingly, on the Monday, having ascertained that Mr. Jeffrey was to dine at home, I set out from Lord Gillies's in a coach, accompanied by Miss Helen Carnegy, of Craigo, as my daughter, and we stopped at Mr. Jeffrey's door between five and six o'clock. It was a winter evening, and on the question, ' Is Mr. Jeffrey at home ? ' being answered in the affirmative, the two ladies stepped out, and were ushered into the little parlour where he received his visitors.

" There was a blazing fire and wax-lights on the table. Mr. Jeffrey had laid down his book and seemed to be in the act of joining the ladies in the drawing-room before dinner.

" The ' Lady Pitlyal ' was announced, and he stepped forward a few paces to meet her.

" She was a sedate-looking little woman, of an inquisitive, law-loving countenance, a mouth in which not a vestige of a tooth was to be seen, and a pair of old-fashioned spectacles on her nose. . . '. She was dressed in an Irish poplin of silver grey, a white cashmere shawl, a mob-cap with a band of thin muslin that fastened it below the chin, and a small black silk bonnet that shaded her eyes from any glare of light.

"Her right hand was supported by an antique gold-headed cane, and she leant with the other on the arm of her daughter, Miss Ogilvy. Mr. Jeffrey bowed, and handed the old lady to a comfortable *chaise longue* on one side of the fire, and sat himself down opposite to her on the other.

"'Well!' said Mr. Jeffrey, as he looked at the old lady in expectation that she would open the subject that procured him the honour of the visit.

"'Weel!' replied her ladyship, 'I am come to tak' a word o' the law frae you.'

"Here followed a long-winded account of a fire which had taken place in a 'kiln and malt-barn' on her property at the 'town end of Kirriemuir.' These had not been insured, but she was determined to 'get damages' from somebody. The case had been already tried in the 'Shirra Court of Forfar,' but it had gone against her.

"The old lady continues—

"'The Minister of Blairgowrie is but a fule body, and advised me no to gae to law.'

"'I think,' said Jeffrey, 'he gave you a very sensible advice.'

"'It was anything but that; and mind, if you dinna gie't in my favour I'll no be sair pleased.'

"After more talk about her lawsuit, Lady Pitlyal drew from her pocket a large old-fashioned leather pocket-book with silver clasps, out of which she presented him a letter directed to himself. He did not look into it, but threw it carelessly on the table. She now offered him a pinch of snuff from a massive gold box, and then selected another folded paper from the pocket-book, which she presented to him, saying—

"'Here is a prophecy that I would like you to look at and explain to me.'

"He begged to be excused, saying, 'I believe your ladyship will find me more skilful in the *law* than the *prophets.'* . . .

"'Maybe,' replied her ladyship; 'but I copied these lines out of a muckle book entitled the "Prophecie of Pitlyal" just before I came to you, in order to have your opinion on some of the obscure passages.'

"Here, then, with a smile at the oddity of the request, and a mixture of impatience in his manner, he read the following lines :—

> 'O'er the Light of the North,*
> When the Glamour breaks forth,
> And its wild-fire so red
> With the daylight is spread,
> When woman shrinks not from the ordeal of trial,
> There is triumph and fame to the House of Pitlyal.'

"The old lady remarks, 'What the "Light of the North" can mean, and "Glamour," I canna mak' out. . . . I begin, however, to think that the prophecy may be fulfilled in the person of my daughter, for which reason I have brought her to Edinburgh to see and get a gude match for her. A' the world ca's her the Rosebud of Pitlyal." †

---

* The "Light of the North" was Mr. Jeffrey; the "Glamour" was herself.

† In the year 1862 I called, in company with our friend Mrs. John Hill Burton, upon the "Rosebud of Pitlyal," then an old lady, in her pretty home of Lavrock Bank.—ED.

"A pause in the conversation now ensued, which was interrupted by her ladyship asking Mr. Jeffrey where she could procure 'a set of *fause* teeth.'

"'*Of what?*' said he, with an expression of astonishment, while the whole frame of the young lady shook with some internal emotion.

"'A set of fause teeth,' she repeated, and was again echoed with the interrogation, '*What?*'

"A third time she asked the question, and in a more audible key, when he replied with a kind of suppressed laugh, 'There is Mr. Nasmyth, north corner of St. Andrew's Square, a very good dentist; and there is Mr. Hutchins, corner of Hanover and George Street.'

"She now rose to take leave. The bell was rung, and when the servant entered his master desired him to see if Lady Pitlyal's carriage was at the door.

"He returned to tell them there was no carriage waiting, upon which her ladyship remarked—

"'This comes of *forehand payments;* they make *hint-hand wark.* I gae a hackney coachman twa shillings to bring me here, and he's awa' without me.'

"There was not a coach within sight. It was by this time past the hour of dinner, and there seemed to Mr. Jeffrey no hope of getting rid of his visitors.

"Her ladyship said she was in no hurry, as she had had tea, and was going to the play, and hoped he would accompany them.

"He said he had not yet had his dinner.

"They then talked of the merits of the actors, and she took occasion to tell him that she patronized the *Edinburgh Review*.

"'We read your buke, sir!'

"'I am certainly very much obliged to you.'

"Here the coach was announced, and, by the help of her daughter's arm and her gold-headed cane, she began to move, complaining loudly of a ' carny tae.'

"The door was closed, and the order given to drive to Gibbs's Hotel, whence they hastened with all speed to Lord Gillies's, where the party waited dinner for them, and hailed the fulfilment of the 'Prophecie of Pitlyal.' Mr. Jeffrey, in the mean time, impatient for his dinner, joined the ladies in the drawing-room.

"'What in the world has detained you?' said Mrs. Jeffrey.

"'One of the most tiresome and oddest old women I ever met with.' And, beginning to relate some of the conversation that had taken place, it flashed upon him that he had been *taken in*. He ran downstairs for the letter she had given him, hoping it would throw some light on the subject; but it was only a blank sheet of paper, containing a fee of three guineas. . . .

"It was not until the day after that he found out from his friend Mrs. George Russell who the ladies really were. . . . He returned the fee with the following letter:—

"*To the* LADY PITLYAL.

"DEAR MADAM,

        "As I understand that the lawsuit about the malt-kiln is likely to be settled out of Court, I must be permitted to return the fee by which you were pleased to retain my services, and hope I shall not be quoted along with the hackney coachman in proof of the danger of *forehand* payments. I hope the dentists have not disgraced my recommendation, and that Miss Ogilvy is likely to fulfil the prophecy and bring glory and fame to the house of Pitlyal; though I am not a little mortified at having been allowed to see so little of that amiable young lady.

"With best wishes for the speedy cure of your corns, I have the honour to be, dear Madam,

"Your very faithful and obedient servant,

"F. JEFFREY."

CHAPTER IX.

1835–1839.

DURING my travels I kept a journal, which I sent home for the amusement of my family. This journal I have by me, and I will quote from it as occasion requires. The first entry is—

"*Banff, November* 16, 1835.—I passed this afternoon with Lord Fife, who showed me his grounds, pictures, and library. Lord Fife, though once a boon-companion of George IV., appears to have many right views, and to be effecting much good. He gives to all classes, both rich and poor, free access to his grounds, and on Sundays to his picture-galleries also; even to the apartments which he himself is occupying. It will sometimes happen that while he is writing in his library half a dozen fishermen and their wives will be walking about the room examining the pictures. He is often much amused at their criticisms.

"Lord Fife provides what I have long desired to see, namely, a kind of reserve of profitable labour as a check to pauperism. His property is so large that a great deal of work may always be carried on with advantage. At present, for instance, besides draining the land, opening new roads, etc., he is erecting a new pier at the neighbouring seaport of Macduff and enlarging the harbour. In these and other occupations he is employing as many as three hundred men and boys, which is a great relief to the district, the fishing season having ended, and farming employment being scarce owing to the approach of winter.

"*November* 17.—Breakfasted with Mr. Pringle, Sheriff-Substitute of Banffshire. I find that one good symptom of the working of the Burgh Reform is that many of the magistrates are taking an active part in promoting education. Objectors to reform, however, are always to be found ; and I was told of an eccentric minister of the Kirk who was so indignant with the provisions of the new Act, that when the first magistrates under it were appointed he omitted to offer the usual prayer for them. This causing complaint and remonstrance, he, the following Sunday, prayed Heaven to 'have mercy on all lunatics, idiots, and the magistrates of this burgh'!

"I was surprised to learn from Mr. Pringle that the Burgh Reform Act did not abolish the old trading rights of burgesses, and that they still exist. He says he is often called upon, much against his will, to order some poor stranger out of the town who is offering articles for sale which a burgess claims an exclusive right to vend.

"At Banff I met Mr. Cameron, the Provost, and had much interesting talk with him. He told me he could distinctly remember going with his father's grieve into the

Highlands to pay 'black-mail' to the chieftain of the district as a security against the 'lifting' of his father's cattle.   This 'black-mail' was paid in kind, chiefly in oatmeal.

"*December* 12.—Left Arbroath by stage-coach in the evening for Montrose. The road runs by the seaside, and we saw the light of the Bell Rock lighthouse. I learnt from the passengers that the contrivance of the floating bell is still used in foggy weather, and that its tolling may be heard at a great distance."

How dramatically Southey has rendered this incident in his poem of the " Inchcape Bell"!

"At Montrose found a letter awaiting me from Lord Panmure, inviting me to take up my quarters at Brechin Castle. Accepted the invitation, and had a hospitable reception.

"*December* 17.—After dinner had a good deal of conversation with Lord Panmure. Though much given to the pleasures of the table, he is a very shrewd man, and a decided Liberal in politics. He mentioned one division in the House of Commons in which Charles James Fox, Lord Grey, and himself had stood alone.

"Speaking of his ancestors, he told me that one of them had taken part in the Rebellion of 1715. 'That Rebellion,' he said, 'was conducted by gentlemen. They were very different from the riff-raff that were engaged in the '45.' His ancestors' *gentlemanly* proceeding led to the confiscation of the family estates. Some years later, however, they were recovered on easy terms ; for when the property came to be sold by auction, any bidding against the suffering family was discountenanced, as in other cases, by the honourable feeling which prevailed throughout the country.

"Lord Panmure had been a keen sportsman, and he talked with relish of his hunting days. I visited a Mechanics' Institute which he had built, and found to my amusement that he had adorned its walls with pictures of hunting and drinking scenes.

"A nephew of Lord Panmure's, whom I met at Brechin Castle, mentioned an odd freak of his uncle's earlier life. A hunting party was collected at the Castle at a time when Lady Panmure was confined to her bed. Lord Panmure laid a wager that he would ride upstairs on the back of a favourite pony and leap over her ladyship's bed! This he actually did."

I learnt, subsequently, of the extraordinary conduct of Lord Panmure towards his own family, including his son, Fox Maule. I was told, however, that in spite of all this he was popular amongst his tenantry.

"*November* 18, 1836.—Left Edinburgh for Queen's Ferry, going round by Dalmeny Park. The house and grounds are among the finest I have seen. I was politely received by Lord Rosebery, who said he would assist me in any way I might point out in carrying my prison measures into effect.

"Left for Culross, a small burgh five miles west of Dunfermline. The chief magistrate being out of town, I sent to the next in authority, a baker, to let him know that I was examining the prison. He sent me word, however, that he could not come, as he 'was busy baking.' At this the gaoler's wife held up her hands, exclaiming,

' Hech, sirs! what na a message for a bailie to send to a gentleman!'

"There appears to be very little crime at Culross, notwithstanding the baker-bailie's limited time for magisterial duties.

"*Glasgow, November* 21.—Dined with Mr. John Kerr (a friend of my brother Matthew's). He inquired particularly after Rowland's post-office plan, of which he is an enthusiastic admirer."

Mr. Kerr soon became a valued friend of my own.

"*Stirling, November* 24.—Went in the evening to dine with the sheriff of the county, who bears the laconic name of Sir Reginald Macdonald Stuart Seton of Staffa, Bart. He is one of the most ceremoniously polite men I ever met with. On our entering the hall he took off his hat and welcomed me to his 'poor house of Touch' (pronounced with a full guttural 'Tough').

"Sir Reginald is a great upholder of Gaelic customs; of course, therefore, he has his pipers. It happened 'fortunately,' he told me, that there was, in addition, an Irish piper that day in the hall. After dinner the Irish piper was requested to play for us. When his stock of wind was exhausted Sir Reginald's own piper began, and the latter certainly made a tremendous noise. His master was much delighted, and by dint of bawling in my ear at last made me understand the question 'whether I did not think the notes very distinct?' Truly a want of distinctness was the last fault I should have thought of finding.

"After the music had ended, and the drums of our ears had had a little rest, we were invited to go to one of the lower rooms to see the servants dance the Strathspey, which they did with much spirit. The next dance was a very pleasing one to witness, for master, guests, and servants all joined in it. I should have joined also had I understood the intricacies of a Scotch reel."

I witnessed a similar mingling of classes on the occasion of a curling-match which took place near Dumfries, in the grounds of a Mr. Leny (the convener of the county), who had kindly invited me to pass a few days with him. The captain of the side on which Mr. Leny played was one of his own livery servants.

At Mr. Leny's house I became acquainted with Sir Thomas Kirkpatrick, the sheriff-depute of the county. He was the last layman appointed to that office, all who followed him being lawyers. I found he had read my report on the prisons of Scotland, and fully entered into my views.

At this same time I paid my first visit to the town of Dumfries, and was kindly entertained at dinner by one of the worthy inhabitants. There was a large party to meet me. We sat down to dinner at four o'clock, where we remained for six mortal hours without any one attempting to move. At last, quite wearied out, I left the table. On reaching the drawing-room I was politely received by the lady of the house, but she expressed her surprise at seeing me *so early!*

I remember that I visited Sir Andrew Agnew at

Lochnaw Castle at Stranraer. He told me of a curious old Scottish Act of Parliament by which the killing of plovers was made punishable, "because," as the Act set forth, "they fly over the Border, and feed on the lands of our natural enemies the English."

In connection with the little port of Stranraer I may mention a story I heard at a later date of Lord Campbell (afterwards Lord Chancellor). He happened to be staying there at the time of the regatta, and was paid the compliment of being created its "admiral." At the dinner which concluded the festivities, Lord Campbell, having no hesitation in the use of "blarney," and a complete command of his countenance, made this astounding declaration : "Gentlemen, in the course of my life I have been so happy as to receive many honours from my queen and country, but I assure you that no honour was ever conferred upon me of which I feel greater pride than the honour of being created admiral of the Stranraer Regatta!"

To return to my diary.

"Shortly after my arrival at Greenock, the son of Mr. Wallace, the Provost and member for Greenock, came to my inn to take me to his father's house. Mr. Wallace is a descendant of the renowned Sir William Wallace. His house and grounds are beautifully situated on the southern bank of the Clyde. After dinner I accompanied Mr. Wallace to a meeting of his constituents, and was much pleased with his manly, straightforward account of his proceedings in Parliament during the previous session. He concluded his address (according to a rule he had laid down when he was elected) by tendering his resignation in the most unreserved manner if his constituents were dissatisfied with the manner in which he had performed his duties. Far from accepting his resignation, the meeting passed an enthusiastic vote of confidence.

" On our way home Mr. Wallace gave me some particulars respecting his struggle in the House of Commons with the Post Office in urging postal improvements, and the good effects that had followed his persevering exertions."

I should mention here that when my brother Rowland brought forward his great measure for a uniform low postage, Mr. Wallace, instead of looking upon it with a jealous eye, gave it his hearty approval.

"*December* 24.—Left Paisley for Ayr. Put up at the King's Arms. Visited the prison, and found it in the good state I had expected. Nothing can be more complete than the change since this time last year. Dirt, noise, and idleness have been succeeded by cleanliness, silence, and industry.

"*December* 25.—Captain Hamilton called on me, and I accompanied him to church. He is very zealous in promoting the improvement of the prison. When I was here a year ago and proposed my remedial measures, he said that if there was any difficulty in raising the necessary funds, he would himself pay every shilling out of his own pocket rather than see my plans abandoned.

"*December* 26.—A verdict of culpable homicide was given to-day by, I believe, a very respectable jury in a clearly established case of barbarous murder ; the reason being evidently their aversion to capital punishment. The judge, foreseeing the possibility of such a verdict, had charged strongly against it, but the jury was resolute. The verdict has made a considerable sensation.

"*Fort George, September* 23, 1837.—This is a strong fortification, standing on a peninsula which juts out into the Moray Firth. It was erected after the Rebellion of 1745, to overawe the Highlands. It is very large, and is capable of holding two thousand soldiers, besides officers and attendants.

"My object in visiting the fortress was to see whether part of it could be converted into a prison for the north of Scotland. I am glad to find that it can easily be applied to this purpose.

"*Inverness.*—Was glad to find on my arrival here that the circuit was not over. Dined with the judges ; sat by Lord Mackenzie, with whom I had a good deal of conversation. He mentioned a striking instance of the confidence which can be placed in the just result of a trial in Scotland. Two men had been charged with murder, but the precognition, or preliminary investigation, made by the sheriff and procurator fiscal, showed that the charge was groundless. Still the public continued to entertain strong suspicions, so that the men were shunned on all sides. Under these circumstances, they came forward and insisted on being brought to the bar and tried for the murder. This was done ; they were fully acquitted, and all feeling against them disappeared."

When visiting the Shetland Islands during the

first year of my appointment, I found that the steamboat which conveyed me was performing her second trip only. The summits of the cliffs were covered with spectators to witness our arrival. I was told that on its first trip some boatmen, thinking that the vessel was approaching too near the coast, put off to warn the sailors of their danger; but when the ship was seen to be making her way right against the wind, they took fright, supposing her to be bewitched, and hurried back.

When out walking one day I saw a miserable-looking man, who, I was informed, was Hare, the associate of Burke, who had carried on the horrible practice of murder in order to get money by selling the bodies of his victims for the purposes of dissection. Hare had escaped by turning king's evidence.

In Lerwick one day I saw a little Shetland pony entering a dwelling-house without ceremony, and was told that it lived there. It always scrambled upstairs, and occupied one of the bedrooms as its stable.

I found that the islanders, at that time, had little intercourse with the rest of the world. The parental tie was so strong that parents were loth to part with their sons even for the whale-fishing. But five or six years later, when the establishment of penny postage had brought facility of communication, the enterprise of the younger generation was not so checked. The number of letters increased at once in England about four or five-fold, but in Shetland it increased thirteen-fold.

The two innovations of steam navigation and cheap postage brought about, indeed, a great change for the Shetlanders. A gentleman whom I knew told me he had once been without news of his family for three months, he being on the main-land, and the winds contrary.

In one of my tours I was kindly invited by the Duke of Richmond to pay him a visit at Gordon Castle. The duke, as I have previously mentioned, had taken an active part in the passing of the Act under which inspectors of prisons were appointed. I was kindly welcomed, and have a very pleasant recollection of my visit.

My host (fifth Duke of Richmond) had been a favourite officer of the Duke of Wellington, and had served under him in the Peninsular War and at Waterloo. A permanent souvenir of his military life remained in his body in the shape of a bullet which had never been extracted.

During my stay at the Castle a dance was given to the tenants, in which I was invited to take part. To this, however, I objected, on the ground that I had never learnt to dance Scotch reels. But my objection was overruled by one of the ladies of the family—Lady Caroline Lennox—who immediately offered to teach me. This she accordingly did, and I hope that at the dance I did not altogether discredit my kind instructress.

In the summer of 1838 a remarkably fine Aurora Borealis was visible in Scotland. I witnessed this phenomenon when staying at Inverary, where I happened to fall in with Mr. Babbage, with whom I was previously acquainted. We passed much of the night together in the open air, enjoying the beauty of the spectacle.

In the course of conversation, Mr. Babbage told me that he was intimate with Sir John Herschel. The two friends were planning a tour in Switzerland, when the question arose as to their possessing the necessary steadiness of head for mountaineering. To settle this important point, they tried the experiment of climbing the scaffold poles of Sir William Herschel's great telescope. When they had reached a height of forty feet, Sir John called out, " Babbage, do you feel at all giddy ? " " Not at all," was the reply; whereupon they resumed their climbing, and without any tremor reached the top, whence they shouted mutual congratulations.

When inspecting some of the prisons in the north of Scotland, I paid a visit, by invitation, to the Countess Duchess of Sutherland at Dunrobin

Castle. I was much impressed by the combination of power and benevolence which her very appearance bespoke, and which all I saw of the management of her great estate confirmed. The countess evidently possessed that first requisite of a ruler, the ability to select good subordinates ; but not content with the exercise of this power, she gave all her tenants the opportunity of personal intercourse with herself. Once every week she held a court, or *levée,* to which all might come (rich and poor) to tender a complaint, offer a petition, or solicit her advice.

The chief employments of her tenants were in the fisheries and on the sheep-farms, but ultimately coal-mining was added to these ; for the countess engaged the services of a geologist to make a careful examination of the ground, which ended in the discovery of valuable beds of coal.

In riding late one evening outside the mail-coach to Perth, I was placed in the greatest personal danger that I ever encountered. The road passes through a glen by a long steep descent. It is bounded on one side by a wall of lofty rock, on the other by a precipice, at the foot of which runs a river, and finally takes a sharp turn to cross the bridge below.

When we began the descent darkness was fast

approaching, but the horses, instead of slackening their pace, increased it every moment. As we dashed along, the coach rocking from side to side, I remonstrated with the driver; but I soon became aware that he had lost all power to stop the horses. The pole-chain had broken. I expected that in a few minutes we should all be hurled down the precipice into the river. In this emergency we owed our lives to the gallant conduct of the guard. He scrambled across the coach, and throwing himself with violence on to the back of the off-wheeler, forced the horse down upon the ground, and thus made a scotcher of its body. The coach reeled and stopped, and we were saved.

Another incident of my stage-coach journeys is of a very different kind. I was travelling in a lonely part of Scotland where there was no habitation within sight, when the guard blew his horn loudly, and, to my surprise, we stopped. Presently I saw a large collie dog come bounding down a hill, making straight for us. When he reached the coach the guard dropped a letter-bag on the ground before him. The dog took up the bag, holding the strap in his mouth, and immediately ran off with it up the hill and disappeared. There was a farmhouse in the neighbourhood, about a quarter of a mile off, and this dog, I was told, always thus fetched the letters for the family.

I remember standing one Sunday night upon the bridge over the Tay near Perth, and witnessing a curiously literal observance of the sabbath. Several fishing-boats were below me, the men's oars standing out horizontally and quite motion-less. Thus they continued till a clock in the city began to strike the hour of midnight, with the first sound of which down went the oars into the water and the boatmen pulled vigorously away.

In the beginning of the year 1838 I received the following letter from my father :—

"Tottenham Terrace, Middlesex, January 10, 1838.
"MY DEAR FREDERIC,

"... Matthew, as perhaps you know, is printing a pamphlet on the parliamentary power of publishing libellous matter without responsibility of the parties concerned. A tremendous prerogative! but pos-sibly a needful one, as Matthew hopes to prove. Rowland is busy at letters to the Earl of Lichfield in correction of the statements which that nobleman made in the House of Lords. You, I presume, are as active in drawing up your annual report. So that 1838 will see the family speaking from the press with a triple mouth. . . .

"God bless you, my dear boy! We shall be so happy to see you here.

"I remain,
"Your affectionate father,
"THOS. W. HILL."

In this year it was decided to introduce into Parliament a Bill for the future regulation of the prisons of Scotland, and I was requested by the Under Secretary of State (the Honourable Fox Maule) to prepare the heads of this Bill.

I had from time to time much intercourse with Mr. Maule, and always received from him kind and efficient support.

The Bill was founded on the remedial measures which I had recommended in my prison reports. One of its clauses provided for the appointment of a body of directors of prisons with authority (subject to the Secretary of State) to regulate all matters relating to Scottish prisons.

At Mr. Fox Maule's request I called upon every Scotch member of Parliament in either House to explain the objects of the Bill, and the chief provisions for carrying it into effect.

Mr. Maule writes to me—

"House of Commons, August 11, 1839.

"Dear Hill,

"By this time you will have struck the wedges away, and the good ship 'The Prison Bill' will have left her cradle to sink or swim in public opinion.

"You may delay your estimate of the House of Refuge. It can easily be got by-and-by, and I have counsel to take before we can move in the matter.

" I have secured that the premises shall be retained at command of Government.

" Let me hear of your first meeting.

" Yours sincerely,

" F. Maule."

Mr. Fox Maule introduced the measure into the House of Commons, and in the usual course the Bill went into committee.   There it received some maltreatment.   Member after member rose to propose some clause inconsistent with the general scope of the measure, and which showed great ignorance of the subject.   At last the Bill reached the House of Lords, and there the treatment was more gentle.   One of the peers, however, objected to the inspector of prisons becoming a member of the Board of Directors, and proposed a clause forbidding such an appointment ; but Lord Aberdeen rose and declared " that for his part he thought the inspector, who had rendered such service to Scotland, would be the most valuable member of the Board," and this declaration at once silenced all opposition to my appointment.

The Bill was passed, and the Board of Directors soon entered on their duties.   Lord Melville was chosen chairman, and Mr. Andrew Murray (Advocate) secretary.

At the request of the Board I addressed a letter

to the chairman on the requisite qualifications of governors and other officers of prisons. In this letter I spoke of the great difficulties I had had to contend with in obtaining the dismissal of bad officers, and urged the Board, on commencing its new avocations, to act with firmness in this matter.

Of such supreme importance, indeed, have I ever regarded the appointment of good officers, that I should expect better results in one of the worst-built prisons, where no system of discipline was pre-scribed, but where there was an earnest and able governor, than in the best-constructed building, and under the most carefully devised plan of manage-ment, where there was an incompetent head.

One very important point, in my opinion, is to leave the selection of the subordinate officers in the hands of the governor, thus securing his full responsibility, and preventing all doubt as to who may be in fault in case of mismanagement.

These and other recommendations were embodied in my letter, which was approved by the General Board, and distributed among the County Boards.

Before this period I had already succeeded in establishing useful labour in many of the prisons of Scotland.

An aphorism of Howard's was, " Make men diligent and they will be honest;" and I have ever considered that the basis of all good systems of prison discipline must be work—steady, active, honourable work—to the exclusion of all artificial and unproductive labour. It was, therefore, with much satisfaction that soon after entering on my official work I saw the last treadmill banished from Scotland.

Work awarded as a mere punishment, and not intended to yield any profit, has a degrading and demoralizing effect. A prisoner may be compelled to do a hard day's work on the treadmill every day throughout his term of imprisonment, and yet be restored to liberty with a fixed determination never to do another day's work as long as he lives. He is let loose on society smarting from the pain of disgraceful punishments, and with a gloomy resolution to revenge himself.

Unless a prisoner acquire habits of industry and a liking for some kind of work, little hope can be entertained of his conduct after liberation ; sooner or later he is almost sure to fall back into crime. But in order to make men, who have been accustomed to an idle, dissolute life, attain to habits of industry and perseverance, they must be supplied with some motive for the change, and inspired with hope for the future. To meet this need I instituted the following system.

All able-bodied prisoners were required to perform an allotted task equivalent to ten hours' labour (the ordinary working day of an honest workman), but all work done beyond this task was paid for at the market rate of wages. The money thus earned was placed to the prisoner's credit, to be expended by him, subject to the control of the governor, either during his confinement in relief to his family, or after his liberation.

Untried prisoners were not compelled to work; but as they were given their full day's wages if they chose to do so, they were almost always glad to work.

Without waiting for the building of new prisons, I was often able to suggest alterations which could be made at a small cost, and which would admit of arrangements for employing the prisoners in useful work. As far as practicable, such prisoners as had learnt a trade were employed at it. This a zealous and intelligent governor would be able to accomplish, even in the face of many difficulties. For instance, in order to give employment to a blacksmith, I have seen a vacant cell fitted up as a smithy.

Writing on this subject recalls to my mind a visit which Sir Charles Napier paid to the Glasgow

Bridewell. It so chanced that I myself was there when he was announced. I offered to accompany him, and we proceeded on our tour of inspection.

When Sir Charles saw the various kinds of work in which the prisoners were engaged, and the industry with which they laboured, he exclaimed, " Why, this is a factory, not a prison !"

" It is both," I replied; and I explained to him the system I had inaugurated of payment to the prisoners for work done beyond their allotted daily task—hence their energy and industry.

" Pay prisoners money !" exclaimed Sir Charles; " I never heard of such a thing !" and he seemed to think they had a very good time of it. But as we proceeded, and the realities of prison-life forced themselves upon him, his face lengthened, and before we parted, his sympathy and compassion being fully aroused, he turned to me and said, " How much do you say you pay the prisoners ? "

" The value of their extra work."

Sir Charles burst out with a growl, " I call that very shabby. The poor devils ought to have every penny they earn !"

The following letters refer to my work at this time :—

From James Stuart Menteth (*Advocate*).

"Closeburn Hall, Dumfries, January 11, 1840.

"My dear Sir,

"Allow me to take the liberty of forwarding to you a copy of the *Dumfries and Galloway Courier* of the 8th inst. In it you will find an able article 'On the Improved Prison Discipline' of the gaol in Dumfries.

"It describes very faithfully the present state compared with the wretched former one, which through your persevering exertions has been put an end to. The present gaoler, Mr. McFarlane, receives all the commendation he well deserves. Not long ago I was over the Dumfries prison with my father, Sir Charles, and we were both highly gratified with the conduct of McFarlane and the discipline he had established, in exchanging idleness in the prison for work. . . .

"We regretted your engagements prevented your taking Closeburn in your way to England.

"I remain, my dear Sir,
"Yours sincerely,
"Jas. Stuart Menteth."

From Lord Ivory.

"Glencone, May 13, 1840.

"My dear Sir,

". . . I shall always be most happy to do whatever in me lies to advance the successful promotion of the business of the Board; and in a more especial manner to cultivate, better than I have hitherto had time to do, my own friendly relations with yourself, whose zeal and enthusiasm in the cause of prison improvement I look upon, as I have always done, as one of the most promising elements of the eventual success of the new system the country possesses. . . .

" Ever most faithfully yours,

" J. IVORY."

CHAPTER X.

1839–1840.

IT was in the year 1839 that I first became acquainted
with Miss Martha Cowper, my future wife. Her
eldest brother Edward Cowper's name was well
known in the scientific world as the improver, or
practically the inventor, of the printing-machine;
for "he may be said to have done for the printing-
machine what Watt did for the steam-engine."*

Mr. Cowper was a man of a most generous disposition, who was ever ready to use his great abilities
in the service of others. To him, therefore, the
knowledge that his printing-machine had largely
assisted in conferring on mankind the benefit of
cheap literature was a source of permanent happi-

---

* See article on Edward Cowper in Leslie Stephen's "Dic-
tionary of National Biography."

ness. His friend James Nasmyth, the inventor of the steam-hammer, thus writes—

" One of the first booksellers who availed himself of the benefits of the machine was Mr. Charles Knight, who projected the *Penny Magazine* of 1832, and sold it to the extent of two hundred thousand copies weekly. It was also adopted by the Messrs. Chambers of Edinburgh, and the proprietors of the *Magazin Pittoresque* of Paris. The Universities of Oxford and Cambridge also used Cowper's machine in printing vast numbers of Bibles and Prayer-books, thereby reducing their price to one-third of the former cost. There was scarcely a newspaper of any importance in the country that was not printed with a Cowper's machine."

Mr. Cowper became professor of mechanics and manufacturing arts at King's College.

" On many occasions he gave Friday evening lectures at the Royal Institution. Like Faraday, Edward Cowper possessed the power of clearly unveiling his subject, and stripping it of all its complicated perplexities. His illustrations were simple, clear, and understandable. Technical words were avoided as much as possible. Intelligent boys and girls could understand him. His choice of subjects, as well as his masterly treatment, always rendered his lectures instructive and attractive. Next to Faraday no one filled the theatre of the institution with such eager and crowded audiences as he did.

" He was one of the most kind-hearted of men ; and the cheerful way in which he laid aside his ordinary business to give instruction and pleasure to others endeared him to a very wide circle of devoted friends." *

From early youth Miss Martha Cowper had taken an earnest interest in the cause of education. Among other efforts she prepared illustrations for a series of popular lectures delivered throughout the country by a Mr. Wilderspin in 1826. There were then no cheap prints or charts illustrating natural history and other subjects such as now adorn the walls of our humblest schools, and Miss Cowper's diagram-drawings were probably the first of their kind.

A few years later Miss Martha Cowper engaged in a literary work for children which became very popular—the *Parents' Cabinet of Amusement and Instruction.* It contained tales, easy articles on natural history and on mechanical science, travels, and short biographies. The idea of such a publication having been originated by Miss Cowper, her friends rallied round her, promising assistance, notably Mr. William Ellis (the ardent promoter of education), who acted as editor, and his wife. Professor Cowper wrote all the articles on mechanical science, and Miss Martha Cowper herself, besides writing some of the most popular tales, wrote all the articles on natural history, for which her

* See James Nasmyth's " Autobiography."

knowledge of the subject, and a constant observation of nature, well fitted her.

Maria Edgeworth, in letters to Miss Cowper, expressed the warmest admiration for the *Parents' Cabinet.* This was the beginning of an interesting correspondence between the ladies. The work passed through many editions. The most recent, under the somewhat altered title of *Happy Hours; or, The Parents' Cabinet*, appeared in 1891, edited by my daughter Constance.*

Before we met I had read Miss Cowper's little tales, and she had read my " Prison Reports." Though widely different performances, these writings had interested us in each other's turn of mind.

Miss Cowper was a special friend of my sister-in-law, Mrs. Arthur Hill. They resembled each other in talent, enthusiasm, and goodness. Miss Cowper assisted in tending her friend through a long and fatal illness. My valued sister-in-law died in October, 1839, but not before the knowledge of our approaching union had given her heartfelt pleasure.

To turn to public events, my brother Rowland's scheme for postal reform was at this time before

* It is a curious fact that while Miss Edgeworth sympathized with my mother in the first production of the *Parents' Cabinet*, her half-sister, Mrs. Butler, should have shown, in correspondence with myself, a warm interest in an edition brought out more than fifty years later.—ED.

Parliament. Owing to my absence in Scotland, I had been able to give him but little assistance in the promotion of his great work. I remember, however, that I drew up the first petition to Parliament on its behalf, signed by the merchants of London. I was in town, and able to be present at the second reading of the Postage Bill, about which I find this short note to my father :—

"House of Commons, Monday night (July 22), 1839.

"MY DEAR FATHER,

"The second reading of the Postage Bill has been carried without a division, and from the character of the debate and other circumstances the measure is as certain of passing into a law as a matter of the kind can be certain.

"The Duke of Wellington supported the Bill, and particularly recommended that Rowland's plan should be adopted throughout. Brougham supported with zeal, and with talent of course, and, what was not of course, without cavils or crotchets.

"Yours affectionately,

"F. HILL."

The year 1840 dawned with the birth of Penny Postage—"the child of Hill affection," as it has been well called. As a full history of it is given in the "Life" of my brother Rowland, by my nephew, Dr. Birkbeck Hill, I shall not enter into so large a subject

in these " Recollections," except so far as it affected
family relations.

In the month of April of this year my marriage
with Miss Martha Cowper took place, and thus
began a career of nearly fifty years of uninterrupted
connubial happiness with a lady of congenial feelings
and views, who essentially aided me in the performance of my public duties, doing with heart and mind
that which only a woman could do.

After my marriage I ceased to keep a regular
diary; but my wife, who possessed the pen of a
ready writer, wrote a journal during the early years
of our married life for the benefit of her own and
my relations in England.

In her journals and letters her wifely partiality
cannot but appear.	I must therefore submit to
insert some praise of myself, or must suppress her
writings altogether.

She writes—

"Edinburgh, May 9, 1840.

"Here I am in this beautiful city, with the old castle
and the fine gardens and the high picturesque houses
stretched out before me.	We arrived at this hotel
(Mackay's, Prince's Street) about three this morning.	I
was tired and weary, but a chorus of birds at that early
hour welcomed me.	The novelty of such a burst of song
in the midst of a city was delightful. . . . The streets are
beautiful, and it is altogether a glorious city; but I do not

know what our Regent Street linen-drapers would say to the odd positions of the shops. Even in the principal streets there are two tiers of shops, so that you have a grocer's under a goldsmith's, a chandler's under a shawl warehouse, and a fashionable shoemaker's under a butcher's, with its agreeable accompaniments hanging over your head as you enter the shop."

We secured some comfortable rooms at No. 10, Castle Street, where my Edinburgh friends soon came to call on my wife. She writes to my father—

' "I think you have heard of Mrs. Fletcher. She is a most interesting woman, full of energy, vivacity, and talent, and her manners are particularly courteous and refined. She is above seventy, but is more youthful and graceful than many a young person.* She has taken a deep interest in the Poor Law question, added to all the other benevolent objects which occupy so much of her time and attention. She spoke earnestly and warmly of Frederic, and this, you know, was very pleasant music to

---

* The widow of Sir Charles Bell described, many years ago, to a friend of ours, her first sight of Mrs. Fletcher, when the latter was a young married woman. It was on the occasion of an illumination in Edinburgh. Lady Bell was seated in a window, and, happening to turn her head, she saw Mrs. Fletcher enter the room with the light of the illuminations striking full upon the turned-back brim of her yellow hat, which gave it the effect of an aureole. "The face," she said, "was like the face of an angel." Lady Bell's last sight of Mrs. Fletcher was in the garden of Mrs. Arnold's home of Fox Howe. Her face, still beautiful in old age, was illumined by the setting sun.--Ed.

me. We are to spend next Saturday evening with this accomplished and discerning lady.

"I had nearly forgotten to tell you that Mrs. Fletcher had just seen a very long letter from Miss Edgeworth to Dr. Alison, giving an animated description of the temperance movement in Ireland. Miss Edgeworth says the good that Father Mathew is effecting is incalculable ; that he is performing wonders, *not miracles ;* that he rigidly refuses all worship of his adherents, and that she considers him the greatest man of his age."

"23. Great King Street, August 10.

"I hope you received the ' Prison Report ' quite safely. The General Board distribute the greater number, but I had the pleasure of sending off nearly fifty. How I wish that Frederic could have put into the report all his thoughts and feelings upon capital punishment, Scottish Poor Law, etc. ! But we must content ourselves that such self-denial is wise, and that he will be able to introduce more and more valuable matter each year."

In September my wife accompanied me in one of my tours of inspection. She writes—

"*September* 10.—Went this morning with Frederic to the wretched old jail in Elgin, which, however, under his directions, has at last been made clean. A fire was in the room where two girls were confined, but no fire could warm such a room in winter. The staircase was outside the old tower. The two girls were but seventeen years old, and would probably be transported for the thefts they had committed. One was a stout, good-tempered looking young woman, decently brought up, but led into evil by bad companions. The other, a thin, spare-looking girl, was a tight-rope dancer belonging to a travelling caravan. Her brother and sister had both been transported. She had never been at school, could not read, write, or sew, scour a floor, reap, or do anything, indeed, but dance. She came into the prison in a state of great destitution four months ago, and is still untried. She looks as if the light of a loving countenance had never fallen upon her. She shrank, and tried to hide herself when we approached her. Oh, the folly of bringing the whole force and machinery of the law to bear upon a poor creature like this, when simple instruction in useful habits and change of the circumstances that had produced the crime would do so much more good ! A few cases of this kind, well made out, would do much to awaken people's minds to the necessity of a house of refuge, where character could be gained as well as good habits confirmed.

"*Banff.*—Miss Cameron (daughter of Provost Cameron) is a good woman, but the lady's broad Scotch and loud voice are somewhat alarming to encounter. She took me to see several schools this morning. The infant school is managed by a most amiable man, named, you would say, for his occupation—Mr. Bairnsfather. My companion was astonished at the learning of the children, ever and anon exclaiming, in a tone of voice which I cannot describe, but which sounded like extreme dissatisfaction, 'Well, to think of the like of that ! There is no bounds to the knowledge of children nowadays.' Then, in the same loud scolding tone of voice, she exclaimed to the lady who accompanied us, 'Well, it's just the most fortunate and extraordinary circumstance that Mr. Hill should have met with Mrs. Hill. It's what I call just providential ! '

" The prison here was in a wretched state before Frederic was inspector. The prisoners would have starved but for the help of two ladies. One fine young man was in for two years for no crime of his own, but because his sweetheart had smuggled some whisky, and he took the blame on himself, though innocent. He literally died for want of proper nourishment, want of air, and the effects of the cold winter without firing. A lady, by hard exertion, got the poor fellow released a few weeks before his death ; but nothing could save him, and he died moaning that he never more could see his native hills or the young girl for whom he had perished. This smuggling case was the more distressing as rich men are living close by whose whole property was made by smuggling.

" *Strathpeffer, Sunday morning, September* 20.—Our windows look out over rocks and sloping uplands cultivated to the edge of the fir-woods, and dotted with numerous cottages thatched with straw, broom, or heather. I took a delightful though lonely ramble up the rocks, and had a fine view of Tor Echelter, the woods of Sir George Mackenzie, and a small lake or tarn. I picked specimens of the grass of pampas, the cotton grass, and the yellow asphodel. All the cottagers were in church at the Gaelic service ; the shepherds' dogs alone keeping watch, and they were so still that I could hear no sound but the wild bee humming over the heather.

"In returning from one of my visits to Mrs. Cameron, of Dingwell, which were always pleasant, her coachman remarked on the beauty of the stars, which on that night were most brilliant. I spoke to him of the shepherd-boy who had spent hours in watching the stars and gaining knowledge about them, and gave him an account of Ferguson's life. I was much pleased with the man's intelligent remark. 'Ah, Mistress Hill, you see it was by minding things and never letting anything pass that he came to be so clever!' It was curious that his remark should be so much like that of the poor black woman that Miss Martineau quotes, who, when Mr. Sedgwick asked her how she could have learnt so much of the laws of some of the States respecting slavery, answered, 'By keeping still, sir, and minding things.' If we could but educate the young 'to mind things,' and 'not to let anything pass,' we should not have complaints of the stupidity of the poor; but we have never thought of training their powers of observation.

"*Inverness, October* 15.—There is so much convenience and comfort at Inverness that one can scarcely imagine the time to be so very recent when the town was without light, without pavement, and without any means of cleanliness. A gentleman of middle age told Frederic that the streets used to be ankle-deep in mud during the summer and knee-deep in winter. He remembered the time when every well-to-do family kept a boy whose express duty it was to go before them and clear a pathway.

"I went but once to the jail, as it is full of workmen altering the place under Frederic's directions. He has persuaded the people here to spend a hundred pounds on the old jail before the new one can be ready. It was most necessary.

"In the course of a week the women will be in a larger room, new windows will be made, means of ventilation created, and gas and water laid on to the highest story; the prisoners will be decently clothed, and separate hammocks (removable by day) provided for them instead of the dirty bedding now occupying the floor. They will be employed in regular work, and books and instruction will be supplied.

"Frederic is most careful to prevent communication from

without. A new window in one of the cells had been made near the floor, thus affording a sight of the street below, but he had it built up again and placed nearer the ceiling. Frederic will not, however, allow a view of nature to be shut out unnecessarily. I heard him giving directions that no blinds should be put up to this same window, in order that the view of the distant Firth, the green hills, and the blue sky might be seen.

"*Monday night.*—Left Inverness for Edinburgh. Rode outside the coach with Frederic part of the way, and much enjoyed the prospect of the woods of Strathspey, now golden with the autumn tints, and their background of huge mountains with rifted precipices coming into life and light under the rising sun. Craig Elachie is a noble mountain. Anderson mentions that the expression, 'Stand fast, Craig Elachie!' is the gathering-cry of the clan Grant, the occupants of this great Strath.

"At Perth, while our fellow-travellers were dining, Frederic ran to the Penitentiary, and I had a long talk with Mr. Hutchinson, the keeper of the jail.

"*Selkirk, October* 24.—Arrived here after a pleasant but cold ride. After dinner we drove to Melrose, stopping at Abbotsford on our way. The sun was setting as we passed through Sir Walter's plantations on the hillsides that he has clothed with beauty. The colours of the changing foliage were exceedingly beautiful, though mournful. Every light breeze scattered the leaves before us, and the Tweed murmured solemnly as it flowed. We both felt the harmony of the scene with our own emotions.

> 'Through his loved grove the breezes sigh,
> And oaks in deeper groan reply,
> And rivers teach their rushing wave
> To murmur dirges round his grave.'

"It was impossible not to think of every line of Lockhart's description of the last journey towards this sweet home—the instant return of reason, and the wild rapture at the sight of the Eildon Hills, and of every dear and well remembered object. Had the lines to Caledonia, in the sixth canto of the 'Lay,' been composed by Scott at that moment, they could not have been more expressive of his feelings.

> 'Still, as I view each well-known scene,
> Think what is now, and what hath been,
> Seems as to me of all bereft,
> Sole friends thy woods and streams were left;
> And thus I love them better still,
> Even in extremity of ill.'

"In the front court, where Scott lingered on the autumn evening of his return, the roses were blooming as they are now, and the same calmness seemed to be spread over the scene.

"On entering the house, the light was so obscured by the painted windows in the hall that it was impossible to examine the curious relics of olden time that crowd the walls; nor did I feel inclined to do so, the whole was so impressive, so part of the living man, that I did not care for detail. The shadow of the magician was a greater relic than aught collected there, and was flung over every part. The beautiful library was filled with splendid tables, antique cabinets, vases, etc.—gifts from poets, and great men, and crowned heads; but they derive almost all their interest from being proofs of the homage paid to genius. Who could curiously examine Greek vases or showy cabinets within sight of the little study adjoining, from whence issued such wondrous spells? The study is precisely as it was left after Scott used it, two days before his death, when, after his arrival from abroad, he desired to be placed at his desk, and wrote a few lines.

"A bed was put up in the dining-room for him near the window, and here he died, with the beautiful prospect he had loved so much in life spread out before him in death."

CHAPTER XI.

1840-1842.

Mrs. Hill's journals continued—Dr. Alison—Infant Felons' Bill and the Honourable Amelia Murray—The Bethunes—William Lloyd Garrison—Mrs. Fletcher and Allan Cunningham—Authorship of "There's nae luck about the house"—Visit to Ayr—The widow of Burns.

"*Jedburgh, October* 27, 1840.—After breakfast I went with Frederic to the jail to settle about the matron's room, the bath-room, etc., and to talk to the women.

"The warder—a very kind-hearted man of fifty—has a most unfortunate appearance. He is tall and very thin, with a deadly white face, red eyes and red nose. We naturally asked whether he was given to drinking. Mr. Boyde, the governor, said, on the contrary, he was an excellent officer, but he had had this strange appearance from childhood. He told me that a poor woman, who came to see her husband who was imprisoned for debt, was so frightened when this man opened the gate that she nearly fainted. She took him for the hangman !

"I left Frederic with the male prisoners and followed my ghostly guide, the warder, to the women's side of the prison, when suddenly, looking at me with the most insinuating expression, he asked, 'Mistress Hill, do you think in the new arrangements there will be room for a

poor turnkey's wife, should he be inclined to marry?'
After thus breaking the ice with me he had some private
talk with Frederic, who sympathized so much with the
poor man's love-story, that he kept his countenance and
never smiled till relating the interview to me, when he
gave the warder the name of the 'sentimental scarecrow.'

"*Greenlaw, October* 28.—Went with Frederic to the
jail. A female prisoner was baking some bread made of
barley and peas flour. I found that the peas gave a bitter
taste to the bread, but in spite of this it is preferred to
oatcake on account of its moistness. Wheaten bread had
been used formerly in the prison, but upon Frederic's
ascertaining that this peas bread was the food of the
country, and that it was pronounced by the doctor to be
wholesome and nourishing, he changed the dietary in
order that the prisoners might not fare better than their
honest neighbours.

"The keeper's wife is to be appointed matron. She
seems to be a very good person. I learnt that several
prisoners had been taught to read (though this has
hitherto formed no part of a keeper's duty). Mrs. Johnson
brought her young son to me who had taught a man,
under sentence of death, to read the New Testament.

"A lad whom I noticed had formerly been a most
unruly prisoner. He was an orphan, and had been
apprenticed to a brush-maker who had ill-treated him.
When he first came into prison he tore his clothes, broke
his porridge-basin, and did all the mischief he could. As
a punishment he was placed in a dark cell, and was even
ironed, but he remained as wild as ever. Mrs. Johnson
told me she saw that all harsh treatment was making him
grow worse and worse. She said to her husband, ' Let's
try to calm him down by kindness.' ' And so, ma'am,'

she continued, 'we smoothed down his nerves a bit, and now he can't behave better than he does, poor lad! though do what I will he won't take to his book.'

"*Edinburgh, October* 31.—Frederic and I met Dr. Alison in the old town. He turned and walked with us for a considerable distance. We congratulated him on the resolution of the town council to petition Parliament for an inquiry by the Poor Law Commissioners into the state of the country. It was delightful to talk to this good man on the progress of his great work. Two months ago, when he seemed a little desponding, I told him I would allow him the same time for its accomplishment that his fellow-benefactor had taken to establish Penny Postage—two years and a half—but he shook his head and said, 'Oh no, he should never be so happy.' Everything, however, looks promising now, and I have little doubt that in the time I mentioned he will see his glorious labours crowned with success. The blessing he will be to Scotland is incalculable.

"*Edinburgh, November* 3.—Mr. Neale, the author of 'Juvenile Delinquency in Manchester,' is a candidate for the governorship of the Edinburgh prison. We asked him to dine with us to meet Mr. Simpson and one or two other friends. Mr. Neale spoke of the new Bill called the 'Infant Felons' Bill,' which has lately been introduced into Parliament. The provisions are very similar to those of the French law, which gives Government the power, under peculiar circumstances, to sentence a young offender to a long term of confinement for his first offence in order to rescue him from evil surroundings. Mr. Neale mentioned the curious fact that this Bill was entirely projected and drawn up by one of the Queen's maids of honour. Upon this Mr. Simpson informed us that its author was the Honourable Amelia Murray, and added, moreover, that she had sent it to him in manuscript to revise.

"The conversation afterwards turned upon an article which appeared in the *Athenæum* for October 24—a review of the memoir of a poor labourer, John Bethune, who was honest, industrious, and self-educated. His story, as told by his only surviving brother, is a most pathetic comment upon the neglect, in this country, of the necessitous poor. All our friends were greatly interested in it, and Mr. Simpson said it should be sent at once to Dr. Alison to serve as an unanswerable argument against Dr. Chalmers' scheme of supporting the poor by the poor.

". . . I have purchased the memoir, and have also procured a copy of the two brothers' lecture on 'Political Economy for the Poor.' They are written in so polished a style that it is difficult to realize the dire poverty which obliged their authors to make use of such materials as grocers' bags for writing-paper. I have written to Alexander Bethune, who is still working as a labourer at Newbury, in Fifeshire, and have received a very interesting letter from him. I have also heard from the minister of the parish, who confirms our opinion of the moral and intellectual worth of the two brothers.

"*November* 15.—Dined with our friends the Wighams, and enjoyed, as usual, the very atmosphere of their well-ordered and cultivated home. We met a Mr. and Mrs. Anderson just returned from Jamaica, and an American gentleman of the name of Collins, a delegate from the Original Anti-Slavery Society, of which the heroic Garrison is the head.*

---

* Twenty-seven years later, when slavery in America had

"Mr. Anderson is a missionary. He and his wife had resided for five years in Kingston. They gave the same account of the 'day of liberation' as has been lately published in *Chambers's Journal* from the Government de- spatches. Some of the delegates from the Anti-Slavery Society went to Jamaica to witness the effect of the abolition. When they returned to America they published an account of it; giving the admirable speech of the governor of the island, Sir Lionel Smith, and describing how well the negroes responded to it by their orderly conduct.

"Mr. Collins mentioned a curious fact respecting the criminal laws in Georgia. He says that whilst there are seventy-three crimes which are punishable by death in the case of a slave, there are only three for which a white man suffers the same penalty.

"*November* 21.—We had a visit this morning from our good friends Mr. and Mrs. Wigham. They brought with them Mr. Dunn, the master of a large Lancastrian school, where six hundred children are instructed, to see my stores of drawings, books, songs for children, etc., and to have a regular lesson from me in the use of these things! At Mr. Wigham's request I gave Mr. Dunn all the help in my power. Memorandums were made of Mr. Grant's bold outlines for teaching elementary drawing, of the sketches of animals for teaching natural history, and of Mr. Hickson's songs for children. Many of these have been introduced into schools from our showing them to friends.

---

ceased to exist, Mrs. Hill had the pleasure of being present at the congratulatory breakfast given in London to William Lloyd Garrison. She was accompanied by her son-in-law, Mr. John Scott, and her nephew, Dr. Birkbeck Hill. The recollection of this joyful and triumphant gathering was an abiding pleasure to her.—ED.

"*January* 16, 1841.—Dined at Mrs. Fletcher's, and passed a very agreeable evening. Her daughter, Mrs. Davy (wife of Dr. Davy, brother of Sir Humphry), is now staying with her during her husband's absence at Constantinople. Dr. Davy has gone there, by the direct invitation of the Sultan, to establish the English hospital system in the Turkish army ; but he almost despairs of effecting much good in the time he can devote to the object, owing to the dilatoriness of the people.

"I had some very interesting conversation with Mrs. Fletcher upon Cromek's 'Reliques of Burns,' and his edition of the 'Nithsdale and Galloway Songs.' I had observed her name mentioned in the notes.

"When Cromek came to Edinburgh Mrs. Fletcher gave him letters of introduction to several of her friends who were admirers and collectors of Scottish song, including Allan Cunningham. She herself furnished him with the interesting account of poor Jean Adam, the authoress of the beautiful song, 'There's nae luck about the house.' Mrs. Fletcher had heard the story while staying with Mrs. Fullerton, an aged lady, living near Greenock, who had formerly been one of Jean Adam's pupils when Jean kept a small school at Crawford's Dyke. Mrs. Fullerton remembered her reading some of Shakespeare's plays with enthusiasm to her little scholars. She also remembered her telling them of her intention to *walk* to London in order to see Richardson the novelist, and the wonderful account she gave them on her return home of her journey.

"Poor Jean had been brought up in penury, and her poetic powers could not keep her above want when she gave up her little school. After wandering about some time she was compelled to seek shelter in the Poorhouse at Glasgow. She died the following day, and all that records the fate of this gifted, tender-hearted woman is the entry of her death in the parish register.*

"In expressing my admiration of the 'Nithsdale and Galloway Songs,' I observed that they were invaluable, not only for their beautiful and vivid imagery, but for portraying the tastes and feelings of a peasantry among whom they had been so carefully preserved from a by-gone age. Upon this Mrs. Fletcher told me a fact which considerably chagrined me. It appears that few of these songs are of the origin that Cromek states them to be; the greater part of the collection are written by Allan Cunningham. When Mrs. Fletcher sent Cromek to Allan Cunningham (thirty years ago), the latter thought that Cromek wished to see specimens of his own poetry; he therefore showed him some. But, to his great mortification, Cromek treated them almost with scorn, saying that it was absurd for any one to attempt to write Scotch songs after Burns. Cromek, however, went on to say that as Burns had created a taste for *old* Scottish song, he should be thankful to Cunningham if he could obtain any fragments for him to publish. Cunningham, in a letter to Mrs. Fletcher, says that the thought immediately came into his head of imposing upon this critic who was so great in his own estimation, but merely for the fun of the thing. He accordingly wrote a few verses and took them the following day to Cromek, who was enchanted

---

* The authorship of "There's nae luck about the house" is a disputed point. In 1810, Cromek, after adopting Mrs. Fuller-ton's evidence as conclusive, changed his opinion in favour of W. J. Mickle, the translator of the "Lusiad," on what seems to be insufficient proof. Messrs. Finlay Dun and John Thomson, in their edition of the "Vocal Melodies of Scotland," published in 1836, attribute the poem to Jean Adam.—Ed.

with them, and besought him to strive to obtain more poetry from 'this rich vein of native talent.'

"Nothing would satisfy Cromek but a thorough examination of all Cunningham's store of old songs—as he supposed them to be—and then he declared they were 'the very things for publication!' Cunningham was amused, and continued the deception, which, he says, was certainly not for the purpose of gaining money, as he only received four pounds for transcribing the poems. He does not pretend to justify the act, but says he does not think it very culpable.

"Allan Cunningham, in another letter to Mrs. Fletcher, which was read to me, describes the interview with Sir Walter Scott when the latter was sitting to Chantrey for his bust. Scott taxed Allan with being the author of the 'Nithsdale and Galloway Songs,' saying, 'Ah, Allan, none but the uninitiated could be deceived. They were too good, *mon*, to be old.' Thus attacked, Allan avowed the truth. He repeats this avowal to his friend Mrs. Fletcher, in order that 'if the matter were to come before the public hereafter, and mistakes were to arise, his secret might be in safe and upright hands.'

"Mrs. Fletcher described to me her first acquaintance with Allan Cunningham. She was staying with a friend in the neighbourhood of Dumfries. This lady said to her on the morning after her arrival, 'Do you see that group of labourers in my grounds preparing to build a new wall ? Well, a poet of no common order is among them. See if you can find him out. He is courting my housemaid, and it was from her that I learnt of his talent. Since then I have given orders for him to have a duplicate key of our library, and, although I can vouch for his not neglecting his work, I understand that he actually sits up half the nights reading.'

"Mrs. Fletcher went to the busy group and quickly discovered the poet. Two or three years later Allan Cunningham came to Edinburgh to improve himself in his trade as a mason. When engaged as a common workman in building some of the houses in George Street, Mrs. Fletcher lent him not only her own books, but procured for him, through Mr. Fletcher, books from the Advocates' Library. At last Allan became assistant sculptor to Chantrey. It was he who obtained from Sir Walter Scott a promise to sit to Chantrey. Cunningham always accompanied his master, and, under his directions, worked much at the bust himself.

"*January* 21.—Mr. George Combe, Mr. Trevelyan, Mr. Robert Chambers, Mr. Simpson, and Mr. Charles Maclaren came to breakfast at our house, and these guests, with my husband at the foot of the table, made as agreeable a party, I think, as ever assembled. For two or three hours the most earnest, philosophical, or playful conversation went on. Everybody seemed happy and animated. . . . Before our party broke up, Mr. Robert Chambers told me that he had read the chapter on 'Saving Societies' in Bethune's 'Practical Economy,' and had prepared an article upon it for the *Journal*.

"The *Journal* keeps up its vast sale of seventy thousand copies weekly. The new edition of *Information for the People* is selling to an amount beyond the most sanguine expectation. Add to all this the valuable cheap books belonging to their 'People's Edition,' their school books and maps, and it is evident that the good the two brothers are effecting is enormous. It is pleasant to see how their labours are appreciated by such men as the Bethunes. But they are valued also by the ordinary class of poor people. The servants here frequently quote from the *Journal*.

"The Chamberses will shortly bring out some cheap music.

"*May* 12.—Last Monday I was at a party at Mr. and Mrs. Robert Chambers'. One of the two 'princes' was there, the veritable grandson of Prince Charles Edward and the Duchess of Albany. He is a highly accomplished, elegant-looking man, and his Highland costume with its jewelled ornaments well became him.

"*Dundee, May* 18.—Frederic up soon after five o'clock, and at the prison till eight. After breakfast I went there with him to examine the female prisoners. The cleanliness in every department does the matron great credit.

"*Arbroath, May* 19.—The jail here is one of the old, badly constructed, badly managed prisons, but it will soon give place to a new one.

"*Perth, May* 22.—Perth delighted me as much as ever. Every approach to it is pleasing and orderly, from the nicely trimmed hedgerows and neat cottages to the beautiful avenues. I went to the prison and saw the female prisoners (twelve in number). All were engaged in profitable work. They spoke with pleasure of their new, comfortable clothing, and were quite proud of their cleanliness. Mrs. Hutchinson, the matron, told me that the improvement in cleanliness has been most striking since the rule of wearing prison clothing has been made imperative. As long as any of the prisoners were allowed to wear their own clothes no amount of care could banish dirt and its consequences.

"*Sunday, 23rd.*—Frederic was at the prison before six o'clock this morning. This afternoon he went to hear Mr. Esdaile preach. Mr. Esdaile is a candidate for the office of chaplain at the general prison. He is a sincere but liberal Christian, and has exerted himself for many years in the cause of education for the poorer classes. Frederic says his language is eloquent and his manner cheerful and persuasive. Frederic also heard him give a lesson in the Sunday school on Biblical geography, and liked his ways to the children. Mr. Esdaile has the general management of two Sunday schools, and has established a library of some magnitude for the use of the children.

"*Morpeth, June* 11.—Mr. Cousins, the keeper of the prison here, told us some interesting facts connected with the separate system. He has a clever lad in the prison, a young pickpocket, who, on first coming, boasted much of his acquaintance among thieves and of his power of detecting a police-officer in whatever guise he might assume. This lad, though he has been only three weeks in prison, and probably never saw a loom till now in his life, has acquired the art of weaving a superior kind of hearthrug, sorting the various colours and arranging them himself. His delight at the effect he is able to produce by his skill and industry is very great. Mr. Cousins said, 'A new ambition seems born within him. He talks of nothing now but of working hard to save up money to buy a loom.' He can now make, in only one day, a rug which will sell for twelve shillings. Mr. Cousins remarked that though few of his young prisoners were as clever as this boy, that all, even the most stupid, were much interested in this rug-making, and all felt a new self-respect on finding themselves able to accomplish the work. He mentioned three instances of prisoners intreating him to be allowed to remain in the prison for a time after their term of confinement had expired, in order that they might earn money enough to buy decent clothes and to pay for their journeys home.

"*June* 16, 1842.—We went to Ayr from Glasgow by the half-past seven o'clock train. A very pleasant ride of forty miles, the last ten of which was along the coast. The day was beautiful, the huge mountains of Arran standing out in such bold, clear forms that they appeared only two or three miles distant instead of fifteen. The sea was of every shade of bright green and deep blue, broken with lines of dancing white foam—no angry surges, but happy spirits of the deep, coursing one another over their vast playground. The sandy shores were diversified by a few villages and one or two neat watering-places. The land is too poor for aught but a scanty vegetation and the wild flowers indigenous to the spot. The dwarf white rose literally covers the ground with stars for miles. Lapwings, dotterels, and sandpipers made the scene lively with motion.

"Upon our arrival at Ayr we spent an hour on the shore, thinking and feeling how one man of true original mind and warm heart had stamped every stone with his image. We had some of his sweetest verses before us, and realized the scene which ' Coila ' describes in the ' Vision,' alluding to the early life of Burns, when

> ' With future hope I oft would gaze
> Fond on thy little early ways,
> Thy rudely carolled chiming phrase,
> In uncouth rhymes
> Fir'd at the simple artless lays
> Of other times.

> ' I saw thee seek the sounding shore,
> Delighted with the dashing roar ;
> Or when the north his fleecy store
> Drove thro' the sky,
> I saw grim Nature's visage hoar
> Struck thy young eye.

> ' Or when the deep green mantled earth
>   Warm cherish'd ev'ry flow'ret's birth,
>   And joy and music pouring forth
>   In ev'ry grove,
>   I saw thee eye the gen'ral mirth
>   With boundless love.
>
> ' When ripen'd fields and azure skies
>   Call'd forth the reaper's rustling noise,
>   I saw thee leave their evening joys
>   And lonely stalk
>   To vent thy bosom's swelling rise
>   In pensive walk.'

"We had a letter of introduction to a Mr. Hall, a great admirer of Burns, and who himself is well worth knowing. He was formerly a small hairdresser in the town of Ayr, but a man of intelligent pursuits. His own beautiful grounds by the side of the Doun enclose the well mentioned in 'Tam o' Shanter,' above which the thorn stood where Mungo's mother hanged herself. Mr. Hall is very ready to show visitors anything connected with the poet.

"We passed the white cottage, of two rooms, where Burns passed his early life, and proceeded to the monument—a very elegant and classical but, to me, a singularly inappropriate testimony of respect to the peasant bard. Terraced gardens surround the building, filled with gorgeous specimens of foreign flowers, all to adorn the memory of him who has made the 'mountain daisy' a flower of more enduring fame than any that greenhouse or hothouse can produce. Within the monument is a table, on which are two glass cases, the one containing his 'Works,' the other the Bible which he gave to 'Highland Mary.' In the first leaf are two or three verses from the Psalms and a few private marks, which conveyed probably some peculiar meaning to the lovers themselves. The

Bible on Mary's death passed into the hands of her brother, who emigrated to Canada. It has since been recovered and purchased from the family. Near to the monument is a small Grecian temple, in which are placed Thom's statues of 'Tam o' Shanter' and 'Souter Johnny.' One cannot but regret that the tender and pathetic features of Burns's Muse have not found a representation, rather than the humorous portrayal of a vice which causes too much misery to be lightly thought of. It is impossible to turn from the cells of a prison which, in nine cases out of ten, drunkenness has been the means of filling, and laugh with full glee at 'Tam o' Shanter's' adventures.

"Mr. Hall told us of a visit from Burns's aged widow, nine years ago, to see the monument. He invited her from Dumfries for that purpose. When it was known in Ayr that she was going to breakfast with Mr. Hall, many of the gentry who were not in the habit of visiting him, requested Mr. Hall as a great favour that they might be allowed to meet her. He replied that he did not know whether this might be agreeable to Mrs. Burns's feelings. Upon going to meet the stage-coach Mr. Hall found a crowd assembled to see her alight, and among them the gentlemen who had wished to breakfast with her. He mentioned the circumstance to Mrs. Burns, and upon receiving her hearty permission he beckoned them to follow to his house.

"Every one admired the erect bearing and the elastic step of the venerable lady. During breakfast she was in excellent spirits, and talked of Burns, of their early days, and of their various visitors of every rank and degree. She mentioned that a neighbour had called recently on her to say that a poor lad, a seller of tapes and buttons, wandering through the country, had set his heart on seeing

Mrs. Burns, and asked whether she might bring him to her house. Permission being readily given, the neighbour returned, bringing the little tape-merchant. There were three or four persons present, and the boy looked anxiously round, and said in a low voice, ' When will Mrs. Burns come ?' He was told that she stood next to him. ' Nae, nae, ye'll no gar me believe *that*. Burns says, " my *bonnie* Jean." ' The poor lad thought that 'bonnie Jean's' charms would be as enduring as her fond husband's poetry.

"Mr. Hall said that Mrs. Burns kept perfectly cheerful till she entered the monument, when she suddenly became ill and nearly fainted. He thinks she was pleased with the superb token of respect to her husband's memory ; but the contrast of life and death, the hard struggles they had gone through, the great need they had felt of the sympathy which was shown too late to save, all over-powered her. She was removed to the open air, and soon recovered.

"We visited the Bridge of Doun. I remarked to Mr. Hall that the people of Ayr ought to preserve it reli-giously. He then told me that it had barely escaped destruction, for, a new bridge being required, the old bridge was actually in the course of being taken to pieces to supply material. This happened during the 'Race week.' A gentleman of Ayr wrote a witty petition in the name of the ' Auld Brig,' and sent it to the gay company in the public ball-room. In half an hour six hundred pounds was subscribed to save the interesting relic. To the honour of the people of Ayr, the subscription was not called for. They felt rather ashamed of their former pro-ceeding, and themselves paid the sum required for new material. Mr. Hall superintended the restoration of the old bridge. Every stone except two was replaced.

"In returning to Ayr we went into Burns's cottage—
'the auld clay biggin.' In a bed in the room in which
Burns was born, where the old roof had nearly fallen in, a
poor old man was lying. He is one of the few now living
who remembers Burns."

CHAPTER XII.

1842–1844.

Scottish Poor Law and Lord Dunfermline—Sheriff Watson's schools—W. M. Thackeray—Secession of the Free Kirk—Procession of ministers—Letter from Mrs. Fry—Maria Edgeworth and Professor Cowper — Debate on Postal Reform—" Field Day."

ABOUT this time the question of the Scottish Poor Law was brought forcibly before the public. In 1840 Dr. Alison had addressed himself to the public conscience in a pamphlet on the "Destitution of the Poor in Scotland," which made a strong impression. Associations were formed in, Edinburgh and in all the large towns in Scotland to inquire into his statements, and to apply to Parliament for a new Poor Law.

Unlike the English, the Scottish Poor Law at that time afforded no relief to any person pronounced by the local authority to be able-bodied, however severe his destitution, or however ready he might be to repay the cost of food and shelter by work. Moreover, every now and then a person was pronounced to be " able-bodied " who was notoriously the reverse. The result of this state of things was, as I have already mentioned, that there were many voluntary prisoners in the Scotch gaols. Even where the imprisonment was of a stringent character, including solitary confinement and hard labour, persons applied for permission to be received within the prison walls, or to remain there after their term of imprisonment had expired. At the Glasgow Bridewell alone these voluntary prisoners sometimes numbered thirty or forty.

I earnestly desired to point out to Government, in my official reports, the urgent need for an efficient Poor Law, but felt doubts as to whether, in my capacity as a servant of Government, it would be permissible to do so.

I recollect a conversation I had on the subject with Lord Dunfermline in the autumn of 1842, of which I find notes in my journal. We were travelling from Edinburgh in order to inspect the Perth prison, both being members of the Board of Directors. I asked for his opinion as to the advisability of my dealing with the question of the Scottish Poor Law in my forthcoming report, observing that as Sir Robert Peel had expressed his opinion that some action should be taken, I thought I might now venture to bring the subject directly before Government. Lord Dunfermline gave me the counsel of a truly canny Scotchman. He advised me to give no formal statement of my views, but suggested that when stating such facts connected with crime as exposed the evils arising from an inefficient Poor Law, I might make "my remarks in such a way as to let them appear to spring spontaneously, and almost to escape from me unawares." For instance, after mentioning the large number of voluntary prisoners, I might say, "Thus the prisons of Scotland are, in fact, serving as Unions."

"After a time," continued Lord Dunfermline, "some member of Parliament, in looking over your report, will come upon this sentence, and, thinking he has made a great discovery, will hurry, full of self-importance, down to the House with the report in his hand, and will start up on the first opportunity, exclaiming, 'Here's a revelation! The prisons of Scotland are serving as Unions!' Upon this, Peel will probably send for the report, and may make a speech of a quarter of an hour upon that one fact. By this means you will not alarm Peel's pride by giving him instruction on the subject of the Poor Laws, and yet will gain your point."

I followed this advice, and felt that I had done

what I could to call public attention to a pressing need. In the end my action, no doubt, did good, but the immediate effect was an order from Government to discontinue the practice of receiving voluntary prisoners, and to turn out those already received. Foreseeing that Government might issue this order, I had strongly recommended in my report the establishment of houses of refuge as temporary asylums for this class of persons. They had already been tried on a small scale and had proved successful. But, unfortunately, Government did not take up the plan with any vigour, and as several years elapsed before a good Poor Law was given to Scotland, many persons remained in the criminal class who might have been rescued.

Meanwhile, men of all shades of political opinion in Scotland were working together for the good cause. Conspicuous among these were Lord Jeffrey and Professor Wilson.

In a letter dated November 3, 1842, I write—

"I have been to-day to hear Professor Wilson give a lecture at the college in favour of the principle of the English Poor Law. He was, in my opinion, more earnest and eloquent than logical ; but it is good to have such a man on the right side, even if he may not give the best reasons for being there."

When I first visited Aberdeen, in 1835, I became acquainted with Sheriff Watson, the founder of Industrial Schools, with whom I formed a friendship which lasted till his death.

The simple and inexpensive means by which great results may be obtained has seldom been more strikingly shown than in the Aberdeen schools. When they had been in existence for a few years the whole county was emptied of its juvenile beggars and young thieves.

After I had left Scotland, Sheriff Watson wrote to me—

"In 1841, while you were labouring to improve our prison discipline, I was labouring to establish schools for the destitute. Our cognate occupations naturally drew us together, and you were among the first to encourage me to prosecute the then doubtful experiment. You always predicted success. . . .

"The importance of industrial school training is now universally acknowledged, and if it were faithfully and systematically carried out, would form a centre of attraction for all classes of the community. It would soon become manifest that the widows' prayers and the orphans' thanks were of more avail in warding off national convulsion than all the purchased batons and bayonets of the empire."

Elsewhere describing the origin of the schools, he wrote—

"As the only local stipendiary magistrate, and every day called upon to deal with juvenile delinquents, more sinned against than sinning, I resolved to mitigate and, if possible, remove this great social evil; and, to that end, proposed to open an Industrial Feeding School, where they would be fed, educated, and trained to habits of industry."

In October, 1841, the school was opened in an old warehouse that had been obtained at a low rent, with ten or twelve boys dragged in by the police. The number of children rapidly increased, till in a few years' time there were four schools in operation—a boys' school, two girls' schools, and a school for both boys and girls.

The children did not sleep at the schools, but returned to their parents in the evening, as Sheriff Watson was averse to breaking the family tie; and such was the effect of good training upon these children, once the pests of society, that in many cases they became the "little missionaries of their home circle."

As many of the boys would become farm-labourers, it was considered well to give them some knowledge of rocks and soils; they were, therefore, encouraged to bring to school specimens of every kind of rock or earth they could find, till, with a little help from their teachers, a very practical, though small, geological collection was formed.

Rough shelves were put up bearing the names of the various strata in their proper order. Upon these the boys themselves placed their specimens. Simple lessons were given on these substances, and on their uses in agriculture and manufactures.

A small museum of natural history was also formed, the powers of observation and general intelligence in the children rapidly increasing under this kind of instruction.

In one instance, where a boy on leaving school had been placed in a printing-office, the head of the establishment wrote to Sheriff Watson—

" He is not naturally clever, but rather the opposite; yet, amid half a dozen boys of similar age, I find this boy decidedly more serviceable in doing various things requiring some exercise of intelligence. In short, regarding the instruction given as a means to an end, I should say the difference between him and others is that he has a more thorough and ready command of the tools that have been put into his hands."

The artisans of Aberdeen, realizing the great benefit to their own families of the withdrawal of a dangerous class from the streets, presented the school fund with a sum of no less than two hundred pounds.

The children were given three meals a day of plain but wholesome food. Deducting the money received for work done, the annual cost per child was only five pounds. My wife, who visited the schools with me, and who, like myself, had a warm esteem and admiration for their founder, wrote an account of them many years afterwards, which appeared in the *Leisure Hour* for December, 1885. The following is taken from this account :—

"When I visited the schools in 1845, the girls' school was in a moderate-sized house with a small garden attached to it.

"It was scarcely possible to believe that those neat little children before me, with the polished hair, clean frocks and pincloths, sewing so diligently, could have been rescued from the worst population of the city. But ·the fact was soon proved to us. A new scholar arrived—a little wretched, ragged girl, whose skin was as dirty as her frock, and whose hair stood out many inches from her head in one great tangle.

"The mistress received her kindly, and told her to go into an adjoining room, where a woman would give her a warm bath and lend her a nice wrapping-gown to wear whilst her own clothes were washed and dried—a work which was done very rapidly. When the child returned to the schoolroom the mistress looked into her great bag of pieces to find some suitable for patching the holes in the old frock. The child was then put under the superintendence of an elder girl, who fixed the patches and showed her how to sew, helping her considerably in this first lesson. The child went home that evening totally changed in appearance, and she, as well as her parents, must have felt the value of the school.

"I was told of one little girl who on her return to her poor home entreated her mother to let her scour the dirty floor, and would never go to bed till she had made things tidy, so that at last the mother imitated the child and became industrious herself.

"Indeed, one of the objects of the founder of the institution was to act upon the parents as well as the children. Once every month they were invited to come to the schools to hear the children sing, repeat poetry, Bible stories and texts, and to look at their writing, sums, and needlework; and sometimes, during the summer, they were invited to a little feast, given by the children themselves, of tea, bread and butter, and fresh lettuces and radishes from their own little gardens.

"Part of Sunday was spent by the children attending a short service at school. The parents were invited to this service, and many came who had never entered a church.

"I heard many interesting anecdotes of the little pupils as I passed from one room to another. One child had been trusted to carry a parcel to a lady who had ordered some needlework, and who would give her eight shillings in payment, to be taken safely back to the schoolmistress. When the lady was counting out the money, after saying some kind words in praise of the work, she was surprised by the child's bursting into tears. On being asked the cause, the child could at first only sob and exclaim, 'I was only minding the differ;' and then she explained that but a year ago she had begged of that lady's servant to give her a 'bawbee.' The servant had found her, early one morning, at the stone stair-head, where she had been sleeping all night, and had driven her away with hard words, and now she was never cold or hungry, and the lady herself was trusting her with 'a' that siller.'"

Sheriff Watson used to describe a visit paid by the author of "Vanity Fair" to one of the schools situated in Sugar House Lane. The sheriff accompanied him, and was somewhat surprised at his total silence during the inspection. On leaving, Thackeray turned to him exclaiming, "If I had attempted to speak to you I should, like a great lubberly boy, have burst into weeping."

In the month of May, 1843, the Established Church of Scotland was rent in twain by the secession of those who formed themselves into the Free Kirk. "It was," to use Lord Cockburn's words, "the greatest event that had occurred in Scotland since the rebellion of 1745," and long before it took place it was the leading topic of discussion in Edinburgh.

One party maintained that owners or patrons of livings had alone the right to appoint the minister, and that moreover they had the right to force him upon the parishioners, provided he were under no legal disqualification, however odious he might be to them. The other party maintained that the parishioners possessed a legal right to reject such a minister.

"But this point was soon lost sight of, absorbed in the far more vital question, whether the Church had any spiritual jurisdiction independent of the control of the civil power. This became the question on which the longer coherence of the elements of the Church depended. The judicial determination was, in effect, that no such jurisdiction existed. This was not the adjudication of any abstract political or ecclesiastical nicety. It was the declaration, and, as those who protested against it held, the introduction, of a principle which affected the whole practical being and management of the Establishment. On this decision being pronounced, those who had claimed this jurisdiction, which they deemed an essential and indispensable part of what they had always understood to be their Church, felt that they had no course except to leave a community to which, as it was now explained, they had never sworn allegiance." *

It was on the 18th of May that my wife and I happened to be walking towards George Street, when we met a procession of black-coated, white-cravatted gentlemen whose countenances one and all were striking, for they bore an expression of stern and melancholy determination. I learnt afterwards that these men had just renounced all worldly prospects, with manse and kirk, to follow the dictates of conscience. They were the seceders from the Established Church who had just left the meeting of the General Assembly.

The name of Dr. Chalmers is intimately associated with this great movement. In his " Life " by

* See Cockburn's "Life of Jeffrey."

Hanna the following account is given of the final scene in the drama :—

" The day of trial at last arrived. For some days previously an unprecedented influx of strangers into Edinburgh foreshadowed the approach of some exciting event. Thursday, the 18th of May, the day named for the meeting of the General Assembly, rose upon the city with a dull and heavy dawn. So early in the morning as between four and five o'clock the doors of the church of St. Andrew's, where the Assembly was to convene, opened to admit the public. As the day wore on it became evident that the ordinary business of the great city had, to a great extent, been suspended ; yet the crowds that gathered in the streets wore no gay or holiday appearance. As groups of acquaintance met and commingled, their conversation was obviously of a grave and earnest cast."

Towards midday the Marquis of Bute, as Lord High Commissioner, held his first *levée* at Holyrood, and on its close proceeded as usual to St. Giles's Church, and from thence, when service was over, to the meeting of the General Assembly at St. Andrew's Church.

" Dr. Welsh, the moderator, entered and took the chair. Soon afterwards his Grace the Lord High Commissioner was announced, and the whole assemblage rose and received him standing. Solemn prayer was then offered up, and, the members having resumed their seats, Dr. Welsh read, amidst breathless silence, the protest of the seceding party. When the reading was finished he laid the protest upon the table, turned and bowed respectfully to the commissioner, left the chair, and proceeded along the aisle to the door of the church. Dr. Chalmers, seizing eagerly upon his hat, hurried after him with all the air of one impatient to be gone. Mr. Campbell of Menzie, Dr. Gordon, Dr. Macdonald, Dr. Macfarlan followed him. The effect upon the audience was overwhelming. At first a cheer burst from the galleries, but it was almost instantly and spontaneously restrained. It was checked in many cases by an emotion too deep for any other utterance than the fall of sad and silent tears. The whole audience was now standing gazing in stillness upon the scene. Man after man, row after row, moved on along the aisle till the benches on the left, lately so crowded, showed scarce an occupant. More than four hundred ministers and a still larger number of elders had withdrawn.

" A vast multitude of people stood congregated in St. George's Street, crowding in upon the church-doors. When the deed was done within, the intimation of it passed like lightning through the mass without, and when the forms of their most venerated clergymen were seen emerging from the church, a loud and irrepressible cheer burst from their lips, and echoed through the now half-empty Assembly Hall.

" There was no design on the part of the clergymen to form into a procession, but they were forced to it by the narrow-ness of the lane opened for their egress through the heart of the crowd. Falling into line and walking three abreast, they formed into a column which extended for a quarter of a mile and more. As they moved along to the new hall prepared for their reception, very different feelings pre-vailed among the numberless spectators who lined the streets and thronged each window and door and balcony on either side. Some gazed in stupid wonder ; the majority looked on in silent admiration.

"Elsewhere in the city Lord Jeffrey was sitting reading in his quiet room, when one burst in upon him saying, ' Well, what do you think of it ? More than four hundred of them are actually out.' The book was flung aside, and, springing to his feet, Lord Jeffrey exclaimed, ' I'm proud of my country ; there is not another country upon earth where such a deed could have been done.'"

One of the self-sacrificing ministers who renounced one of the best livings in Scotland, was Mr. John Ainslie, brother of my valued friend and connection, Mr. Daniel Ainslie, of the "Gart" Callender.

Large funds had to be raised for the support of the poorer ministers, but contributions flowed in rapidly and the necessary money was obtained. Two advocates of Edinburgh (both of whom I knew), Mr. Graham Spiers and Mr. Menteth, gave up each one-third of their yearly income to this fund. The latter gentleman is spoken of highly and affectionately by Lord Cockburn in his " Circuit Journeys."

The correspondence of myself and my wife at this time brought us some letters of general interest. A mutual friend sent me a copy of a letter from Mrs. Fry to Mr. W. Allen, the Quaker philanthropist and friend of the Duke of Wellington. It was written in the autumn of 1842, and has not, I believe, appeared in print.

"I think you will be interested to hear that we got through our visit to the Mansion House with much satisfaction. After some little difficulty that I had at arriving from the crowd, which overdid me for the time, I was favoured to arrive, and when led into the large drawing-room by the Lord Mayor I felt quiet and at ease.

"Soon my friends flocked round me, and I had a very satisfactory conversation with Sir James Graham, and I think the door was opened for further communication on a future day; it appeared most seasonable my then seeing him.

"I then spoke to Lord Aberdeen, and the door was opened for his helping us, if needful, in our foreign affairs.

"During dinner for about two hours, when I sat between Prince Albert and Sir Robert Peel, we had deeply interesting conversation upon the most important subjects: with Prince Albert, upon religious principle, its influence upon sovereigns, etc.; its importance in the education of children, and upon modes of worship; *our* views respecting it, etc.; why I could not rise at their toasts, not even at the one for the queen; why I could rise for prayer, etc.; also on the management of children generally; on war and peace; on prisons and punishment. And I had the same subjects, or many of them, with Sir Robert Peel. I think I hardly ever met with so cordial a reception from all parties and different ranks. The kindness shown me was extraordinary.

"After dinner I spoke to Lord Stanley about our colonies, and I think I was enabled to speak to all the men in power that I wanted to see.

"I shook hands very pleasantly with the Duke of Wellington, who spoke beautifully, expressing his desire to promote the arts of peace and not of war ; he said he was not fond of remembering the days that were past, as if the very thought of war pained him. I could not but feel that it is good for various persons of various descriptions to be brought together ; it promotes peace and love, and removes much prejudice and party feeling."

Letter from PROFESSOR COWPER *to his sister,*
MRS. HILL.

"97, High Holborn, May 3, 1844.

". . . A short time since I called at Mr. Lestock Wilson's to see Miss Edgeworth. It was at breakfast-time. Her younger brother was in the room when I arrived, and presently Miss Edgeworth came in. I bowed and introduced myself at once, and at once we were acquainted. She is a very little woman, but although so advanced in life, is full of spirit and cheerful good temper. We talked and chatted at 'railroad speed.'

"I then asked her if she would like to see King's College.

"'To be sure I should. I should like to see every-thing.'

"*E. Cowper* (in a joking cheerful manner). 'I hope you will excuse my having sent the card of admission to my lecture on Telegraphs to Mr. Wilson instead of directly to yourself. I did not know whether your health was such that your friends would allow you to go out in the evening.'

"*Miss Edgeworth* (laughing). 'Oh, hang my friends! I will go everywhere in spite of them all.'

"'Well, sister,' said young Edgeworth, 'you know you have promised Mr. Wheatstone to go to King's College to-morrow at two o'clock.'

"*Miss Edgeworth.* 'To be sure I have.'

"*E. Cowper.* 'Well, then, I will have the pleasure of showing you my room, and how we teach mechanical things in a college.'

"Accordingly she came, and Wheatstone entertained her in George the Third's Museum for two hours and a half. She then came into my room and stayed about half an hour. Then I said I was sure she must be fatigued, and so said her friends the Beauforts; but she said, 'Oh no! oh no!' but I said, 'Really, I will not show you anything more.'

"She was very much pleased. She liked my coarse models extremely. 'The coarser the better. I can see them and understand them well.' I explained the Jacquard loom to her, and then she asked, 'Ah, but how are the cards made?'

"'Why, ma'am, you are as bad as Prince Albert; for when I showed him the Jacquard loom he asked me precisely the same question.'

"*Miss Edgeworth.* 'Then Prince Albert is a very clever fellow.' And all this passing as lively and quick as the chat of an evening party.

"I showed her the Parlour Press, and presented one to her, and she insisted on having my name written on it by myself. I gave her also the cards showing the complementary colours, and a little movable diagram showing the principle of the Jacquard loom, and we parted glad to have met each other.

"I showed her also the model which I had made of her father's telegraph, and then she became thoughtful and seemed to call up old recollections. 'Yes, that is it; that was what he used, and I thank you for mentioning it in your public lectures.'

"I said, 'It will always be in this room, so that every student who comes here will know it to be your father's.'

"Yesterday week, at the Royal Institution, I found the 'Life' of her father left there for me—a present from her, with her own writing within the cover. 'Maria Edgeworth to E. Cowper, Esquire, with her thanks for the notice of her father's telegraph and his kindness to herself.'"

Since the establishment of penny postage in January, 1840, the reform had met with persistent opposition from those in authority at the Post-Office. The result was that in July, 1842, when the Tories were in office, my brother Rowland was dismissed from his post at the Treasury. No man but himself could carry his great plan, as a whole, into effect, and in dismissing him, his measure was, to use his own words, "handed over to men who had opposed it stage by stage, whose reputation was pledged to its failure, and who had unquestionably been caballing to obtain his expulsion from office."

These men had thus gained their point for the time being, but meanwhile leaders of the Liberal party came forward with expressions of strong indignation for the injustice done, and with offers of assistance. The public conscience began to be aroused.   Cobden, describing the feeling evinced in Scotland, wrote to Rowland, "The heather's on fire."

On the 10th of April, 1843, a petition for inquiring into the state of the Post-Office, proposed by my brother and in his own name, was presented to the House of Commons by Mr. Baring,* and on the following night Mr. Hawes gave notice that Sir Thomas Wilde would call the attention of the House to the same soon after the Easter recess. Various delays occurred, but finally the matter came before the House on the 27th of June.

"The motion of which Sir Thomas Wilde had given notice was for a select committee, 'To inquire into the progress which had been made in carrying into effect the recommendations of Mr. Rowland Hill for Post-Office improvement; and whether the further carrying into effect of such recommendations, or any of them, will be beneficial to the country.'"†

It can easily be imagined with what anxiety we looked forward to a debate so important to the prospects of postal reform. I was in Scotland at the time, but my friend Mr. James Simpson, who happened to be paying a visit to London, promised to send me the earliest tidings.

* Late Chancellor of the Exchequer.
† See "Life of Sir R. Hill," by Dr. Birkbeck Hill.

His letter, addressed to my wife, is as follows :—

"41, Doughty Street, June 28, 1843.

"MY DEAR MRS. HILL,

"I promised a few lines with my impressions on the *field-day*. It passed off yesterday, and was a triumph. The Liberal House, and notoriously the country, are too decidedly with Mr. Rowland Hill to have made it safe for Sir Robert Peel to have refused the committee. It was conceded, in fact, though in a different form, for *decency's sake*.

"It would have done your heart good to have witnessed the generous support of the Liberals, and the shouts with which the mention of Mr. Rowland Hill's words were received; the hearty condemnatory cheers with which Wilde's Post-Office *exposé* was answered; the decent silence of the other side ; but, above all, the prophetic declaration of Sir Robert Peel (made tauntingly to the Liberals) that Mr. Rowland Hill ought to be made Secretary of the Post-Office at once—an appointment which will certainly take place one day.

"The discussion and its publication all over the country is invaluable. It makes the temporary eclipse all the better.

"It was delightful to see the Hills of three generations in the House—from the venerable head with his black silk cap in the Speaker's gallery, in gradation of Matthew, Edwin, and Arthur, down to the youths from Bruce Castle and Hampstead.

"I am

"Affectionately yours,

"JAMES SIMPSON."

My father also writes on the occasion—

"44, Chancery Lane, June 28, 1843.

"MY DEAR FREDERIC,

"... I went into the Speaker's Gallery at the House of Commons, and had the pleasure of hearing a noble speech from Sir Thomas Wilde on the question that so closely concerns us all. ...

"It was delightful to me to hear the speakers uniformly speak highly of your brother. Mr. Baring, who knew him best, gave him a very high character indeed. This we know he well deserves, but not all men have their just merit acknowledged.

"Mr. Goulburn* complained, however, of his letting out the secrets of the prison-house ; rather a dangerous admission that there was that which could not bear the public eye. One good stroke amused the whole House. The Post-Office had made a vaunting return of the sums transferred by means of money orders. It stated it at eight millions per annum, adding the sums paid out to the sums paid in. Your brother Rowland, who sat under the gallery, whispered to a member that it seemed that the water which ran into a pipe and that which ran out, put together, made the water that ran through the pipe. Mr. Goulburn had unfortunately quoted the Post-Office document, thinking it favourable to his case ; but the pipe's comparison had reached Mr. Baring, who put it out in good style and raised a roaring laugh. ...

"I remain

"Your affec^te· father,

"THO. W. HILL."

* Chancellor of the Exchequer.

Rowland's health, which was never robust, suffered from the continued strain put upon his powers at this time.

Harriet Martineau wrote to me in the spring of 1844—

"I am glad to hear your glorious brother is going to be quiet at Croydon. He must complete the glory of his achievements by preserving, if possible, health and at least a buoyant and cheerful spirit till he is wanted again to carry out his entire scheme. That day must come. Meantime entire rest seems to be his duty. I do wish it could be found in foreign travel; its effects are so marvellous in recruiting an overwrought mind and nerves too much tried. I trust his worldly fortunes will soon have grown beyond the limits of all anxiety, and then perhaps his family will urge him to go abroad.

"Pardon this freedom if it seems to you excessive; but you would hardly think so if you knew that he has written to me with a kind confidence which seems to authorize my saying what I think to his affectionate brother."

Two years later I received the following note from Rowland :—

"Reform Club, November 25, 1846.

"DEAR FRED^c.,

"I have accepted the offer of Government of an appointment as Secretary to the Postmaster-General. The appointment to be permanent.

"The engagement has much to recommend it (I shall be in close communication with the Postmaster-General and the Treasury). . . .

"The appointment is avowedly for the purpose of carrying out my plan.

"In haste,

"Yours affect^{ly}.,

"R. HILL."

CHAPTER XIII.

1845–1847.

DURING the long reign of the Peel administration I
had much petty opposition to contend with from Sir
James Graham, the Home Secretary, and earnestly
did I desire the return of the Whigs to power, not
only as a benefit to the nation at large, but especially
in connection with my work of prison reform.   As
long as Lord John Russell had been my official
chief, my hands were left completely unfettered.

My wife wrote to her eldest sister on December
20, 1845—

"I write a hasty line to express my heartfelt joy at
Lord John's having accepted office. I have been in the
most painful suspense since Frederic left me for Glasgow.
I had no means of learning the truth till an hour ago.
Most earnestly I hope a long reign is before the Whigs.
The very last act of Sir James Graham has been to

16

attempt to undo half the good that has been done in Scotland in prison discipline, by urging the directors to assimilate their rules to those of the English prisons—that is, to 'introduce *penal* or useless labour and flogging, and to diminish the power and responsibility of the governor.' All these he calls '*great improvements.*' Fortunately he has overstepped the law, and told us to break both the spirit and letter of the Scottish Prisons Act."

In April, 1846, I made a tour of inspection in Northumberland and Durham, which counties, as I have before mentioned, formed part of my district. I wrote to my wife from Newcastle—

"At a small prison in this neighbourhood I found the keeper in perplexity how to act. A prisoner (the only one in the gaol) had fortified the door of his cell on the inside, so that the keeper could not enter. The keeper asked me whether he should break open the door. 'By no means,' I replied. 'Let the man alone until hunger compels him to ask for food ; when, in order to get it, he must, of course, pull down his barricade. Then give him food, but very sparingly, and for some time afterwards keep him on short allowance.' This advice the keeper followed, and he had no further trouble.

"I told you I had gained over one of the county magistrates—the chairman of the visiting justices, with whom before I had had strong differences of opinion. How do you think I obtained his good will and favourable opinion ? By not wearing a nightcap! When we met we began, as in duty bound, to speak of the weather, and I remarked that I had still the remains of a cold. 'A cold!' he said. 'Do you wear flannel?' 'Yes.' 'Do you

wash in cold water every morning from head to foot ?'
'Yes.' 'Do you wear a nightcap?' 'No.' 'Then you
ought never to have a cold ; and I can't imagine how you
caught it.' After this explanation his tone became friendly,
and he invited me to drink tea with him, which I did."

A little later I went up to London in order
to join my brother Arthur previous to our taking
a tour on the Continent together, and also to be
present at a public dinner to be given to my
brother Rowland.

I wrote on June 19—

"At Wolverton, where the trains stop some time for
refreshment, a gentleman in my carriage having got out
heard that Ibrahim Pacha was in the refreshment-room.
He ran to get a peep at him, and found him, to the amazement of all beholders, with a loaf in one hand and a roll
of butter in the other, plastering and eating as fast as he
could !

Frank (the husband of my sister Caroline Clark), who
came up also for Rowland's public dinner, told us a good
story of the Pacha at Birmingham. It appears that the
skeleton of a great whale is exhibiting there just now,
and Ibrahim and his suite went to see it, and got inside.
No sooner did the showman see Ibrahim within the
skeleton, than he rushed out of the shed, locking the door
behind him, and blowing his horn proclaimed to the crowd
that the great Eastern Pacha was to be seen inside the
whale. He doubled the price of admission, but the place
was at once crammed with people, and the showman
reaped a capital harvest. To the additional delight of the

spectators, the grand Pacha, who was trying to make his escape, was found stuck between the ribs of the whale."

The following are extracts from the letters which I sent home from Switzerland :—

"*Chamouni.*—A mile's walk and a further descent over the *débris* of the mountain brought us to Loeche Bad, a place where there are natural hot baths, much frequented by the French and Swiss, but not by the English. The temperature of the water is brought down artificially to blood-heat, and people remain in it *six* or *eight* hours a day! They wear large gowns, and bathe in company without regard to age or sex. They have little floating trays before them, on which you see books, flowers, coffee, etc. Strangers are admitted to see the bathers, and when we went there must have been sixty or seventy in the water, all very merry and some very noisy; many of the ladies with their hair dressed, or wearing fine caps. Two were playing the game of 'Fox and Goose,' and some were amusing themselves by squirting water, which they do with much dexterity. Arthur gave great satisfaction and excited cries of 'Bravo' by making them a low bow; and, indeed, our entrance on to the platform was greeted with general cheers. . . .

"Arthur, who feels the heat much more than I, is in the habit, when he comes to a public fountain, of dipping his umbrella into the water, and then walking off with the dripping umbrella over his head, to the amusement of the bystanders.

"*St. Gothard.*—One of the daughters of the landlord of the Grimsel Hospice (where we are this morning) is the only handsome girl or woman we have yet seen in

Switzerland. I should think an English girl would have a dozen lovers within an hour of her arrival at any place in this country. What can be the cause of so sad a dearth of personal beauty in a land of so much natural beauty? Whatever it be, I trust that it will be ultimately removed.

"*Meyringen.* — Yesterday we witnessed the grandest natural sight, at least the finest combination of grandeur and beauty, which I ever beheld—the fall of the river Aar and of a tributary stream from a height of two hundred feet into a fine mountain gorge. The extraordinary character of the fall is caused by the circumstance of the two streams dashing against each other and uniting about halfway down. The Aar, from its volume and weight, strikes against the tributary with such force as to cause a great portion of it to rise again nearly to the top in the form of splendid clouds of spray producing beautiful rainbows. The waters disappear in mist, coming in sight again in one clear unbroken column.

"*Lucerne.*—Left for the Righi. On the road we came to a chapel erected on the spot from which Tell is said to have shot the arrow which killed Gessler. In the book in the chapel, in which strangers are invited to write, Arthur wrote, 'Tell won the liberty of his country by his courage, may his posterity preserve it by mutual love;' a hint of which the Swiss appear to be much in need. . . .

"The most striking object at Lucerne is a monument by Thorwaldsen to the memory of the Swiss Guard killed by the populace of Paris when defending Louis XVI. It is shown to visitors by one of the few members of the Swiss Guard who effected their escape and are still living. I think it is the finest and most impressive monument I ever saw. It is cut out of the hard face of a large rock in a secluded situation, with a quiet pool of clear water before it and surrounded by trees. The figure represented is a wounded lion in the pains of death, trying, even at that moment, to protect a shield on which are carved the royal arms of France. There is a wonderful combination of dignity, majesty, and affliction in the lion, and the whole monument strikes you as grand in conception and most successful in execution."

During my absence my wife wrote to me from our Edinburgh home, 55, Inverleith Row, of things public and private. In one letter she says—

"The opening of the noble railways excites much good feeling. In the account of the grand opening of the Paris and Brussels line, I saw it mentioned that King Leopold stood at the station on his frontier to receive and welcome the first train, containing two thousand visitors! The Berwick railway was opened last Monday. The good folk from Princes Street go for the bathing to Portobello in seven minutes!"

Again she writes—

"June 28, 1846.

"I write with a light heart. The delightful news reached Edinburgh by yesterday afternoon's mail of the passing of the Corn Law Bill in the Lords without a single vote against it, the thorough defeat of the Irish Coercion Bill by 173 votes, and the return of good men and true to that power which they had made a blessing to their country.

"Really the world seems to me twice as full of pleasant prospects! How we love to associate nature with our feelings! Last New Year's Day, the morning after your departure for London, I saw the sun rise with great beauty over Arthur's Seat. It was at the time of the potato failure, and, feeling deeply interested in all Cobden's appeals for untaxed food, I earnestly wished that the next New Year's Day the blessed sun, the ripener of our countless stores, might rise upon a new era of free trade. Peel's great measure had not then been proposed. Just now, as I recalled these feelings, I went involuntarily to the window, and there over Arthur's Seat stretched a rainbow brilliant with hope fulfilled!

"How I wish that the mighty dead could see the change of opinion upon subjects affecting the happiness of mankind! but, though all unknown to us, they may be partakers of our joy in their wondrous state.

"I do not think I shall tire you by mentioning again how often our three little girls talk and think of you. I met them by accident out walking with their nurse. They were shouting your name that you might hear them! Flags have been painted more than a week to welcome your return. 'Only to get ready, mamma,' said little Nora."

Later in this year I find the following entry in my diary :—

"*November* 5.—On Tuesday I breakfasted at Mr. Wigham's with a party including Mr. Lloyd Garrison, Mr. Frederick Douglas (the slave who effected his escape), Mr. George Thompson, Professor Pillans, and others. Mr. Garrison and Mr. Douglas are both prepossessing in their appearance, and are evidently men of strong intellect. At Mr. Wigham's request Mr. Garrison gave an account of the present state of the anti-slavery question in America. He said that it had made, and is making, rapid progress, and he appeared to think that the way in which the abolition of slavery will be ultimately brought about will be by the Northern States (for at present they scarcely deserve to be called Free States) insisting either on the repeal of the Fugitive Slave Law or the dissolution of the Union."

My wife, who met Mr. Douglas at Mr. Wigham's house during the summer of this year, thus writes of him—

"Mr. Douglas is self-educated and highly intelligent, and his adventures, which he related to us, are extremely interesting. He is lecturing for the cause of emancipation. In a book which he has published he speaks of a 'dialogue upon slavery' which he had read when only twelve years old, and which strongly impressed him. He did not know the author's name, but from his description I felt certain that it was Mrs. Barbauld's 'Master and Slave.' When I spoke to him on the subject he said he would give the world to read the story again, and that he had tried everywhere to procure it, but in vain. I told him I would send him 'Evenings at Home,' and I have just sent him a copy for his eldest son, a little lad of seven. It is pleasant to think how Mrs. Barbauld's nervous, energetic reasoning fired the heart of the poor, brave young negro."

To return again to my diary.

"*November* 5, 1846.—On Tuesday I dined at Mr. George Combe's, where there were present Archbishop Whately, his chaplain, Dr. West, Mr. Robert Chambers, Sir George and Lady Mackenzie, Mr. and Mrs. George Combe (the latter a daughter of Mrs. Siddons), Mrs. Crowe (author of 'Susan Hopley'), and two or three other persons.

"Archbishop Whately spoke of a conversation he had with Lord Melbourne after the passing of the Bill for the abolition of negro slavery. On leaving the House of Lords together Lord Melbourne said to him, 'Well, my Lord Archbishop, now it is over it is very well, but I think it would have been better if they had left it alone and not made so much ado about it. Every civilized country has had slaves, and why should not we? The Greeks had slaves, and the Romans had slaves.'

"We afterwards continued the conversation about Lord Melbourne in the drawing-room. I asked what was the cause of his success with the Queen, and the influence he obtained. To which the archbishop replied that it was certainly not by flattery, for he did anything but flatter. He was exceedingly frank, and unhesitatingly gave expression to his thoughts, whatever they might be. He supposed that the straightforwardness of Lord Melbourne, and his odd but clever mode of putting things, was pleasing to the Queen. He was, besides, a man of perfect good temper, of varied and extensive knowledge, which he acquired apparently without effort, and generally of sound judgment.

"The conversation next turned to the pleasure of companionship, either in person or act, even in cases where there is no oral communication. Archbishop Whately told a story of two neighbouring gentlemen who used each to go into a bower in his garden to smoke a pipe after dinner. They never exchanged a word, but they always came out exactly at the same time, and when the first was ready to light his pipe he made a signal by waving his handkerchief to the other, and, on receiving a signal in return, they both began to smoke. The pipe out, they got up, bowed to each other, and walked into their houses."

Among our Edinburgh friends were two sculptors whom I have not yet mentioned—William Brodie and John Steele.

My wife had occasion, in 1881, to write the following account of the former :—

"Mr. Brodie was a working plumber in Aberdeen when we first saw him in 1846. He was fond of art, and attempted at all spare moments to model small bas-relief subjects, generally portraits. In these he was very successful. He executed an excellent likeness of Sheriff Watson while the sheriff was presiding in court.

"It was not possible to see Brodie and his wife in their own home without being interested in them, and without wishing to further Brodie's desire to become an artist. His little house of three rooms and a 'lean-to' was a model of a working man's home, and proved how much refinement was consistent with very small means. I shall never forget the little parlour. A bird sang in the window over a stand of flowers, in the midst of which was a globe of gold-fish. Prints of good subjects, bas-reliefs, and small copies of Raphael's 'Cartoons' were on the wall. A violin was on the table, the property of a friend working under the same master-plumber, and a piece of poetry written by another comrade.

"Among those who encouraged Brodie's dawning genius

were Sheriff Watson, Mr. and Mrs. John Hill Burton, Mr. Nimmo, Lord Murray, and ourselves. Brodie's master was induced to spare him for a month that he might visit Edinburgh. Before he arrived Mr. and Mrs. Burton and Mr. Nimmo had procured him twenty commissions for bas-relief portraits, at twenty-five shillings each. At the end of the month he had many more commissions, so he went back to Aberdeen, gave up plumbing, and brought his family to Edinburgh. He now studied art systematically, and by the kindness of a gentleman named Buchanan he was sent, a few years later, to Rome.

"His wife has proved as true a helpmate in prosperity as in the struggles of early life. She has seen her husband fully appreciated, and his portraits of the noble and the good spread over the land." *

William Brodie is said "to have made more portrait busts than any other sculptor;" amongst these were four of the Queen, and one of Lord Jeffrey. He executed the marble statue of Lord Cockburn in the Parliament House, and that of Sir David Brewster in the quadrangle of the University, and, later on, the colossal statue of the Prince Consort at Perth.

I remember a remark of Mr. Brodie's about brain work and manual work. He said that when he was a plumber he imagined that handicraftsmen were the only hard workers, and that the work which is purely from the brain could be nothing but

* Mrs. Brodie has died since the above was written.

amusement. But when he became a sculptor he found, to his astonishment, that his early struggles as a mechanic, however severe, could not compare with the hard and exhausting labour which now came to him as brain work.

Brodie was a full member of the Royal Scottish Academy, and when he died, in 1881, that body voted him a public funeral. My wife writes again of him—

"Not only the Scottish Academicians followed the illustrious artist to the grave, but distinguished men of all professions, and friends from all classes. The grand procession winding its way to the Dean cemetery evinced the wonderful contrast between Brodie's situation in early life, and his distinguished position at its close; but the *man* was the same, ever keeping his own character pure from the temptations of ambition. He was the same earnest Christian at the end as at the beginning, feeling that the Creator of all beauty was the God of truth. The minister who preached the funeral sermon, who had had long and intimate intercourse with him, said he 'never left William Brodie without feeling he had received help from him both for this life and the next.'"

Mr. Steele (afterwards Sir John Steele) was the sculptor of the statue of Scott in the Princes Street monument. This established his position as a leading sculptor, and he afterwards made important statues of the Queen, the Duke of Wellington, the

Marquis of Dalhousie, etc.   He was a most simple-minded man, like many of our best artists, and a general favourite.

In the year 1846 he visited Rome.   In passing through Paris he went to the bank of the great financier Lafitte to get cash for a banknote for ten pounds.   On his homeward journey, after crossing into France, he lost his portmanteau—no surprising event to occur to our art-loving but unpractical friend.   But the means which he took to recover it were indeed surprising.   Recollecting that Monsieur Lafitte, at whose bank he had changed his ten-pound note, was at the head of the Ministry, he wrote a letter to him, and, prefacing his request with an account of his important banking trans-action, asked the Minister to have a search made for the portmanteau.   He enclosed a drawing of it, showing all its straps and buckles!   Lafitte received the letter while entertaining a party of friends, who were amused beyond measure at the *naïveté* of the young artist.   On arriving in Edinburgh, Mr. Steele told us, with his wonted simplicity, what had happened, and great was our mirth at his recital. For some time afterwards when any of us met him we asked what news he had of his portmanteau. Indeed, the poor man was much twitted about it.   But presently he was able to turn the laugh against *us*. The amused Lafitte had actually set all the police to work, and the portmanteau arrived bodily in Edinburgh, with a note from his private secretary conveying the Minister's congratulations to Mr. Steele on the recovery of his lost property !

CHAPTER XIV.

1847–1850.

In the spring of 1847, Mr. Crawford, one of the inspectors of English prisons, died, and this causing a vacancy, I determined to apply for an English district. I considered my work in Scotland to be, in the main, finished, and now, after twelve years' residence in that country, I desired to be once more settled within reach of my aged father and of my brothers. My health also at that time had suffered from overwork, and a change of scene was deemed advisable. My application was successful, and thus my official career in Scotland came to an end. So much, however, had I become attached to the country and its inhabitants, that to quit them was felt by me as a severe wrench.

The following is a short summary of the reforms

in the Scotch prisons which I had been able to effect.

1. At the time of my departure all the prison buildings were well adapted for their purpose, and the "separate system," with certain limitations, had been established.

2. There was not in any prison a single bad officer.

3. In every prison there was industrial occupation, more or less productive, to the exclusion of all artificial labour. The use of treadmills and cranks had been entirely abolished.

4. Every prisoner who did more than his allotted task was allowed the value of his overwork (subject to the control of the governor in its disposal) ; and thus a means was provided to the industrious on leaving gaol of making a fresh start in an honest career.

5. The general conduct of the prisoners was good, although flogging was entirely abolished.

6. The cost per head of the prisoners was comparatively small. To take the last complete year of my superintendence as a guide, the average cost was £16, whilst in England it exceeded £25.

Before quitting the subject of the Scotch prisons, I would again lay stress upon the great importance I attach to productive labour. How can a permanent habit of industry be acquired by a prisoner but by associating pleasurable and honourable feelings with industry, and painful and dishonourable feelings with idleness ? But hard labour is, at the outset, often made degrading instead of honourable, by forming part of the sentence of punishment awarded to some of the worst offenders. In Scotland, at the time I am writing of, no one was ever sentenced to "hard labour," but every prisoner was set to work as a matter of course, and had a daily task assigned him representing ten hours' labour. The prisoner was employed, if possible, at his own trade, or, if ignorant of any, he was taught a trade.

In proof of the success of the system of payment to prisoners for voluntary work done beyond their allotted task, I will quote the following passage from my last report on the prisons of Scotland :—

"With the value of their overwork some of the prisoners assisted in maintaining their families, while a great number earned money for a decent suit of clothes, or had a small fund with which to support themselves on leaving prison until they could get work. In one instance a little boy in Glasgow prison, who had previously been a great source of trouble to his mother, was enabled, when his mother fell ill, to send her a pound, which, by great industry, rising frequently as early as three in the morning, he had earned. In another instance a prisoner of Aberdeen, a blacksmith, obtained money enough, not only to assist his family whilst he was in prison and to fit up a forge for himself on liberation, but to repay the person whom he had injured the whole amount of the loss which he occasioned him, which was £25. And in a third case, at Edinburgh, a young man who was an engraver, not only improved himself in his profession while in prison, but earned money enough to pay his passage to America, and thus to place himself in a position far removed from his former scene of disgrace, where he might obtain a new character, and where, in fact, he was afterwards heard of living respectably."

A governor of one of the prisons writing to me on this subject remarked, "*Very few prisoners who earned much money under this rule ever returned to prison.*" The money was, of course, given out with much caution. It was generally put into the hands of the overseer of the parish where the discharged prisoner lived, the superintendent of police, or the churchwarden, to be used in the best way.

My esteemed friend Mr. Brebner, governor of the Glasgow Bridewell, of whom I have already spoken, may be said to have lost his life in the advocacy of the great cause of industrial prison-work. He overtaxed his strength in preparing his voluminous evidence on this subject for the Prison Board, taking scarcely any rest for some nights previous to their meeting. Just as his evidence was to be given he was stricken with apoplexy, and died in my arms.

Mr. Brebner was so highly esteemed that the Town Council of Glasgow voted him a public funeral. He was followed to the grave by crowds of all classes, and the police in attendance recognized many who had formerly been in Mr. Brebner's charge as prisoners.

I began the inspection of my new district in England in the summer of 1847. It comprised the whole of the north of England and also of North Wales, to which an eastern district was afterwards added.

Few of the reforms which I had carried out in the Scotch prisons had found their way into those of England. Treadmill and other unprofitable labour was in full force. No motives were given to industry, and voluntary work for payment was strictly prohibited. Any money given to a prisoner on his discharge was purely a matter of charity, and depended chiefly, like almsgiving in general, on the degree of destitution.

In most of the English prisons I found the inmates either associated together, with some attempt at classification, it is true, but under very inefficient superintendence, or collected in larger bodies and subjected to the "silent system." This system I have always considered to be very pernicious. I write of it in my report for 1847—

"When prisoners are brought together it will, I think, be generally admitted that they should really associate as human beings, and not be doomed, as under the 'silent system,' to eternal silence, with their heads and eyes fixed, like statues, in one direction ; and that all attempts to enforce such a system, and to carry on such a warfare with nature, must be productive of endless attempts at deception on the part of the prisoners, and lead to much punishment. Again, that by turning the officers into constant organs of punishment, the system must greatly weaken their moral influence, and tend to prevent that feeling of respect and attachment which it is so desirable to create. The object of discipline in a prison, so far as relates to control, ought to be to curb only the bad passions and evil propensities, and not to destroy the social feelings, and stifle desires which are in themselves innocent. When, therefore, prisoners are placed together, although neither idleness nor disorder of any kind should be allowed, I would never recommend that they should be forbidden to look at each other, or, at stated periods and in a quiet tone, to converse."

The "separate system," I found, was but little in use in the English prisons. Though strongly opposed to an unlimited use of this system, I consider it greatly superior, even when carried to excess, to the indiscriminate association of prisoners or to the "silent system." The plan which I look upon as the best is complete separation in the first instance (though in some cases for a very short period only), gradually followed, according to circumstances, by judicious classification, the amount of association increasing or diminishing as it is found to be beneficial or otherwise.

Speaking of the clothing of the prisoners in England, I write—

"The use of party-coloured clothing continues in many English prisons, carrying with it a degrading badge, opposed to that feeling of self-respect which, in the process of reformation, it is so important to create and preserve."

On my first inspection of the prisons of North Wales I found that several governors, as well as under-officers, were unfit for their posts. I write to my wife on April 12, 1848—

"I have very little doubt that the governors at Beaumaris and Carnarvon will be dismissed, and most assuredly the one at Ruthin ought to follow. All these men have been many years in office."

I found that the chaplain of one of the Welsh prisons was addicted to drinking. On my laying the case before the magistrates, they assured me that they were aware of the fact, but that, being on social and friendly terms with him, none of them liked to tell him to resign. I offered to undertake the task, and my interview with the reverend gentleman ended in his placing his resignation in my hands. He thanked me for having as much as possible spared his feelings, and said he hoped that whenever I returned to that neighbourhood I would come and dine with him !

In this same year (1848) I write to my wife from York—

"I am scattering the poor matrons before me in all directions. I had to recommend the removal of one from Durham, of another from Northallerton, and I see I shall have to recommend the removal of a third from here. This prison, although there is a well-meaning man for governor, must hitherto have been a sad place of corruption, little superintendence and no work. No wonder that there should be attempts to escape. Six prisoners I find under a charge of conspiring to attack some of the officers with a view to breaking out of prison.

" *Hull.*—The good people here seem to think that they have a 'commissioner of all work' among them ! I have no slight task at the prison, but, in addition to that, I have been applied to by the chairman of the Watch Committee to make suggestions for the improvement of the police ; another gentleman has begged me to take up the question of the want of a stipendiary magistrate at Hull ; a third has assured me that the application of endowments for education here requires investigation, though he 'was afraid such inquiry did not come *strictly* within my province ;' and I had yesterday a message to inquire whether it lay within my power to examine into the state of the drainage in the suburbs of Hull !"

I write of a visit to Richmond, Yorkshire—

"I got up early and went to see the old castle—a fine ruin in a commanding situation. My guide was one of those persons who have a stock phrase which they use on all occasions, without much regard to its appropriateness. With him everything was 'according to history.' 'What is the height,' I inquired, 'of the fine old keep?' 'According to history,' was his reply, 'it is ninety-nine feet.' I suggested that it would be well to check history by letting down a piece of string, but he did not understand my drift. Walking on, we came to a part of the battlements where the hill, at the top of which the castle stands, descends precipitously to the river beneath. 'A pretty steep descent this,' I remarked. 'Yes, sir,' he answered, 'according to history it is almost perpendicular;' an answer which so tickled me as nearly to throw *me* off the perpendicular.

"After receiving various other pieces of information 'according to history,' I left the castle and went to see the ruins of an abbey, which you reach by a very pretty walk of about a mile by the side of the river. By this time I was ready for my breakfast, and returned to the inn. A gouty commercial traveller came into the breakfast parlour. It appeared that he belonged to the wine trade, and the gout of this worthy martyr had, no doubt, been brought on by his setting an example which he wished all his customers to follow. A gentleman asked him what kind of night he had had. 'Much better than usual,' he replied, 'owing to my having drunk four glasses of brandy and water before going to bed. And I suppose,' he added, with perfect gravity and with the air of a man who is trying to make up his mind to a disagreeable thing—'I suppose I must do the same to-night.'

'After meeting the Mayor of Richmond and one of his

fellow-magistrates, I found I had still time on my hands before the train started, and went into the market-place. A market, especially in a country town, is always to me a place of interest and attraction, partly owing, no doubt, to my having been in the habit, when a boy, of accompanying my mother to market and carrying her basket. I like the clean, healthy-looking, country people, the odd medley of fruit, poultry, pigs, ironware, drapery, baskets, bonnets, shoes, tubs, and clocks, the quacking of ducks, the cackling of geese, and the neighing of horses.

"In a distant part of the market-place I observed a young man standing on a chair and addressing those around him. I found that he was a 'cheap-jack' selling chemical concoctions of various kinds, which he displayed in a sort of tray or pedlar's box suspended from his neck. He had lost his right arm, and was therefore obliged to perform his experiments with his left, often making use of his mouth also. He was very young—not more, apparently, than eighteen or nineteen—had an intelligent countenance and the command of fluent language. In his address there was a strange mixture of sound sense, odd extravagance, and error. When I arrived he was dilating on the virtue of a powder for fumigating rooms, and demonstrating its action by making a puff of smoke with a bad smell. For this valuable concoction I find, on the undoubted authority of my 'cheap-jack,' a Parliamentary grant of £5000 has been awarded to our friend Dr. Southwood Smith! The honour of inventing another recipe he assigned to our friend Dr. Nichol, of Glasgow, who, I find, has no sinecure, either in lecturing or travelling ; for, in addition to his labours as an astronomer, it appears that he is professor of chemistry in the Universities of Edinburgh, Glasgow, Aberdeen, and St. Andrew's !

"By-and-by our young friend began to speak of the post-office, and urged upon his simple country auditors the necessity of preserving the important secrets in their letters by means of his 'sympathetic ink,' which, he stated, was invented by a distinguished member of the 'Anti-poke-your-nose-into-other-people's-business Society!' 'No doubt,' exclaimed the young orator, 'when Sir James Graham was charged with the base act of opening people's letters he denied the deed. Like Banquo, he shook his *hoary* locks and said, "You cannot say I *done* it!" But it *was he* who gave his secret orders to have it done. How much custom, gentlemen,' continued the vendor, 'would any railway company have if they advertised that all parcels sent by their railway would be pried into? And who,' he demanded, his eloquence rising with the occasion, 'who would send his letters through the channels of Government if he knew that they were to be *subjugated to a fiery ordeal in the dark chambers of the post-office?*'

" *York.*—I wrote to you last night, and must be very brief now, as I am just starting for the prison, and much of the little spare time which I had has been taken up by my most loquacious landlady. She has been explaining to me, at great length, why, notwithstanding her husband is now worth £2000, she continues to wear a short-sleeved gown in the morning—a practice which is 'part of her nature, and which she would not give up, no, not if she possessed the Queen and all the Indies!'"

In this year (1848) the French Revolution took place. The excitement spread all over Europe, and was evinced even in this country by riots and other disturbances. Fears were entertained of a

French invasion, and, my mind being thus directed to the subject of national defence, I conceived the project of a reserve force. My plan was to engage a number of well-disposed men, to have them efficiently armed and drilled, to pay them adequately when on duty, and to give them a small pension in old age. These men were to hold themselves in readiness to leave their various employments for service on the shortest notice. Thus a well-trained force would be at hand in all parts of the country to quell tumults, or to aid in resisting invasion.

I wrote and published a pamphlet on this subject, entitled "A National Force for the Economical Defence of the Country from Internal Tumult and Foreign Aggression." It was favourably reviewed in the *Examiner, Globe,* and *Spectator* newspapers. No such reserve force has, to this day, been established for inland duty, but in 1852 the Government brought before Parliament a project for establishing a naval reserve, and Mr. Bernal Osborne, in the House of Commons, charged the Ministers with having adopted my plan in its spirit, though without acknowledgment.

Among the letters I received on the publication of my pamphlet is the following, from my friend John Hill Burton, the historian :—

"20, Scotland Street, Edinburgh, April 12, 1848.

"MY DEAR SIR,

"I was agreeably reminded of you the other day by receiving from you a copy of your able pamphlet, which I was glad to see receiving immediate notice in the *Examiner.* In accordance with its principles, it occurred to me, while we were hearing all the rumours of the threatened catastrophe in London, that the special constables were more to be relied on than the troops, and that some day or other it may turn out a mistake to suppose that mere discipline and isolation will make men taken from the dregs of society, as too many of our soldiers are, the firm friends of order and property.

"It might have been wished—and I have heard other people who approve of your principle say the same—that you had gone more into detail, but I suppose official duties left little time at your disposal, and you thought justly that it would be a good service to publish the outline.

"Yours ever,

"J. H. BURTON."

The following is to my wife from our genial friend Mr. James Simpson. It is remarkable that in it he foreshadows the great Volunteer movement.

"33, Northumberland Street, Edinburgh, March 8, 1848.

"MY DEAR FRIEND,

"Your letter and Mr. Hill's pamphlet are just received, and both have given me much pleasure. We are truly happy to observe your good spirits, indicating that all is well with you.

"The Cheap Defence plan is so good that I think it

must be adopted. I have been myself, in society, advocating the training of every young man to the use of arms, but did not think of paying and clothing them. This last, however, may be necessary to obtain a *certain* available force. The ranks would be filled by competition ; and I do not think that the force may not have added to it as many volunteer corps of *gentlemen* as will clothe themselves and bear all their own expenses.

"The remarks on the tyranny of unions are excellent. There are no greater tyrants than the lower classes, and *they* complain most loudly of tyranny. . . .

"Mr. Edwin's pamphlet much delighted me. His plan, too, is excellent. The Hills for ever! Think of good Mr. Hill senior's interest in the French news at his age! That wonderful event will turn to good, I trust.

"With love and esteem,

"I am yours affectionately,

"JAMES SIMPSON."

The following extracts are taken from letters to my wife during my tours of inspection :—

"Manchester, March 28, 1848.

"There was a capital meeting last night at the Free Trade Hall. I never attended a public meeting at which there was so much earnest, logical, and eloquent speaking, and I have no doubt it will have a very beneficial effect. The modest application of the West Indian planters for permission to take two millions a year out of our pockets was met as such impudent demands ought to be met. Cobden spoke excellently, as did Milner Gibson, Bright, and Colonel Thompson. . . ."

"Ipswich, May 8, 1849.

"On Sunday I passed a pleasant evening with Mr. Allen Ransome at his father's—a fine old gentleman, physically, mentally, and morally. On our arrival we found him in his drawing-room with his family, his servants, and some of their children, reading to them interesting accounts of Ragged Schools; and it was evident, by the respectful yet unembarrassed way in which some of the servants made remarks, that the whole household were living on friendly terms, but with proper subordination.

"Mr. Ransome has more than a thousand men in his employment, engaged chiefly in the construction of agricultural implements and railway carriages, and he speaks in high terms of the conduct of the workmen and of the spirit of harmony between them and their employers. He says that he believes that the money which an employer expends in increasing the comforts of his workpeople is generally his most productive capital."

"Norwich, September 23.

"Bishop Stanley's funeral ceremony was very impressive, and so was the memorial service and sermon to-day. The sermon was in the best possible taste, and full of good matter, and the choir and organist seemed to throw their whole soul into the sublime music. The grave is in the nave of the cathedral, and around it were assembled a great number of children, in whose instruction and training the bishop had taken a personal interest. The grave is so placed that at a certain hour of the day, the sunlight, coming through a painted window, will fall upon it.

". . . I passed a very pleasant evening at Mr. Leigh's parsonage. He said that the late bishop would have entered warmly into my views and have thoroughly supported me."

"September 25.

"I have avoided the subject of cholera in my letters, but I will mention for your comfort that I believe it to be a mistake to suppose that cholera is accompanied by pain. At Wakefield prison the surgeon told me, when I expressed surprise at not seeing the indications of pain in the faces of the patients, that he always considered it a good sign when there was pain, and that it was torpor and insensibility they had to contend with."

"Lincoln.

"On Sunday I dined between the cathedral services with one of the county magistrates, Mr. Fardell, who knew Matthew when he came this circuit; and, by the way, I have Matthew's old lodgings. I was remarking to Mr. Fardell on the youthful appearance of most of the county magistrates at the meeting last week, and was surprised to hear from him that most of them had been put into the Commission of the Peace when they were mere infants; and that till lately this was a common practice, just as children used to have commissions in the army and navy."

"Lincoln, June, 1850.

"I have heard a good story about the consultation of the jury that had to try a Dr. Snaith some years ago on a political charge, Matthew being the doctor's counsel. It appears that, except one, the jury was composed of Tories, all disposed to bring in a verdict of guilty, and that when they retired, the foreman (father of one of the county justices with whom I have been dining) went up to the dissenting juryman and addressed him somewhat in this fashion : 'Sir, we had best understand one another.

I have been a soldier, and have passed twenty-four hours in a ditch, with nothing to eat ; so you have no chance of beating me, and you had better give in at once.' To which the other replied, ' What you say is very likely, but I have been a sailor, and I once passed three days and three nights on a plank in the middle of the sea, with only a crust of bread to eat the first day, and with nothing for the other two ; so I suppose I can hold out as well as another.' The foreman, in alarm, cried out, ' By Jove, there's no beating that ! ' He sent off immediately to his medical attendant, got a certificate from him that his life would be endangered if he were kept long without food, succeeded thereby in obtaining the dismissal of the jury (which had the effect of an acquittal), and arrived at home only a few minutes late for the family dinner."

" Manchester.

"Mr. John Shuttleworth told me that at the exhibition in 1839 of the Mechanics' Institute here, a man one day demanded admission in so noisy a manner that it was evident he was intoxicated. Some of the directors who were present refused to allow him to enter, but a respectable mechanic, himself a director, gave it as his opinion that the man was quite capable of conducting himself properly if they appealed to his good feelings. He further offered to accompany him round the rooms. The man was allowed to enter, and the sudden decorum which he evinced, as his good-natured guide pointed out the various interesting objects, was truly remarkable. He stayed two hours, and when he left the exhibition he turned to some of the directors and expressed his regret at the violence and rudeness of his conduct. He requested permission to bring his wife and son the following Saturday, stating that his son was a fine likely lad, and would enjoy the sight of so many curious and beautiful objects still more than he had done. Permission being granted, he brought his wife and son, and remained even a longer time than the previous Saturday. He said he feared he was too old himself to take advantage of the classes of the Mechanics' Institute, but that his son should become a member, and he immediately paid down the subscription. On leaving the hall he again expressed his regret at his former conduct. The wife was observed to linger behind, but as soon as her husband and son were outside the door, she suddenly turned to the directors, and, with a voice tremulous from emotion, said she knew not what gentleman she had to thank for admitting her husband, but that whoever it was she felt most grateful to him. That evening was the first for years that her husband had returned home sober, or that he had expressed any wish to give her pleasure. She stated that during the twenty years she had been married she had never been to a public place of enjoyment, and said how happy she had felt with her husband and son in looking together at such beautiful things!"

CHAPTER XV.

1850–1851.

AT this time I was engaged in writing a book upon "Crime, its Amount, Causes, and Remedies," which appeared before the public in 1853, with Murray for its publisher. This work recorded the information I had gained and the opinions which I had been led to adopt during my sixteen years' inspectorship of prisons. I have had no reason to change these opinions, and it is a matter of much satisfaction to me to see the modern school of scientific penologists bringing forcibly before the world such subjects as the hereditary nature of crime, the relation of crime to insanity, and cognate matters to which I gave my support so many years ago.

I cannot state what I consider to be the fundamental principles of our dealings with crime and criminals better than by quoting from my book.

18

"The leading principle of the criminal law of Britain, like that of most other countries, as I understand it, is to deter from crime by awarding punishment for different offences in proportion to their magnitude.

"The objections to this principle appear to be insurmountable. In the first place, it is one which it is impossible to carry out with anything like accuracy, öwing to the infinite variety of circumstances which increase or diminish the guilt appertaining even to the very same act, or which indeed make the commission of an apparently small offence really more culpable sometimes than that of a great offence.

"Much, no doubt, is done to meet these inequalities by the latitude given to the judge who passes sentence, but that is *pro tanto* an abandonment of the principle on which the laws are constructed.

"But even if it were possible to draw up a list of offences according to their real turpitude and their injury to society, and to prepare a corresponding scale of punishment, it appears to me that it would not be wise to act on such a system.

"The object of punishment being the prevention of crime, that punishment cannot be well fitted for its purpose which, after the infliction has terminated, allows an offender to be let loose again on society, without regard to the cause of his offence, or to the fact whether such cause has been removed; and without reference even to the possibility that the offender may have been hardened and rendered worse by the very punishment itself.

"This objection seems fatal to the plan of meting out doses of punishment as cures for specific crimes. No doubt it is necessary, with a view to the deterring effects on other members of society, that a person should suffer by the commission of crime, and that his condition should be rendered worse than that of the peaceable and honest man ; but this has been ordained by laws superior to all human edicts.   Not to dwell on the unhappiness of a life of crime, even while the offender is at large, I maintain that the natural consequence of crime in the withdrawal of the offender from the privilege of mixing with society, which he has abused, and his confinement until he can be safely restored, more fully carries out this principle of punishment than almost any other plan that could be proposed ; for in proportion to the length of the habits of crime and heinousness of the offences committed would, in general, be the period necessary for effecting a cure, and consequently the duration and amount of the punishment.

"Whether, therefore, we try to suppress crime by the mere infliction of punishment according to the number and magnitude of the offences committed, or whether we try to stop crime by curing the criminal, or, where complete cure is impossible, by improving him to the greatest possible extent, the natural and self-regulating punishments which God has instituted and pointed out appear to be the best and most accurately adapted for securing that the amount of punishment shall be in proportion to the offence committed.

"But who is to determine the fact of cure ? and who the precise means by which a cure is to be effected ?   I would submit that those only are fully qualified to do this who are entrusted with the charge of the offender, who have time to study his character, to watch the effect of the different influences brought to bear upon him in the formation of new habits ; and who have opportunities of gradually relaxing the system of discipline, and of trying the new powers of their moral patient to resist those temptations to which he would be exposed on his return to society.

"No one thinks of sending a madman to a lunatic asylum for a certain number of days, weeks, or months. We content ourselves with carefully ascertaining that he is unfit to be at large, and that those in whose hands we are about to place him act under due inspection, and have the knowledge and skill which afford the best hope for his cure, and we leave it for them to determine when he can safely be liberated.

"Those best acquainted with the subject know that between lunatics and criminals the difference is often but slight. Perhaps it may be ultimately found by cautious experiment that a somewhat similar process may be safe and expedient in the treatment of criminals, and that while it is still left to the courts of justice to determine on the guilt or innocence of the accused, and on the necessity of their withdrawal from society, it may be assigned to those entrusted more or less directly with the reformatory treatment to determine the time of release; subject, however, to a most competent, well-appointed, careful, and responsible supervision and control such as ought to be invariably exercised in the case of mad-houses; and subject to the proviso that no amount of subsequent good conduct should be considered sufficient to warrant the liberation of a person who had ever been guilty of deliberate murder.

"It is perhaps natural that Englishmen should regard with a jealous eye the introduction of a power to subject any of their countrymen, however criminal, to an imprisonment not limited, in the ordinary way, to a certain number of months or years; and it is fitting that such a change should be gradual, and that its operation should be carefully watched. The feeling from which such jealousy arises was manifested on the first creation of an efficient police; yet no one now thinks of pointing to the police as the infringers of liberty—that is, as the infringers of the liberty of the peaceful and honest—for the more the liberty of the turbulent and dishonest is restricted the better; the freedom of the malefactor being the bondage of the just. And such, I am satisfied, would, in time, become the general feeling regarding an arrangement for securely detaining every offender, when once caught, until there is a rational prospect of his living honestly and peaceably. In truth, had this practice, so conformable to common sense, the advantage which the sanction of time and experience causes, instead of having to contend with the hostile feeling attendant on novelty, any one who should propose to abandon such a system, and to enact that, without regard to an offender's moral condition, he should, at the end of a certain fixed period, be let loose again on society, would probably be regarded as little better than a lunatic."

My brother Matthew adopted these opinions on the subject of the indeterminate sentence, and warmly advocated them in some of his charges as Recorder of Birmingham. The following passage is from a charge delivered in December, 1856:—

" Surely all who give themselves the trouble of mastering the subject, must feel that what we ought to aim at is, to prevent criminals once apprehended and convicted from being so placed as to have the power of offending again, until we have some proof that their dispositions and habits are changed for the better. And if the discipline of the gaol should fail to produce its intended effect, then is it not unquestionably right that the seclusion of the prisoners should continue even if it last for their lives ?

"Ages ago this island was infested with wolves ; a dire calamity, as all conversant with the history of those times well know. What should we have thought of the sanity of our ancestors if, after giving a reward for each wolf caught, they had, when a certain number of months or years had elapsed, opened the dens and restored their wolves to liberty ? And yet I am sure that you will feel that, as between wolves and burglars, the latter are by far the more dangerous beasts of prey."

The importance of the principle of the indeterminate or indefinite sentence is now widely recognized. Mr. Havelock Ellis, in his preface to an "Account of the New York State Reformatory of Elmira," by Alexander Winter, F.S.S., writes—

"The first step in the rational treatment of the criminal is the introduction of a bracing moral training. This can only be effected by means of what is called the indeterminate or indefinite sentence. To allow a man to stagnate in prison routine until a capriciously fixed day arrives, as a *deus ex machina,* to open the prison door, is the height of absurdity. The prisoner must win his freedom by his own exertions. Not until he has shown himself capable of living a fairly human life may he safely be liberated. It cannot be too frequently or too emphatically asserted that the indefinite sentence is the foundation of the rational treatment of the criminal. It is worthy of note that this has been recognized in the foundation of the International Association of Criminal Law, a society made up of criminologists from all parts of the civilized world. Wherever that fundamental principle is neglected, the best prison system is condemned to hopeless routine and sterility. Wherever it has been introduced, stagnation is impossible."

Again Mr. Havelock Ellis, in his able work entitled " The Criminal," writes of the indefinite sentence—

"It has been adopted by several of the American States, such as Massachusetts, Ohio, Pennsylvania, and Kansas, and it was introduced at the famous State reformatory of New York at Elmira, by an Act passed in 1877. This Act took from the courts the power of definitely fixing the period of confinement in prisons until, in the opinion of the managers of the reformatory, they may be let out on parole for a probationary period of six months. To an Englishman, Frederic Hill, belongs the honour of first suggesting this fruitful reform, the indeterminate sentence ; and his brother, Matthew Davenport Hill, vigorously supported the principle. In 1886, Garofolo—independently, it appears—advocated indefinite imprisonment in a pamphlet entitled ' Criterio positiva della penalita,' published at Naples ; and in his great work, ' La Criminologie,' he wisely and consistently advocates the abolition of the definite sentence of imprisonment. In Germany it was advocated in 1880 by Dr. Kraepelin, a well-known authority on these matters ('Die Abschaffung des Straffmasses,' Leipsig) ; and in 1882 Professor von Liszt, of Marburg, supported it with the weight of his authority. This fruitful reform, which sprang up almost at the same time, and

with apparent spontaneity, among the Anglo-Saxon, Latin,
and Teutonic races, although of such recent growth, needs
little advocacy. It is so eminently reasonable that to
state it seems sufficient to ensure its acceptance. When
its advantages are generally known and realized it will
undoubtedly spread in the same way that it has already
begun to spread in the United States."

In the prison of Elmira, already alluded to, I have
always taken a deep and, I may say, a personal
interest. Mr. Brockway, the founder of the institution, still presides over it. Mr. Winter writes in
his account of Elmira—

" The institution, owing to the astonishing capacity for
work and the vigilance of its originator and conductor,
has been worked up from quite small beginnings, with a
hundred and eighty-four inmates, to a physical, intellectual,
and, above all things, a moral sanatorium of over a
thousand inmates, unique of its kind in the world. This
steady growth clearly shows what confidence the institution
has won amongst the administrators of the law and in the
opinion of the public by the satisfactory solution of the
problem which it set itself to solve. . . . In nearly all
the states of the Union Brockway's System has more or
less contributed to a reform in legislation and in institutions
for criminals in general.

" . . . The success of the institution does not depend
merely on a formal fulfilment of the law or of moral duties,
but upon a power of discretion and judgment based upon
a wide knowledge of the world and of men ; upon an
entirely special study and understanding of the outward as
well as the inward man. For this reason special care is

observed always in New York in the election of members of the tribunal or board of managers. They are no retired military officers, but men from amongst the people—men who themselves know the struggle for existence, and who understand the problem, not merely theoretically, but practically. On the other hand, no judge, or court of justice, is in a position to form a better or more trustworthy judgment of an offender, both in regard to the defects of his external and internal faculties, or to say when he is brought into a normal condition, than a man in the position of the general superintendent. Brockway is not only conductor of the establishment; he lives amongst the inmates; he lives and thinks with them, with each individual. Without suffering the discipline to be in the least relaxed, he is in close individual relationship to them, and, in the truest sense of the word, is at the same time friend, minister, and prison-master.

"The reformatory is a compulsory school and training institution for its inmates. This compulsion, however, it must be understood, is only intended to arouse the individual, and to compel him by his own efforts to recognize and improve his defective faculties; and it depends exclusively and solely on the will, industry, and behaviour of the individual in question, whether and at what time he is promoted or liberated, or on the other hand degraded into the third or actual criminal grade. The regaining of his freedom is a prisoner's only aim and aspiration; it is constantly before his eyes, and is a miraculous force that never ceases to impel him, and it is able to arouse the most insusceptible and dormant character." *

---

* See "The Elmira Reformatory," by Alexander Winter, F.S.S., published by Messrs. Swann and Sonnenschein (1891).

That the fear of an indefinite *loss* of liberty is the most powerful of all deterrents to the criminal at large, may be proved by the fact that American convicts will go down on their knees in the dock to implore the judge not to send them to Elmira. I learn this from my friend Mr. W. M. F. Round, for many years the corresponding secretary of the Prison Association of New York, himself an ardent worker in the cause of penal reform.

The Elmira system of training the "will-power" of the prisoner, and inspiring him to aid in the work of his own reformation, is in accordance with principles advocated in my work on "Crime," as follows:

"If a prisoner has been subdued merely by fear, and by a force not addressed to his reason, the probability is that, on the pressure being withdrawn, even for a short time, he will resume his old practices, and that with a fresh spirit of hostility and recklessness. So, also, if he has been treated, though not with harshness, yet like a child in leading-strings, without any cultivation of the powers of self-control, and still less those of virtuous self-action, although he may conduct himself in an exemplary manner in prison, and leave with a sincere desire thenceforward to live honestly and respectably, he will be so wanting in the power to provide for himself and to resist temptation, as probably soon to fall again into crime."

Captain Maconochie, the zealous and able advocate of improved prison discipline, wrote in his book entitled "Crime and Punishment"—

"If we look abroad into ordinary life, we cannot but be struck with the resemblance which our present forms of secondary punishment bear to everything that is most enfeebling and deteriorating, and how directly opposed they are to those forms of adversity which, under the influence of providential wisdom, reform character and invigorate it. Slavery deteriorates; long seclusion deteriorates; every condition, in a word, more or less deteriorates which leaves no choice of action, requires no notice but obedience, affords no stimulus to exertion beyond this, supplies the wants of nature without effort with a view to them, and restores to prosperity, through lapse of time, without evidence that such restoration is deserved.

"What improves, on the contrary, is a condition of adversity from which there is no escape but by continuous effort, which leaves the degree of that effort much in the individual's own power, but if he relaxes, his suffering is deepened and prolonged, and it is only alleviated and shortened if he struggles manfully—which makes exertion necessary even to earn daily bread—and something more, prudence, self-command, voluntary economy, and the like, to recover prosperity."

Captain Maconochie recommended that for sentences to a fixed period of imprisonment should be substituted sentences to a fixed amount of labour. This he proposed to measure by marks, and hence the name given to his system. These marks were not only to serve as the price of the prisoner's freedom, but as a means of obtaining various privileges, amongst others that of assisting his family. In 1854 Captain (now Sir Walter) Crofton based his system of convict discipline upon this plan of Captain Maconochie's, adapting it to the provisions of the Penal Servitude Act. He brought the Irish prisons, as is well known, into a state far superior and widely different to those of England, introducing, besides reformatory treatment, graduated liberation.

The principle of the Mark System is adopted at Elmira.

I have already referred to my observations on the connection between crime and insanity. Mr. Havelock Ellis remarks in the " Criminal "—

"Sometimes crime seems to be the method by which the degenerating organism seeks to escape from an insane taint in the parents. Of the inmates of the Elmira Reformatory, 499—or 13·7 per cent.—have been of insane or epileptic heredity. . . .

"We are now learning to regard the criminal as a natural phenomenon, the resultant of manifold natural causes. We are striving to attain to scientific justice. We are seeking in every direction to ascertain what is the reasonable treatment of the eccentric and abnormal members of society in their interest, and in the still higher interests of the society to which we belong."

I quote again from my book—

"By the abolition of revolting punishments and by confining the object of the statute to the protection of

society and the cure of the offender, the propriety and
reasonableness of the law would eventually become so
evident that public feeling would be strong in its support,
and all unwillingness to give evidence would disappear.
Thus nearly all parties in a court of justice would have
the same object—the arrival at the truth ; instead of the
hall of justice being degraded, as too often it is, into a
kind of mental boxing-ground, where witnesses are insulted
and browbeaten, and where the prisoner, to his surprise,
sometimes finds that any arts of trickery and deception
which he may have practised are outdone by the well-
dressed gentlemen around him, in their power of twisting
evidence, distorting facts, and implying with well-feigned
simplicity the truth of that which they know to be false.

" As criminals, like other ignorant people, have generally
great confidence in their good luck, any chance of escape
of conviction much diminishes the fear of the consequences
of their acts."

And they are perfectly aware of the reluctance felt
by juries to bring in a verdict which will produce
a sentence of death.   Were this penalty changed to
that of life-imprisonment, murderers could no longer
count on reluctance to convict, and " the excited
interest now often shown in them, with all the *éclat,*
romance, and heroism of crime, would fall to the
ground."

Lord John Russell, when speaking on this
subject, remarked—

"When I consider how difficult it is for any judge to
separate the case which requires inflexible justice from

that which admits the force of mitigating circumstance, how invidious the task of the Secretary of State in dispensing the mercy of the Crown, how critical the comments made by the public, how soon the object of general horror becomes the theme of pity, how narrow and how limited the examples given by this condign and awful punishment, I come to the conclusion that nothing would be lost to justice, nothing lost in the preservation of innocent life, if the punishment of death were altogether abolished."

In the same speech Lord John Russell alludes to the bad effect of public executions. They, happily, no longer exist, but the brutalizing effect of an execution is but diminished, not banished. The cheap newspapers carry the account of the final scene of disgrace and pain far and wide, and it is eagerly read by all who are attracted by baneful excitement. Mr. Havelock Ellis remarks in the "Criminal," "Perhaps the most powerful reason in favour of the probable disappearance of capital punishment is the humanizing influence that would be exerted on the community generally."

In dealing with the argument so often used by those who uphold capital punishment, that it has a deterrent effect upon crime, I show in my book that it has, in fact, an entirely opposite effect.

"It must be remembered that an example of punishment is also a *suggestion to crime,* and that the greater the display of the first the more does the idea of the second fasten on the mind. It is notorious, as a general rule, that any act to which the public attention is powerfully attracted, whether it is a murder, a suicide, or other deed of an exciting kind, is likely to be followed by similar acts. In truth, there are always many people whose reason has so slender a control over their feelings, that no sooner is an idea connected with their strong predispositions forcibly presented to their mind, than the feeling becomes unconquerable, and it takes its course regardless of consequences."

Public opinion against capital punishment seems to be gradually gaining ground. I have myself lived to witness great changes. Within my lifetime men were hanged for stealing five shillings' worth of goods ; and when Sir Samuel Romilly's Bill for the improvement of the criminal law and the abolition of this monstrous evil was introduced into the House of Lords in 1810, the Archbishop of Canterbury, together with eight bishops, voted against it, as did also the Lord Chancellor, Ellenborough. The latter, speaking in the name of the Bench generally, declared that no man's property would be safe if the measure were carried. It was not until the year 1826, long after the death of Sir Samuel Romilly, that his reform, brought forward now by Sir Robert Peel, was finally passed through Parliament and became law.

CHAPTER XVI.

1851–1852.

THIS year (1851) was the year of the Great Exhibition, the first Crystal Palace, in Hyde Park. My wife and I were present at a lecture delivered by my brother-in-law, Professor Cowper, in the building on the completion of its erection. I will give a short extract from the account which appeared in the *Illustrated London News* for January 4. Grave doubts had been entertained whether the light iron pillars would be able to sustain the weight of the vast roof.

"The last day of the year 1850, the one on which Messrs. Fox, Henderson, and Co., contractors for the building, were to have given up possession to the Royal Commissioners, was not inappropriately chosen for the private visit of the members of the Society of Arts, who collected together in large numbers to listen to Professor

Cowper's truly lucid explanation of the scientific construction of the Great Industrial Palace.

"'Let us begin with the columns,' he said, 'which are
not solid, as if of brick or stone, but hollow—that is,
tubular; and here science at once decides that this is the
stiffest and strongest form for a given quantity of material.
. . . Perhaps there are some critics present who, on looking at the columns of this building, may consider them
weak; let me, however, respectfully request of such critics
to test their own power of judging of these columns by
mentally estimating what these four quills—one inch in
length—will bear.' (Here Mr. Cowper placed the four
pieces of quill in a vertical position between two boards,
the upper one being adjustable by hinges, and then placed
weights on the upper board just above the quills until
they reached 224 lbs.) This beautiful and conclusive
experiment drew forth loud applause.

"He concluded his lecture with these words: 'There
is no doubt that when our friends from the Continent visit
this splendid palace they will be perfectly astonished at
the preposterous notion of retaining the trees within it!
But they may learn a lesson from them, and that not an
unimportant one. Some of our intending visitors have
been amusing themselves of late years with planting trees
of liberty, which withered and dried up, and were finally
uprooted. Now, we are not a people very fond of emblems,
but I look upon those trees as real trees of liberty; they
prove beyond doubt that *we* do not live under a despotic
Government. The people—right or wrong—wished these
particular trees to remain. A thousand trees were cut
down in Kensington Gardens some years since, and not a
word of complaint was uttered; but John Bull had set his
mind on these six or eight trees in particular, whether

they spoiled the building or not; and there they are standing proofs of the attention the Government pays to his wishes. We might carry our imagination further, and say these trees represent the liberties and rights of various classes and opinions, and all that is required is that each tree of liberty should be so pruned and trained as not to overshadow or injure its neighbour, while the magnificent arch above, like our glorious constitution, is comprehensive enough to include and protect them all."

In this year an important change in my official life took place. My brother Rowland greatly desired my assistance at the Post-Office. He writes in the " History of Penny Postage "—

"I proposed that I should have as assistant secretary some one in whom I had entire confidence, and who would be able to take my place in my absence. My wish was to obtain the appointment for my brother Frederic. . . . Although he was able to accomplish a good deal (in his English district), he found among the country justices of the peace, who have the general charge of the county prisons, far more of *vis inertiæ* than he had encountered in Scotland. In the belief that in the Post-Office, in conjunction with myself, he should have a new and wide field for the exercise of his knowledge of the principles of government and his powers of administration, and that he should be able to render me effectual assistance, he was ready to accept an appointment, should it be made, as assistant secretary."

This appointment was made, and I entered upon my new duties in the month of June. Amongst the kind and cordial letters which I received upon this occasion were letters from Lord Truro and Mr. C. P. Villiers, and also from many persons officially connected with prisons, from whom I took a reluctant farewell. It would have been impossible to me, however, to bid farewell to the subjects of prison discipline and the laws affecting criminology. By connecting myself with the Law Amendment Society, I was able still to work for reforms in these and kindred matters, with men of influence and power in the land. I also joined philanthropic bodies as they were started—such as the Metropolitan Discharged Prisoners' Aid Society, the Reformatory and Refuge Union, etc.

I now finally settled my family at Hampstead, where my brother Matthew had lived for many years, and where my brother Rowland was also now settled. At Hampstead, too, were living my wife's eldest sister, Miss Cowper, and her near relative Mr. John Lepard, whose house had ever been a second home to our children. We were within easy reach of Tottenham, where my aged father lived, in the near neighbourhood of his sons Edwin and Arthur, who inhabited Bruce Castle. My dear mother had died in 1842, but my father lived to the advanced age of eighty-eight years.

I must mention that in March, 1850, my sister,

Caroline Clark, with her entire family, left England for South Australia. Her husband and herself desired a better climate for their children, two of whom they had lost by consumption. My nephews and nieces have visited England many times since then, but my sister and her brothers never met again, though a close and regular correspondence between us, till her death in 1877, kept the knowledge of each other's interests unbroken.

On Christmas Day, 1849, my father, then eighty-six years old, presided at a complete family gathering in the ancient hall of Bruce Castle, where we sat down to the Christmas feast, a party of fifty. My eldest daughter distinctly remembers this event, and the rush of all the little ones when their beloved grandfather inadvertently walked under the mistletoe.

His sympathy with children may be seen in the following letter to my second little girl, who had sent him a birthday present:—

"Bruce Terrace, April 25, 1849.

"MY DEAR LEONORA,

"Your affection for me, which you show in so many ways, makes me quite happy. I thank you for your pen-wiper, and the more as you have made it yourself.

"I thank you for your wish that I may live a 'billion of years.' I am not sure whether you mean a French billion,

that is a thousand millions, or an English billion, that is
a million of millions. . . . But, my dear girl, I could
hope to make your heart glad by assuring you that I have
a confident, though humble, expectation of many more
years of life than you have named or could name—not,
indeed, in the present world, but in a world of far greater
happiness than you and I can think of. This hope I hold
fast through a firm belief in the goodness of the great
Creator. . . . That He may ever preserve you and yours
is the earnest prayer of your affectionate grandfather,

" THOS. W. HILL."

Writing to my wife, he says—

" Accept my sincere thanks for your thorough sympathy
in all my feelings. Of these, thanks to the Author of
my being, the vast preponderance is enjoyment. I could
wish for better sight and better hearing, but have so much
to be grateful for that it is not without compunction that
I turn so much as a thought on these lost possessions.

" How happy, my dear daughter, are you in all your
relations — children, husband, sisters, brothers ! The
children here are coming home ever and anon, delighted
with lectures from our talented relative Mr. Cowper.
Relative I call him, for we are all ingenious in tracing
an alliance which it is an honour to possess."

In March, 1851, my father became very ill, and
the illness proved fatal. In a diary kept by me
at the time I write—

" *May* 1.—Martha sat some time by my father, describing
to him the ceremonies that were to take place at the

opening of the Industrial Palace that day—the prayer for increased good will and intercourse between the nations; and how the assembled multitudes, collected from so many nations, were to sing Hallelujah to the great Creator who had endowed them with the faculties that had produced this wonderful Exhibition of mind and talent. Tears, Martha said, rolled down his face as he ejaculated, 'Thank God, thank God, for living to see this day! I cannot see this noble Exhibition with my actual vision, but to hear of it is a great blessing. This real peace-meeting! I cannot join them with my voice, but I can in my heart.

> "All people that on earth do dwell,
>   Sing to the Lord with cheerful voice."

I leave the world bright with hope. Never, surely, has God's government of the world been so clear as at the present period.'"

He was gratified at thinking how many of his family and friends had assisted in the great work of the Exhibition, and had sent contributions to it. He spoke of Edwin's envelope-folding machine, and Julian's ventilating-pump; of Follett Osler's crystal fountain, and Mr. Cowper's printing-machine.

On learning of my appointment to the Post-Office my father evinced much joy, and expressed his satisfaction that henceforth Rowland and I should be working together.

One day, on the window of his bedroom being

opened, he composed some verses which he dictated to a friend.   They commence thus—

" Aura veni.

Come, gentle breeze ! come, air divine !
Comfort this drooping heart of mine.
Ah, solace flows with Heaven's own breath,
Which cheers my soul that sank in death.
The works of God all speak His praise ;
To Him eternal anthems raise."

On the 13th of June, the day of my father's death, my diary records—

"At half-past one, when Rowland, Martha, and myself were sitting near him, he took a hand of each of us in his, and, placing it near his heart, kissing it and pointing upwards, with a radiant expression of intense love and happiness, was evidently contemplating a future meeting with us and all his family.

"At about half-past eight my dear father expired without a struggle."

I received many letters of sympathy upon the death of my father.   Mr. Charles P. Villiers wrote—

"I had only the pleasure of seeing him upon a few occasions, but I remember well the impression he made then upon me by the simplicity of his manner and the justice and intelligence of his observations.   I learn from you with great satisfaction that he did, as his end was approaching, refer to me as one of those who felt an interest in the success and welfare of his family.   He only, I assure you, justly appreciated my feelings.".

An old pupil, Henry Sargant, wrote—

" I am now merely putting into words what has been my opinion ever since I was capable of forming one for myself—that he was emphatically the best man I ever knew, of a constant, loving, noble nature."

Mr. John Jones, the surgeon who attended my father through his illness, wrote to me—

" Your father's death has deprived me of a dear and highly esteemed friend. It is thirty years since I first entered Hazelwood school, and with very little interruption I have kept up a close intimacy with the late Mr. Hill. I shall never forget the pleasant and instructive hours I have passed in his company. His energy of character, his enthusiasm, his hopefulness, his benevolence, were remark-able. He sympathized deeply with all that was good and true. Then what an intellect, what memory, what powers of reasoning ! . . . For years I had loved him, but never so much as when he lay in placid resignation on his death-bed."

The Law Amendment Society was the initiator of many legal reforms. In this year (1851) it advo-cated improvements in the patent laws, putting an end to the very heavy legislative charge for every new patent, and substituting a moderate scale, especially for patents terminable (unless continued at the instance of the patentee) at the end of a few years. The Bill on this subject, which was ulti-mately carried through Parliament, was founded on the report of a committee of which I was a member, as was also Sir Frederick Bramwell.

I was very desirous that the society should make a further recommendation to Parliament to appropriate a certain sum of money for the purchase of any patent which the commissioners of patents might deem it expedient for the public to acquire, so as to admit the free use of an invention where it would be of service to the people at large. I so far carried the committee with me as to obtain the insertion in their report of a recommendation that a trial of my plan should be made. But this recommendation was not adopted by Parliament. Had it been adopted it would have put an end, in such cases, to the harassment of inventors from fraudulent attempts to invade their patents. From my personal acquaintance with Professor (afterwards Sir Charles) Wheatstone, who was largely concerned in the introduction of the electric telegraph, I knew this harassment to be so severe as sometimes to throw him upon a bed of sickness.

Speaking of Professor Wheatstone, I may mention that he was a member of a small society of which my brothers Edwin and Rowland and myself were members. We used often to breakfast together for the discussion of various subjects, principally economic. Dr. Nield Arnott, Mr. Chadwick, Dr.

Carpenter, and Mr. Wentworth Dilke were also members. The meetings of this little society, which, with the approval of Mr. Helps, we termed " Friends in Council," were to me, and I believe to all the other members, a source of much pleasure. Our most frequent house of meeting, by the pressing invitation of its owner, was that of Dr. Arnott, whose inventions are well known to the public.

Dr. Arnott's friends, who knew his simple and kindly nature, were surprised at his remaining so long a bachelor. When he told me of his approaching marriage, I remarked that we had wondered why he did not marry long ago. His answer was, "*I hadn't time !*" I believe, however, that the circumstance admitted of a more romantic explanation.

After their wedding Mrs. Arnott was duly ensconced in the doctor's house in Regent's Park, but she confided to Mrs. Rowland Hill that when she attempted to arrange her garments in the ample wardrobes which furnished the bedrooms, she found them filled already with stoves and other inventions of her husband's !

One of Dr. Arnott's first scientific exploits was accomplished when, as a young man, he held the post of surgeon on an East Indiaman. A violent storm off the coast of Africa put the vessel in danger, and the peril was increased by the fact that the

From the portrait

captain's chronometer had got out of order. Happily the young surgeon had studied science with its applications as well as the classics at Aberdeen University, and to the delight of the captain he was able to repair his chronometer.

When Dr. Arnott wrote his book upon " Natural Philosophy " his friends objected to its bearing such a title, in the fear that it might suggest to the public that his attention was not sufficiently fixed upon subjects strictly medical, which might injure him in his profession. To get over this difficulty he called his book " Arnott's *Physics*."

When I first went to the Post-Office two mutual insurance societies in the London office, one called the " Widows' and Orphans' Annuity Society," the other the " Letter Carriers' Burial Fund," had fallen into difficulties owing to miscalculations in the rates of payments and premiums, and other causes. I was able to rescue them from their liabilities by inducing the Postmaster-General, Lord Clanricarde, who readily entered into my views, to ask the Treasury to grant us the appropriation of some of the " Void Order Fund," and some of the money in " dead letters," which amounted to a very large sum. With this money an insurance office of undoubted stability, the " Atlas," was induced to take the Post-Office Societies' liabilities on itself.

The Money Order Office was the first department placed under my charge.   I was able to further the development of the system in various ways, and after a time introduced work by contract into one part of it.   The head of this branch was entrusted with the selection of his own assistants and with fixing their pay, and for his own remuneration was allowed so much per thousand on all money orders issued or paid at the central office.   By this arrangement, without the least sacrifice in the quality of the work done, an immediate saving was made of nearly half the cost.

Early in 1852 Charles Dickens came to inspect our " Money Order Office," and I had the pleasure of acting as his guide.   He described what he saw in an article in *Household Words* for March 20 of that year, from which I now give a quotation. When I read this article I was astonished to find how many little incidents had impressed themselves on this distinguished writer's mind—incidents which had passed before me unnoticed, but of which I instantly recognized the truthful description.

"The Central Money Order Office is in Aldersgate Street, hard by the Post-Office.   It is a large establishment—large enough to be a very considerable post-office in itself.

"The room in which the orders are issued and paid

has a flavour of Lombard Street. It has its long banker's counter, where clerks sit behind iron gratings with their wooden bowls of cash and their little scales for weighing gold, and vistas of pigeon-holes stretch out behind them. Here, from ten o'clock to four, keeping the swing-doors on the swing all day, all sorts and conditions of people come and go. Greasy butchers and salesmen from Newgate Market with bits of suet in their hair, who loll and lounge, and cool their foreheads against the grating, like a good-humoured sort of bears ; sharp little clerks, not long from school, who have everything requisite and necessary in readiness ; older clerks in shooting-coats, a little sobered down as to official zeal, though possibly not yet as to cigar divans and betting offices ; matrons who *will* go distractedly wrong, and whom no consideration, human or divine, will induce to declare in plain words what they have come for ; people with small children which they perch on edges of remote desks, where the children, supposing themselves to be for ever abandoned and lost, present a piteous spectacle ; labouring men, merchants, half-pay officers ; retired old gentlemen from trim gardens by the New River, excessively impatient of being trodden on, and very persistent as to the poking in of their written demands, with tops of canes and handles of umbrellas.

"The clerks in this office ought to rival the lamented Sir Charles Bell in their knowledge of the expression of the hand. The varieties of hands that hover about the grating, and are thrust through the little doorways in it, are a continual study for them—or would be, if they had any time to spare, which assuredly they have not. The coarse-grained hand which seems all thumb and knuckle, and no nail, and which takes up money or puts it down with such an odd, clumsy, lumbering touch ; the retail trader's hand, which chinks it up and tosses it over with a bounce; the housewife's hand, which has a lingering propensity to keep some of it back, and to drive a bargain by not paying in the last shilling or so of the sum for which her order is obtained; the quick, the slow, the coarse, the fine, the sensitive and dull, the ready and unready; they are always at the grating all day long. Hovering behind the owners of these hands, observant of the various transactions in which they engage, is a tall constable (rather potential with the matrons and widows on account of his portly aspect) who assists the bewildered female public, explains the nature of the printed forms put ready to be filled up, for the quicker issuing of orders and the greater exactness as to names; and has an eye on the unready one, as he knots his money up in a pocket-handkerchief, or crams it into a greasy pocket-book.

"An Irish gentleman (who had left his hod at the door) recently applied in Aldersgate Street for an order for five pounds on a Tipperary post-office, for which he tendered (probably congratulating himself on having hit upon so good an investment) sixpence! It required a lengthened argument to prove to him that he would have to pay the five pounds into the office before his friend could receive that amount in Tipperary."

Lord Clanricarde was succeeded as Postmaster-General by the seaman, Lord Hardwicke, who brought nautical ideas to the Post-Office, and thought to inaugurate a sort of man-of-war's discipline therein! He directed that the "clerk-in-waiting" at St. Martin's-le-Grand, when he took charge at 4 p.m., should be duly informed that "*All's well,*" and that when he went off duty next day at 10 a.m. he himself should solemnly report, *"All's well"*!

Lord Hardwicke, on beginning his reign, gave orders that all letters directed to the " Postmaster-General " should be reserved for himself to open. He consequently reached his rooms to find a gigantic pyramid of official communications, which the clerks, no doubt, had piled up in high glee! I believe that one day's trial of this arrangement quite sufficed his lordship!

CONCLUSION.

BY THE EDITOR.

CHAPTER XVII.

1853–1893.

Married Women's Property Bill—Letters from Mrs. Grote and Lady Byron—Various economic subjects—Postal reforms—Napoleon III.—Kossuth—Pulszky—Lords Canning and Elgin—Visit to Egypt—Work in Hampstead—Mrs. Hill—" Elmira "—F. Hill's opinions quoted during the prison labour struggle in the United States.[1]

THE substance of the foregoing recollections was jotted down by my father from time to time, and put into my hands to edit three years ago, as I have already mentioned in the Preface. He has approved the additional matter which I have been able to introduce, owing to the discovery of contemporary letters, diaries, etc. He now, at the age of ninety years, puts the pen altogether into my hands that I may briefly wind up the story of his life, and attempt some personal recollections of the "league of brothers," as they have been well named.

To resume the narrative where my father left off. In 1854 an agitation was commenced to arouse public attention to the injustice of the existing laws respecting married women's property. Two ladies, Miss Barbara Leigh Smith and Miss Bessie Raynor Parkes,* published a pamphlet which gave "A Brief Summary in Plain Language of the Most Important Laws concerning Women, with a Few Observations thereon." Before its publication my father's eldest brother, the Recorder of Birmingham, examined it and vouched for its correctness.

The attention of many persons being thus drawn to the subject, practical action followed. The Law Amendment Society took up the matter. Petitions were sent in to Parliament, and many men and women of enlightened views gave themselves up to work for the abolition of laws which, especially among the poor, were bringing about countless evils.

My father was dealing with the subject at the Law Amendment Society. He writes, "I had the warm sympathy and active co-operation of my dear wife. She enlisted in the cause many women whose support gave it dignity and strength, such as Mrs. Jameson, Mrs. Fletcher, and Mrs. Grote."

* Afterwards Madame Bodichon and Madame Belloc.

I find my mother's name in the first list of female petitioners, which includes, besides those just mentioned, the names of Harriet Martineau, Elizabeth Barrett Browning, Mary Howitt (secretary of the London Committee), Mrs. Cowden Clark, Mrs. Gaskell, Mrs. Carlyle, Lady Kay Shuttleworth, Mrs. Robert Chambers, etc.

Miss Barbara Leigh Smith, writing to my mother on matters of business connected with the petition, says, "Your letters are always thoroughly sympathizing, and do me good." Mrs. Grote's first letter is characteristic :—

"Mrs. Grote has received the communication which Mrs. F. Hill wished Mr. Lewin to hand to her, and begs to assure that lady of the readiness with which she will append her signature to the accompanying petition whenever it is judged advisable to put it round for that purpose. Few subjects have more occupied Mrs. Grote's mind and attention than the injustice practised towards women, especially in all that relates to property ; and she would feel further interested in the endeavour which is now making in favour of her sex, if the petition were so framed as to include a prayer that *all kinds* of property falling to married women, by bequest or otherwise, might be secured to them absolutely. And she would, further, wish to renounce on the part of married women that odious semblance of 'compensation' called 'non-liability for debt.'

". . . Mrs. Hill may rely on Mrs. Grote's co-operation

in the honourable efforts she is making whenever it suits her to invite it."

Lady Byron writes to a member of the family—

"It was a great satisfaction to me to learn from your letter that the Law Amendment Society had taken up a question which I think better left to generous-minded men than brought forward by women themselves. Whatever legislation may effect *protectively*, I must rely more on education *preventively*. The use of one means should not set aside the use of the other."

The Married Women's Property Bill met with much opposition and mutilation, and many years passed before the measure was carried. Still the attention of the public had been called to the injustice of the existing laws, and legislative concessions gradually followed. It was not, however, until the year 1882 that the present law, which puts the husband and wife on an equality as regards property, finally came into being.

Among other measures initiated by the Law Amendment Society, at which my father laboured as a member of its council, were the law of limited liability and a reform in the law of evidence; the latter measure was strongly urged by Mr. Pitt Taylor (a member), in his well-known work on "Evidence," for admitting the testimony, for what it is worth, of the parties themselves, at that time

strictly excluded. So far as civil cases are concerned, the law was altered in accordance with
Mr. Pitt Taylor's views; but in criminal cases his
recommendation has not been adopted in England,
although it has been adopted in America.

Some years later the Law Amendment Society
was incorporated with the Social Science Association. At my father's suggestion the society took
up the subject of labour and capital, and in 1870
he was one of a band of lecturers who attempted
to spread a knowledge of political economy with
a view of preventing strikes and lock-outs. Professor Stanley Jevons, Dr. Hodgson, Mr. R. H.
Hutton, and Professor Thorold Rogers were the
other lecturers. My father's subject was the
"Identity of Interests of Employers and Workpeople." The following year, in a paper read at
the congress of the association, after recommending
industrial partnerships and lamenting the loss of a
quarter of a million sterling in the Newcastle
strike, he alludes to the efforts of the society to
enlighten the public on these subjects by itinerant
lecturers, paid or honorary, and regrets the want of
financial support which crippled their undertakings.
He concludes as follows :—

"Let us hope that a practical people like the English
will not allow matters of such momentous importance to

drift about as chance may direct, but that they will make a vigorous effort to weed out error and implant truth; so that gradually, yet surely, for waste and comparative poverty, may be substituted thrift and increased wealth; and for discord, harmony."

In 1872 my father came back to one of his old subjects, and wrote upon " Prison Labour " for the International Prison Congress held in London. Other economic or political subjects engaged his attention. In 1878 he wrote upon " The County Franchise Difficulty : how Removable ? " A quotation from Shakespeare given on the title-page sufficiently suggests his line of argument—

> "Take but degree away, untune that string,
> And, hark, what discord follows ! "

He approved of the extension of the franchise to women, and worked for some years on the committee of the original society for promoting that object.

Such were the subjects at which my father worked in his leisure hours, and at which he has continued to work till within the last few years.

At the General Post-Office a minute may be seen of the improvements which he introduced and carried.   Many of these relate to the reorganization of routine business; to improvements in the ventilation of the old Post-Office; the utilization of available space, which deferred the expense of building; precautions against fire, etc.; but some of them are of wider interest. In 1854 he made a suggestion, which was adopted, that an annual report should be submitted to Parliament by the Postmaster-General. This report he wrote himself for fourteen years. He also suggested the quarterly publication of a Postal Guide. This first appeared in 1861, and its editing was superintended by him till his resignation in 1876. Later on he proposed the introduction of " Postal Notes," now called " Postal Orders," and although he did not succeed in inducing any Postmaster-General to introduce the measure, he was permitted in 1875 by Lord John Manners (now Duke of Rutland) to take preliminary steps for its accomplishment. The measure was developed and carried after he had left the service.

His introduction of the " Contract System " has already been alluded to. This he promoted especially in regard to the Packet Service; *i.e.* the conveyance of foreign and colonial mails, the management of which was transferred from the Admiralty to the Post-Office in 1860. This Department was under his direction for seven years. By promoting open competition and the non-renewal of subsidies the efficiency of the service was largely augmented, producing a great increase of revenue together with a great decrease of expenditure. The details may be seen in the official records of the Post-Office, and also in Sir Rowland Hill's "History of Penny Postage." Into this branch of the service, as into all others under his direction, he carried the principles of free trade. Although he effected a considerable reduction in foreign and colonial postage, no arbitrary cheapening of rates was ever inaugurated by him, but he laboured to give the public the greatest good for the least possible cost in a *self-supporting* service.

In some private memoranda my father writes—

"With respect to the contract system I may state that my brother (Sir R. Hill) highly approved of its introduction, and expressed it as his opinion that, if it were carried to the extent of which it was capable in the Postal Service, an annual saving to the country would result of probably not less than a quarter of a million sterling. Not my brother only, but the Right Honourable W. H. Smith, when Financial Secretary of the Treasury, expressed a favourable opinion of the contract system.

"This system, it may be observed, is consistent with the practice of granting pensions after a certain length of service; since that object can be obtained by the periodical retention of a small part of an officer's salary.

"Another matter in which my brother and I agreed (indeed, I do not recollect anything in which we did not agree) related to the competitive examinations by the Civil Service Commissioners. We regarded the introduction of these examinations into the Post-Office with much regret. Their tendency, we were convinced, is to fill the ranks of the officers with mediocrity; mediocrity, that is, as regards the qualifications which are essential for zealous and efficient action. They are opposed to the great principle that those who are responsible for the success of any business should have the choice of its officers; seeing that they have the greatest interest in a good selection, and possess the fullest knowledge of the qualifications required. Had the acquisition of one of the dead languages been insisted upon in my brother's time for admission to the Post-Office, Rowland himself, the author of the greatest postal measure ever effected, would most certainly have been excluded. How long would a private firm, which allowed some other authority than their own to choose their clerks, keep out of the *Gazette?*"

Again writing of the Post-Office my father says—

"By no alteration originating with myself was injury done to any existing officer; provision being always made to prevent this. And I believe the same may be said of the far greater alterations effected by my brother."

During his long official life my father encountered those disappointments and frustrations in the accomplishment of good which are more or less common to all who have "a great thing to pursue." This at times even caused his health to break down ; but, as his nephew, Dr. Birkbeck Hill, writes, "he regarded the slightest approach to vindictive feeling as both wrong and foolish." In never letting "the pure benevolence of his soul be for one moment clouded over by resentment," he had the faithful assistance of his wife. No woman could be more keenly sensitive regarding her husband's interests than our mother, but she ever conquered her own feelings and cheered him by keeping his mind fixed on the good he had actually accomplished. But while our father met personal trials in this spirit, nothing could exceed his indignation and his readiness to do battle with those who oppress the weak, or who, by the pursuit of their own selfish ambition, "lower the standard of public morality." We have often been told that when Napoleon III. accomplished his *coup d'état* our father marched into Bruce Castle exclaiming to the assembled family, "That scoundrel has done what I always said he would do!" On April 19, 1855, my father wrote—

"To-day there has been a grand procession to escort the Emperor Louis Napoleon to the Guildhall. Many of our officers went to the top of the Post-Office to witness the procession ; and I was asked if I would not go, but I replied that I had been so long an inspector of prisons that the sight of a rogue had ceased to be any novelty to me."

Writing in later life of the events of this period, he says—

"In a conversation which I had with Kossuth, who was brought to my house by our mutual friend Mr. Pulszky, I learnt that it was his intention to apply for military assistance to the French emperor. I endeavoured to dissuade him from doing so, reminding him that, by his acts, Louis Napoleon had shown that he was not to be trusted, and remarking that even if he promised to support the Hungarian cause, he would be sure to abandon it whenever he thought it to his interest to do so. Unhappily, I did not succeed in altering Kossuth's intention.

"When the boast reached my brother Matthew's ears that, in fighting against Austria for the liberation of Italy, 'France went to war for an idea,' he remarked, 'Yes, for two ideas—Nice and Savoy.'

"A few years later Monsieur Berrier, 'Batonnier' of the French Bar, was in England, and was present at a meeting of the Law Amendment Society. He made an eloquent and feeling speech, urging us 'to keep in its full blaze the torch which was burning so dimly in his own country—the torch of freedom both in law and politics.'"

I well remember my father's regular attendance at the evening meetings of the Law Amendment Society. He used to talk to us children, even when very young, about his work there, and explain to us the reforms that he was assisting to promote. We always felt that we were giving up the pleasure of his company for a good cause.

With a further view to our sharing in his interests and pleasures, he was in the habit of marking, and afterwards reading to us, passages in books or newspapers which he thought might interest us. This habit has remained unbroken. He wrote to my mother on May 27, 1852—

"In an article on 'Sir Roger de Coverley,' in the last number of the *Quarterly Review*—an article well worth reading—I came to this passage, of which I thought you would like to have a copy. It might be well to placard it in our nursery. 'One swallow will not make a summer out-of-doors ; but one face invariably cheerful, one temper never ruffled, one heart always affectionate, makes a summer in a house.'"

Happening to come upon this letter in recent years, my father had several copies made of the quotation, and gave them to friends who had families of children.   One of these friends versified the lines as follows :—

> "' One swallow does not make a summer '—that is clear ;
> But within the house to find
> One cheerful face and kind,
> One temper always sweet,
> One heart in love complete,
> Makes summer all the year."

My father wrote in August, 1858, from Normandy, where he had taken his eldest daughter for her first visit abroad—

"We met Mr. —— again at the chateau d'Arques. . . . What a charm there is in the manners of a true gentleman or gentlewoman !   Ease, refinement, self-respect without egotism, an evident desire to please, ready to converse, but ready also at the proper time to be silent.   How careful we should be, as I hope we are, to cultivate such manners in our children !"

It is impossible to do more than allude to a few

of the men and women of mark that my father was acquainted with in his later official or private life. He knew Lords Canning and Elgin as Postmasters-General. He wrote of Lord Canning—

"He showed me kind consideration, and was always ready to consider any measure which I thought would promote the public good."

And of his successor—

"Every one who was acquainted with Lord Elgin must, I am sure, have regarded him with great esteem and respect. In his previous office of Governor-General of Canada he had done good service, and, in one of my conversations with him, he told me that a treaty which he had there negotiated, between the English Government and that of the United States, was the only treaty he knew of which had not led to disputes. This he accounted for by observing that neither the American negotiator nor himself had made any attempt to overreach the other, but that both had gone into the discussion with freedom and candour."

Intercourse was also renewed with the present Duke of Argyll, who had formerly sympathized in the work of prison reform in Scotland, and who became in turn Postmaster-General.*

* The late Duchess of Argyll, when Marchioness of Lorne, obtained permission to become a regular visitor to the female prisoners at Inverary. In her application to my father she said she desired to visit them "not as a patroness, but as woman to woman."

At Hampstead my father and mother counted amongst their friends Mrs. Jameson, Mrs. Chisholm (the indefatigable promoter of emigration), Miss Mulock, and the Hungarian patriot Mr. Pulszky, with "his brave and admirable wife." Their Scotch friends did not forsake them. Mrs. Wigham visited Bellevue. Though now elderly, she shared her host's enthusiasm for early walks, and allowed him to take her to the top of Hampstead Heath at six in the morning to see the sun rise! John Hill Burton generally made his appearance unexpectedly, just as, in accordance with our early hours, the family was going to bed. He was said to divide his spare time, when in London, between ourselves and Carlyle.

In 1870 my father bought a house in Thurlow Road, to which we removed, giving it the name of Inverleith House, after our old Edinburgh home.

Upon retiring from the Post-Office, in 1876, my father paid a long visit to Egypt. He was accompanied by my eldest sister, and they stayed at Ramleh with my sister, Mrs. John Scott, and her husband, then a judge in the International Courts at Alexandria. My father followed his habits of early rising, and of taking long walks during the day, as regularly in the land of the Pharaohs as he did at home. A southern sun and burning

sands had no effect upon him. Stories of his performances were repeated amongst our friends, and
grew as they were repeated, till at last it was
reported that he had walked the seven miles from
Cairo to the Pyramids, made their ascent, and
walked back, and all before breakfast!

His visit to his daughter and son-in-law introduced him to many of their friends, some of
whom became valued additions to his acquaintance.
Amongst these was General Gordon.

It has been a great satisfaction to my father that
his son-in-law, Mr. Justice Scott, has been in a
position, both in India and Egypt, to carry on the
work to which he himself had devoted his early
manhood—the work of Penal Reform.

After my father's official life ended he was
haunted by a serious dread that he should have
" nothing to do." I may truly say that from that
day forward, never, for one half-hour, has such a
misfortune befallen him. Besides his work at the
various societies in London of which he was a
member, he became a guardian of the poor in
Hampstead, a Church trustee, and a member of
charitable committees. He had assisted his friend,
the Rev. H. F. Mallet, in starting the Hampstead
Branch of the Charity Organization Society some
time previously.

The next subject which he took in hand was the improvement of the Vestry.   He writes—

"I found on inquiry that the election of the Vestry was in the hands of a mere handful of persons, the general body of ratepayers taking no part in it, and that many of the Vestrymen were unfit for their duties. Having consulted my friends Mr. Bond and Mr. Finch, we decided to take the matter up, and at the next election to try to secure the appointment of at least one thoroughly good man, in the expectation that such a member would at once obtain great influence.

"Our intention having become public, at the next election a large number of ratepayers were present. We succeeded in our object, and, by repeating the attempt for some years, we effected a great change in the character of the Vestry and in its proceedings."

The following paragraph in the *Pall Mall Gazette* of December 29, 1887, is supposed to refer to my father :—

"The assailant of the Vestries who signs himself 'S. P. D.,' to-day makes a notable admission. He says, 'I am happy to say that I know Hampstead and its Vestry, and if Hampstead were a sample of the rest of London, what a different place London would be!' Now, why is Hampstead better than the rest of London? It used to be as bad as, or worse than, the other Vestries. The reason is that in Hampstead, some time ago, there arose one just man, in whom civic virtue was not extinct, who set himself deliberately and with religious purpose to revive a higher standard of municipal morality in his district. His success was marvellous. If forty just men like him were to be found in all London, all the Vestries would be like Hampstead, and then 'what a different place London would be!' But you must first catch your just man before anything can be done."

In the month of February, 1882, my father planned and organized a public dinner in honour of the police force of Hampstead. Writing on this subject, he says—

"My object was twofold: first to give a well-earned tribute of respect to our force, and next to set an example which I hoped would be followed elsewhere. I was also desirous of showing the detractors of the police in general that their statements and opinions met with no response in the respectable part of the population."

The appeal for subscriptions met with so cordial a response, that after paying all expenses the committee were enabled to hand over to the directors of the Police Orphanage more than a hundred pounds. My father's old friend, Mr. James Marshall, J.P., took the chair, Colonel Henderson attended, and the whole proceeding went off most satisfactorily. Shortly afterwards a similar tribute was paid to the police of Kilburn.

My mother had not my father's bodily strength to enable her to undertake regular charitable or philanthropic work. But her help and sympathy were ever ready for those who *could* work—especially

*Mr. and Mrs. Fredric Hill, and their daughter Constance
from the portrait group by Ellen G. Hill*

in any matter connected with children. Her own grandchildren were a source of constant delight to her. She followed the school-life of the eldest into every detail, and inspired him with her love of natural history.

To the end of her life she maintained the strong interest which she had shown in the first years of her marriage with the erring and unfortunate members of the human family. In 1878 she wrote a paper for the Prison Congress at Stockholm on "Prison Discipline." She took a keen interest in the New York State Reformatory of Elmira. The letters and papers respecting it which she received, lay on her bed within a few days of her death, in 1887. Her portrait, as well as that of my father, hangs on the walls of Elmira.

It is remarkable that my father is not the only survivor of those connected with the first establishment of inspectors of prisons in 1835. His former colleague, Dr. Bissett Hawkins—also a nonagenarian — refreshes old memories by exchanging letters with him once a year; and the Right Honourable Charles P. Villiers, the "Father of the House of Commons," who promoted my father's appointment, is still able, although his senior, to engage in public duty, and retains his warm feelings towards the Hill family.

My father has always taken a lively interest in the extensive work of his friend Mr. W. M. F. Round, corresponding secretary of the Prison Association of New York, of whom mention has already been made. In the autumn of 1888 the prison system of that State received a severe blow. A reactionary party, the so-called "Labour Reformers," carried the election of a man as Governor of New York under whose rule the "Yates Prison Bill" was passed, which put an end to all productive labour in prisons.

Mr. Round writes to my father on October 7, 1888—

"The infamous 'Yates Bill,' which we thought we had killed, but which was passed in an extra session of our New York Legislature, has thrown our whole prison system into chaos. . . . We know that under its operation the prisons will become a burden to the people such as they have never had to bear before, and crime will increase."

A great struggle now began for the repeal of the "Yates Bill." Mr. Round again writes—

"I should be very glad if you would permit me to publish that part of your letter of August 29, in which you have most wisely referred to the operation of the Bill in the Elmira Reformatory. . . . You will see that I ventured to quote your opinions in the *Herald*, and have done so again in my 'Princeton' article."

In a letter dated January 28, 1889, he describes the severe and unremitting contest into which he entered to obtain the passing of a "reasonable Prison Bill"—a contest which we found afterwards, in its strain upon his health, had nearly cost him his life.   He goes on to say—

"I am trying with all my ingenuity to make it possible to run over to England this spring, and one of the principal motives is a desire to take in fresh draughts of inspiration from your counsel and enthusiasm."

Three months later the repeal of the "Yates Bill" was carried.   I learn from Mr. Round that he quoted my father's opinions in support of productive prison labour before the Judiciary Committee of the Legislature of New York.   He wrote to him on April 25, 1889—

"We passed to-day, in the Legislature of New York, an ideal Prison Bill, which provides for classification and much else that is good—a considerable extension of the Elmira plan—and makes a prison system of which any country may be proud. *Your words to me have helped in this battle*, by which we have won a victory of justice over political chicanery.   I am almost ready to sing my 'Nunc dimittis.'   You have fought many such battles, and you know how I feel."

CHAPTER XVIII.

1853–1893.

My father has had occasion to speak more frequently of his brothers Matthew and Rowland, owing to their work being of a public kind, than of his brothers Edwin and Arthur; but enough has been said of these latter to suggest their leading characteristics.

For thirty years his brother Edwin held the office of Comptroller of the Stamp Department at Somerset House, where his mechanical talents came into play. His many contrivances are amusingly described in the *Daily News* of November 3, 1871. The writer of an article, entitled "Under Somerset House," says—

"Once fairly underground, and it is as if we were in the cave of an amiable magician. Doors open of their own accord; stamps of fabulous value are created out of waste-paper by a wave of the hand ; wooden arms and limbs are moved by unseen agencies, and classify documents with inconceivable rapidity and unfailing exactitude. Bundles of valuable deeds . . . walk gravely into the room unaided, and present themselves silently to be stamped. Other mysterious contrivances for lessening human labour abound . . . ingenious inventions of the Comptroller of the Stamping Department."

Here his "wind-proof doors" were first used. He set his ingenuity to work in their invention for the sake of a rheumatic porter at the Wellington Street entrance.

My uncle's bedroom was a museum of curiosities, affording much amusement to all who were allowed to inspect it. A network of cords stretched across the bed-head and ceiling. If at night the blankets pressed upon him too heavily, he could, as he lay, pull a string, with a sort of claw at the end, which grasped the bedclothes and relieved him of their weight. Again, if he awoke early and wanted to know the time, he could pull a cord which opened the shutter to admit the light, and by pulling another cord he could shut it again, and so on !

His work on currency has been spoken of already. Other economic questions interested him. He wrote papers on "Criminal Capitalists" and analogous subjects for the National Congress on Reformatory and Penitentiary Discipline held at

Cincinnati in 1871, and also for meetings of the
British Association and the Social Science Association. In these papers he maintained that criminal
enterprise requires capital for its development as
much as honest labour, and that if those who
harbour criminals and receive stolen goods were
effectively dealt with by the law, theft and burglary,
as an organized business, must fall to the ground.
A simple illustration of the truth of this position
may be seen in the fact that burglaries are little
feared in country places or at the seaside, where
it is difficult to dispose of loot.

My uncle Edwin had a most kind heart, as may
be guessed from his care for the rheumatic porter.
He carried his sympathy for pain or discomfort
to an extreme point. When his children were
young, and complained of a tight frock or an uneasy
shoe, out came his penknife to remedy matters
by a good slit! He was as simple as " Dominie
Sampson " with regard to his own clothes, and his
wife managed their renewal in much the same way
as that recorded in the case of the " Dominie."
When her husband's black velvet waistcoat, or any
other garment, was getting shabby, she took it
away overnight and put a new one in its place,
the metamorphosis remaining alike undiscovered !

One hot summer day my uncle Edwin was

walking in Kensington Gardens, absorbed in argument, with his brothers Rowland and Frederic. A gardener happened to set down a pail of water within his reach. To cool his feet he put first one leg into it and then the other, gesticulating and arguing all the time, while the gardener stared in amazement!

He was especially fond of arguing upon his favourite subject, which his old friend Mr. Kerr of Glasgow called "that infernal currency;" but his mind turned also to a very different enjoyment. The same friend said of him that "he was astonished at the correctness of his memory in quoting passage after passage of poetry, and at the almost girl-like ardour with which he recited them."

I have myself a vivid recollection of his repeating to us Mrs. Barbauld's hymn, "Come! said Jesus' sacred voice," and of the deep feeling with which he gave the lines.

Of all his brothers, Arthur most resembled my father in personal appearance, in character, in sentiments, and even in the habits of daily life. The personal likeness between them was so great at one time as to cause my father to absent himself from gatherings of old pupils at Bruce Castle, owing to the inconvenience of being mistaken for the head of the school.

My father wrote of this brother, " I have never known any one who had a greater devotion to duty than Arthur. Let him be but convinced that duty marshalled him in a certain direction, and no obstacle could deter him from moving onwards." We have heard it related that the very day after the death of his young wife he took his place in the schoolroom, supported by the reverent behaviour of his sympathizing pupils.

Both these brothers laid down strict rules for their daily conduct. These included rising for a very early walk, regardless of weather, taking exercise at regular intervals throughout the day, and being abstemious in their food. Wine they took only when ordered to do so by their "medical adviser." Brandy-and-water being prescribed for my uncle Arthur when he was an octogenarian, he refused to have sugar in it, "lest he should grow to like it"! Both strongly disapproved of the Game Laws, and in consequence never ate game. Both felt repugnance to see women engaged in heavy bodily work, and each in his own house assisted the female servants in such acts, among others, as carrying up the filled coal-scuttles. The lives of both brothers were patriarchal in simplicity, and yet both entertained a fear, often expressed, of becoming "fastidious" and "luxurious"!

My uncle Arthur injured his eyesight, during
the struggles of early life, by working at the
acquisition of Greek, in addition to his long day's
labour as a teacher. He thenceforward set himself
to lay up in his memory a store of matter which
he might turn to for mental food when unable to
use his eyes. His knowledge of Shakespeare was
remarkable. He often had as many as five whole
plays "by rote" at the same time, either of which
he could recite without reference to the text, though
the well-used volume was drawn from his pocket
and placed within his reach. One of my earliest
recollections of this beloved uncle is hearing him
recite *Coriolanus* in our parlour at Bellevue when
I was a very little girl. His dramatic power was
great, and all the characters he represented seemed
to live and move before us. It was, of course,
only in after-years that I could appreciate this
great power. Some idea of it may be given
by saying that his rendering of the character of
"Rosalind," in spite of every disadvantage of a
man's voice and outward appearance, remains, and
ever will remain, unrivalled in our memory. I last
heard him recite scenes from *As You Like It* when
he was an old man past eighty. A large green
shade was over his eyes, he wore fleecy gloves
and felt top-boots to keep out the cold of a

winter's evening, and screens were arranged to protect him from the glare of lamps and fire; but as soon as his lips opened everything that we looked upon vanished, the forest of Arden appeared, and Rosalind, in all the charm of youth and beauty, stood before us!

Perhaps the most remarkable feat of memory achieved by my uncle was when, in his eighty-fifth year, he translated Horace's " Ars Poetica." He knew the long Latin poem by heart, and translated it line by line during wakeful hours at night. He retained his translation in his mind, and dictated each portion, the following morning, to his faithful friend and sister-in-law Miss Maurice.

A member of Parliament who used to visit him, in company with Mr. Justice Scott (an old Brucian), expressed his astonishment at " Mr. Arthur Hill's wide and exact political memory."

The recollection of the talks with him as we walked up and down the long passage at Bruce Grove, where he took his regular exercise, is a precious possession. His sympathy was ever keen with young and old, and his nature ardent with enthusiasm or righteous indignation to the last. His " ripe wisdom," as a humble friend described it, has helped many a one in the difficulties of life.

My uncle Rowland was less known to the

younger members of the family than his brothers,
owing to his delicate health and absorbing occupations, but among our recollections of childhood we
have pleasant memories of his sympathy on more
than one occasion. He took a special interest in
the little plays which we wrote and acted, and
came with our aunt to witness their performance.
We always prepared a seat of honour for him,
adorned on one occasion with a gigantic "penny
postage stamp" of our own painting. He also
took an interest in my eldest sister's artistic efforts,
remembering, no doubt, his own boyish successes
in that direction.

My eldest uncle, Matthew, ever held the honoured
position of head of the family. As my sisters and
I grew old enough to pay visits we were invited,
by the kindness of our aunt and cousins, to their
beautiful home at Stapleton, where we saw much
of him, and were proud that he liked to have us
with him. Later on these invitations were extended to my sister Nora's husband, then a young
barrister, for whom he had a special liking.

Speaking of this uncle, Dr. Birkbeck Hill
writes—

"One of the brothers had by nature a hot temper.
He was as a boy 'jealous in honour, sudden and quick in
quarrel.' He was the first of them 'deliberately and

seriously to adopt the maxim that treats all anger as folly. . . . Having arrived at a principle, and that while yet a youth, he strove earnestly and with great success to reduce it to practice.' "

In his advanced age the internal fire only burned brighter and stronger for this self-conquest. It was never fed by paltry or personal wrongs, but by the great wrongs of mankind, which to the end of his life he set himself to combat and redress.

His youthful enthusiasm, his wide literary knowledge, his racy anecdotes and witty sayings, were a delight to us, his nieces, and made a stroll with him up and down the green terrace at Heath House a coveted treat.

In appearance he was more portly than his brothers. My aunt, Mrs. Baines, used to say of him, " I like his broad waistcoat; it is as large as his heart!" We remember his fine sonorous voice as he read the lessons in church, and, on one occasion, his reading at home the second chapter of the Book of Joel, while his deaf wife sat by him, holding his hand and following the text.

Between my uncle Matthew and my father there was necessarily strong sympathy, each having at heart the same subject of Penal Reform. As is well known, my uncle turned his mind especially to the juvenile delinquent, for whose redemption he accomplished so much.

Dr. Birkbeck Hill writes of the Hill brothers—

"As they trusted each other for aid in case of need, so at all times did they look to each other for counsel. The affairs of all were known to each. At every important turn each sought the judgment of all. . . . This curious league of brothers was due to many causes. From childhood they had been steadily trained up in it by their parents. They had long lived together under the same roof. Each had a thorough knowledge of the character of all the rest, and this knowledge resulted in a thorough trust. They had all come to have a remarkable agreement on most points, not only of principle, but also of practice. The habits of one, with but few exceptions, were the habits of all. He who had ascertained what one brother thought on any question would not have been likely to go wrong had he acted on the supposition that he knew what was thought by all."

Indeed, the Hill brothers' similarity of tastes as well as of opinions was a subject of pleasantry with the younger generation. At one of the merry Christmas gatherings at Bruce Castle, a plot was laid to inquire privately of each brother which of Sir Walter Scott's novels he preferred. All five answered, "Old Mortality"!

Dr. Hill goes on to say—

"They were all full of high aims—all bent on 'the accomplishment of things permanently great and good.'

There was no room in their minds for the petty thoughts of jealous spirits. Each had that breadth of view which enables a man to rise above all selfish considerations. Each had been brought up to consider the good of his family rather than his own peculiar good, and to look upon the good of mankind as still higher than the good of his family."

In a notice upon the death of Thomas Wright Hill, which appeared in the *Spectator* for June 21, 1851, it is remarked—

" All the brothers, like their father, are publicly useful men ; and by a sort of confederacy of talent, accordance of opinions, and unity of sentiment, strengthen each other in their several departments."

Their father's words, written to his son Frederic in 1842, have been verified : " The union of my children has proved their strength."

INDEX.

THE END.

PRINTED BY WILLIAM CLOWES AND SONS, LIMITED, LONDON AND BECCLES.

J. D. & Co.